Crema Crimewave

A Coastal Coffee Mystery

Kate Montgomery

MAGNOLIA MANUSCRIPTS PRESS

For all the women who've dreamt of more.

Contents

Prologue

Chandra screeches to a halt in the driveway, nearly stalling her Jeep. She sprints to the door, fist raised.

I whip the door open before she can pound on the it, saving my new shell wreath from impending damage.

"Did you get it?" she squeaks out breathlessly, pushing past me into the house.

"Duh! Why else would I have told you to come?" Scowling, I feign irritation at her question, making room for her to come in and kick off her shoes.

"I can think of dozens of reasons. Now, fork it over!"

Spinning to the table, I grab a tattered yellow envelope. When I spotted it in the mail, I'd torn into it with the energy of a raccoon in a fast-food dumpster. Only the front remains intact, the Florida state seal visible in the upper left corner. I present it to Chandra with the flair of a prized trophy.

Unceremoniously, she rips it from my hands and peels the crumbled letter from the battered envelope. She reads through it, murmuring under her breath, quickly works down the page. The seconds tick by at the pace of minutes. I don't know that I've ever seen her read this slowly. Anxiety courses through me and I clamp my hands over my mouth. Partly a nervous gesture, partly to keep from shrieking.

"Oh my word..." Chandra meets my eyes and grins broadly.

"Can you believe it?!?" I shout, voice strained and tears stinging my eyes. Instead of answering, she reaches for my hands, changes course, then grabs me by the elbows. We bounce up and down in place. From outside looking in, we must resemble kids on a trampoline. The dogs have no idea what is happening but gleefully join right in, dancing around us on their hind legs.

Once we've burned off some energy and collected ourselves somewhat, I reach for the letter and press it to my chest.

"Do you really think I can do it?" For weeks, I've been asking my husband, Brad, the same question. At all times of day or night. This morning, I woke him up at two o'clock to double check. He reassures me that I can do anything I set my mind to and trying new things helps me grow. Each time, I am given a temporary reprieve from the weight of imposter syndrome and can let myself revel in the win.

Rather than answering, Chandra leans back with her arms folded tightly over her chest. Glowering at me, she utters a low growling sound. A sure sign that she's frustrated.

"Fine!" Emphasizing so it sounds like, fine-*uh*, I turn my back and walk to the kitchen. The smell of coffee draws me in, plus it will clear my mind. Moments ago, I was filled with excitement for the future. But at this second, I feel something closer to dread.

Who in their right mind, thinks that I, Graciella Frances Larkin, is capable of this?

"Cees, you got this shug," Chandra reassures, pulling two mugs off the shelf.

1

Coffee Queen

My hands shake as I slide the overly full mug onto the counter.

The heavy foam jiggles as it inches toward Wren. She leans across the counter and inhales deeply.

"It smells heavenly! Can you make me one next?" she pleads, deftly placing the mug on her circular tray. In response, I flash her a double thumbs up. Anyone who prioritizes coffee is my kind of people.

As she twirls away on glittery yellow skates, she pumps her fist in celebration. Today, her blonde and purple hair is pulled away from her face in thick Dutch braids that hang nearly to her waist. With each push of her wheels, she glides toward her newest table, braids swing in unison with each stride, almost like they're waving.

Feeling on top of the world, I turn back to the coffee bar and behemoth of an espresso machine. I gather my dark, heavy curls off my neck, fanning to cool myself. Wrapping my hair into its usual bun will keep it out of my face and most importantly off my neck. The AC may be on, but it has to be close to ninety degrees outside. The small space I work in heats up quickly.

Humming softly, I wash my hands thoroughly, no health code violations on my watch, thank you very much, and set to work cleaning the frothing wand and pitcher. While the half and half makes a creamier version of a latte, it is slightly messier to clean up than whole milk. Despite that, breves are quickly becoming a favorite of mine and a handful of our regulars.

A throat clears behind me, and I turn to see the cafe's owner, Sebastian Acosta. He flicks on his million-wat smile, the one that makes my best friend Chandra Boudreaux weak in the knees, and asks, "How's the coffee bar, today?"

"Hey Seb! If it was any better I couldn't stand it."

"I hope that means this is going well?" he says, continuing to beam ear to ear. I forget that not everyone was raised with a grandfather who loved colloquialisms.

"Today feels like I'm starting to get a handle on my lattes and breves," a hint of pride edges into my voice. I've been at Azúcar for three months and only this week got the upgrade to this section of the coffee bar. My days of only making drip or iced coffees have ended, at least I hope they have.

"A success! I knew you would be great here," he says sincerely, a light slap of his palm on the counter emphasizes his point. He gestures to the machine, and I gladly begin his coffee. Every day, he requests a double shot with three sugars.

I believe him too. Despite dating Chandra and spending a ton of time with my husband and I, Seb takes his business very seriously. The child of Cuban immigrants, he dreamt of owning a restaurant since childhood. His grandfather told stories of the cafes lining the streets in Old Havana and the sense of community they brought. Running Azúcar is that dream in action. When he offered me the job in his cafe, I considered it an honor. He took a chance on an unemployed, amateur sleuth with a marketing degree, trusting me to craft coffees for his beloved customers. This cafe is his home, and he views the staff as family. Not in that sickly sweet, cover-up the toxicity way either. He genuinely cares for each person on his team and the community we serve.

Seb's attention is taken when a dapper man enters and calls his name. Arms open wide, they embrace in a greeting. I'm reminded again why I loved coming here as a customer. It has that feeling of visiting old friends.

Returning to my task at hand, I steam half and half, then set to work measuring espresso to pull a double shot for Wren's coffee. The squeak and faint whoosh hint at her return. I take my time tamping and inserting the portafilter in the machine. With a satisfying snap, the extraction begins. Watching the smooth, caramel coffee hit the cup, I shimmy back and forth. After a run of dead shots early last week, my confidence took a hit. I take a second to celebrate that beautiful crema forming and know, this shot is pure perfection.

Wren squeaks to a halt as I turn with a steaming coffee, in her favorite mug. It's bright purple with the logo of her roller derby team-The Salty Beaches. Dropping to a barstool, she hooks her skates on the lower rung and reaches wiggling fingers in my direction. Sipping her coffee like the life-giving beverage it is, she clicks her wheels together in delight.

"Girlfriend! You may be our new breve specialist!" She crows between sips.

Resisting a impish grin forming, I bow dramatically to hide my face. How many times can one person smile over a cup of coffee? Fairly sure I've maxed out that limit for the day. And I've been here for an hour. Changing the subject, I ask what the kitchen has on deck for our lunch. Wren runs through a few choices and offers to set aside whatever I pick. No matter how good the rest sounds, I'm an absolute sucker for a classic Cuban sandwich. Which is good, since I'm averaging two a week.

Over the next hour, a steady stream of mid-morning customers flows in. Today brings a mix of our regulars from local businesses and tourists in town for the final weeks of the busy summer season. In a flash of bittersweetness, I realize Snowbird season is nearly upon us, representing the true end of our summer. With the change in season, we will gain a new set of regulars. Those who return yearly, fleeing colder northern temps to savor the warmth of a Florida winter.

For today, I focus on what the current customers are excited about. Despite my joy in the recent latte successes, I am pleased that most order flavored cold brews or our house specialty— coladas. The tiny but powerful Cuban coffees are a hit amongst the locals. Before I realize it, we're running low on milk, and I dash to the back room, asking Seb to watch the counter for a moment

Laden with a gallon of milk, cream, and another bag of beans, I hear chatting as I approach the counter. Noting the familiar voice, I pick up my pace.

Linda Langston, my neighbor for the last five years, stands across the counter from Seb. She's surrounded by a small gaggle of women. All are well dressed in pressed slacks and twin sets. Linda stands out with a brightly colored pair of ceramic earrings. Today, she has flamingos that coordinate with her blush pink top and white capri length slacks. They bob and swing as she collects orders to relay to Seb. The effect widens my smile.

Linda's book club has arrived for their post-meeting coffee. She meets with a group of retired teachers and librarians monthly to discuss their latest read. Mostly they prefer thrillers or romances, even better when combined into one novel. This month is a billionaire romance with a nanny and a murder on a train. Over the last few weeks, she's been catching me up when we have coffee on the porch. I will say, my tastes run toward mysteries, cozies, and classics. But, to support her, I listen with rapt attention and discuss her theories on who may be the culprit.

Wren appears at the counter with a to-go order for two cold brews with caramel and coconut cold foam. I mentally add that to my list of drinks to try for myself. Linda must be on the same wavelength. She and one of her friends change their orders to match. With fourteen drinks to make, Seb offers to stay behind the counter to help me catch up. I gladly accept the help. He takes half the orders, leaving the rest to me.

Wren and Linda cross the restaurant to the patio, arms linked with their heads together. On book club days, we block off a section of the patio for the ladies to meet. I would have loved to have her stick around and chat, but sadly, I need to focus. Disappointing Linda with poorly made drinks does not appeal to me.

Working as quickly as possible, I start with the to-go orders and am halfway through Linda's. A line of steamy, creamy lattes, breves, and coladas await pick up from the counter. I'm steaming milk when I hear a loud thump, followed by several more and a shout. Assuming it is simply staff moving around in the kitchen, I carry on, adding the milk to another latte, this one with a dusting of cinnamon to finish it off. As I reach for the cinnamon shaker, the sound of glass shattering stops me in my tracks.

2

Losing History

The entire restaurant freezes in an instant. No one seems to be able to quickly identify the source. Heads spin left and right, frantically checking the windows.

Within seconds, gunshots echo down the street. Followed up quickly by shouting and screeching tires.

Our guests flee from in from the patio. A dozen tumbling bodies crash through the crowded restaurant, frantically seeking safety.

In a flash, Seb launches himself over the counter and sprints for the open door.

Struggling to free myself from my apron, I grab my cell phone from under the counter and rush after Seb without a second thought. Several patrons are calling 911, so I call Chandra. She answers on the second ring.

"Yello," she mutters, obviously distracted. I hear her radio tones in the background.

"Gunshots!" I squeak, squeezing between tables. "At the cafe…" She disconnects before I can give any details. Not that I had much to offer but I could have told her a little more. Clearing the tables, I run out the door.

Brad. He needs to see this and I need him. He answers with a finger pressed to his lips and audio muted. I assume he's in a meeting and mouth, "gunshots" while simultaneously muting my end, his clients won't want to hear the chaos on the street. He leans off camera for a second, then returns with a shouted, "Are you okay?" I nod and flip the camera to give a view of the street, as I burst onto the sidewalk and turn toward the commotion. The bakery next door is in shambles.

The antique plate glass window is destroyed, shards of glass resemble a mouth with jaggedly sharp teeth. It looks mon-strous—fractured and leering. Tears spring to my eyes when I see the shop owner, Bernice Jenkins peering around the edges, a hand-kerchief pressed to her face. Malcolm Deluca, her grandson, stands in the street, arms folded over his head. He stares in disbelief at the disappearing car.

Coming back to myself, I turn to watch the fleeing vehicle and snap screenshots frantically. Praying that the photos contain enough detail to identify someone or something. I mentally catalog- black sports car, two doors, soft top, missing passenger taillight. There's a sticker on the driver side bumper, I can't make it out, other than it is light in color. Maybe white? Definitely a Florida plate. Two large forms are visible in the car, I would guess they are male by the size but cannot be sure. The one takes up most of the front seat, he's got to be huge in person.

Once the car is too far away, my attention returns to Mrs. Jenkins. She stands frozen in place, crying silently, leaning heavily on a cane. I rush to her side, crunching my way through the glass littering the sidewalk. In the bright afternoon sun, it sparkles like diamonds, the effect in opposition to the destruction surrounding us.

"The police are on the way," I offer reassuringly, guiding her into one of the undamaged chairs. My hand snakes around her thin shoulders. She leans into my waist, her entire body quakes, beyond the point of tears in this moment. I fold her against me and silently nod at Brad. He blows a kiss and disconnects. Seconds later, my phone pings with an incoming text.

On my way. Be safe. Te amo.

Instead of responding, I heart his message. Now, I sag into Mrs. Jenkins. Brad is on his way. I'll be okay. We'll be okay. She tightens her grip around my waist, and I rub her back in a small circle.

The distant wail of police sirens breaks the oddly silent morning. All movement and sound outside has ceased.

"How did they know to come?" she asks in a muffled, small voice.

"We called," I reassure her, intentionally keeping my voice low, "I *think* most of our customers called within seconds of hearing the glass and gun shots."

"I'm not even sure what happened." Shaking her head, Mrs. Jenkins leans back in the wooden chair, it creaks beneath her. With one hand, she wipes her eyes with the pale-yellow handkerchief. I notice the floral pattern edging the cotton square. While the color may have faded with years of use and washing, the stitching remains vibrant. It strikes me as an item my grandmother would have loved. "I don't know what to tell the police. It was all so fast and so loud." I'm used to seeing the matriarch of downtown and the change hits hard. She seems so frail.

"Don't worry about that for now. Tell them what you can re-member, it will be enough to get started." She nods shakily and pats my hand.

"Nonna!" Malcolm's voice booms through the remnants of the bakery. He rushes to her side and falls to his knees. She switches from needing to giving comfort. She pulls him to her and murmurs quietly into his dark hair. I turn back to the broken window to give them privacy.

The sirens are closer and my time is limited before the bakery is a full-scale crime scene. The clock is ticking and I snap photos of everything. In the words of Chandra, it's all important. The broken window, bakery case filled with crushed bread and glass, overturned tables, cash register hanging open, a baseball bat.

How had this much been destroyed in a matter of seconds? Approaching the window, the damage becomes clearer. The hand lettered sign is one of the landmarks in the neighborhood. An original from 1951 when the bakery opened. Gerardo's is a staple in the area and a common spot for out-of-town visitors on the weekend. How many times have I walked past this sign and stopped to stare at the vintage lettering? I've admired the shimmering gold letters of "Gerardo & Sons". It truly is an icon. This shop represents a moment in the past; the family has lovingly carried on traditions for many generations. The idea of the window surviving decades of hurricanes, only to fall victim to a random robbery is heartbreaking. These are the parts of old Florida that we lose bit by bit.

"CiCi, could you help us?" Malcolm asks, his voice has dropped in volume but remains thick with emotion. He's pulled a chair next to his grandmother and sits with one arm wrapped tightly around her shoulders.

"Of course!" I respond eagerly, desperate to help with whatever they need. "What can I do?"

"We know you have experience helping the police," he says cautiously. "Nonna is nervous to speak with them. She hasn't ever had to speak with police, and I think it's upsetting her as much as this." Using his free hand, he gestures at the interior of the shop. "Would you be able to sit with her when she has to answer questions?"

"I'm happy to! I'll stay with you the whole time," Crouching in front of Mrs. Jenkins, I grasp her hands in mine. "There's no need to be nervous."

Before I can finish, a voice cuts me off, "What are we nervous about?" Seb has rejoined us.

"Mrs. Jenkins is a little nervous to speak with the officers," I explain, trying to convey that he should take over. I do one of those jerk my chin and bug my eyes moves, hoping that he gets the point and I don't look like I'm having a seizure. Thankfully, he seems to get the hint.

"Nah— my girlfriend is coming. She's the best and will make sure you're okay," Seb reassures Mrs. Jenkins. I notice the pride and delight in his smile when he talks about Chandra.

"I'll second that," I say heartily. Chandra is highly skilled in getting people to open up, for better or worse. She's just the person to talk with Mrs. Jenkins. Now, to try to figure out how she can be assigned to this case may be a different story. Since our last cases earlier this year, her assignments have changed. Granted, I am not 100% sure what all she does now. But maybe that change will be in our favor?

In an effort to distract her from the current circumstance and because I am nosey, I ask about the history of the business and how long ago it was found.

"My parents, Gerardo and Juanita, opened the bakery in 1951. Both come from long lines of bakers in Italy. Their parents lived in the same neighborhood and owned similar but different enough shops. My father's family focused on bread and savory pastries. My mother's family focused on sweeter pastries— cakes, cookies, biscotti. Their marriage wasn't one of conflict, they shared a love of baking and caring for the community," pausing to dab her eyes, "They decided to move to the US in 1938. Thankfully they made it here before the war began in Europe. It was a terrible time for many they knew, some were never heard from again." After a moment, she continues with a wistful smile, "My father went to work at local bakeries while my mother practiced her skills at home. This helped them both gain an understanding of local culture and what baked goods the locals enjoyed. Mama sold bread and pastries from her kitchen for years. Following the war, they'd saved enough money and gained enough skill to open this small bakery and storefront. It became a family affair. All nine of us children took turns helping when and where we could. My oldest brother and I loved it the most. But life gets in the way, and he wasn't able to run the business. In 1985, my husband and I took over the bakery. We loved continuing on the family tradition and keeping the past alive for the neighborhood." She again stops and dabs her eyes. "Until now, that is..."

3

Grounds for Involvement

The deafening shriek of sirens brings us back to the current situation. Slamming doors and thumping boots herald the arrival of the officers. Furthering the cacophony, there are the shouting voices and squawking radios as the team enters the bakery. I stand with my hands raised, facing the incoming flood of law enforcement. Silently, I wait for them to approach me. Running at them will do nothing to make this less stressful for any of us.

A cell phone buzzes on the table beside us, I spot Brad's picture on the screen. Seeing his smiling face, even for a moment boosts my confidence and soothes me. Everything will be okay, and he'll be here soon. Intentionally slowing my breaths, I step forward when the officer gestures to me.

"Name and address please," he barks, his face is strained with a deep line between his brows.

"Graciella Larkin, 47 Flamingo Way, Palmetto Breeze," I recite quickly. Pausing he looks at me intently. Meanwhile, I study his nametag, Officer Brandon Malloy. "But, you can call me CiCi."

"You Chandra's friend?" he asks in a thickly Southern drawl. Is that a little south Georgia I hear?

Nodding way too aggressively, I chirp, "Yep!" while dropping my hands down. "Sure am!"

"Huh. She's on her way, but what are you doing here?"

"I work at the cafe next door. I'm a barista," leaning past us I point to the brightly colored umbrellas. "We heard the glass shatter and gunshots. I ran over here to see what happened."

"You ran *toward* the gunshots?" incredulity drips from his voice, the frown returns. Pretty sure he's doubting my honesty and sanity.

"Well, why wouldn't I?" I am equally shocked. Who wouldn't run to see if someone needed help?

"To start with, most folks hide when they hear gunshots. Like all of those fine people—" he turns to point at the customers peering at the scene from our patio, safely tucked inside.

"You'll learn quickly, she doesn't do what most people would," a bayou accented, female voice calls out. We turn to see Sergeant Chandra Boudreaux picking her way through the glass and debris.

Seb appears from nowhere and escorts her to us. "She seems to attract trouble wherever she goes." In all fairness, she seems to attract it and I follow in her wake. But that's for another time.

"Hey pot, nice to hear you ribbing the kettle," I retort. She winks, then gestures for me to continue with Officer Malloy.

"About fifteen minutes ago, I heard some bumping noises and raised voices, quickly followed by breaking glass. Before making it outside, I heard three gunshots, fired rapidly, then squealing tires. Unfortunately, I didn't get a look at the perps, but I did get a few photos of the vehicle and license plate." Despite smiling when I used the word *perp*, Chandra seems generally pleased by the details I share. "Can I grab my phone?" pointing the table next to us. Officer Malloy nods. Unlocking it with a quick glimpse at the screen, I present the photos snapped earlier. Thankfully, the photos are clear, but I wish it would have caught their faces.

Officer Malloy takes my phone and records the vehicle make, model, and plate number in his notebook. He radios in the details, requesting officers in the area be on the lookout for the vehicle and suspects involved in an armed robbery.

Hearing the description gives me a cold chill, shivers run down my spine and spread out as goose bumps. Rubbing my arms, I attempt to dissipate the sensation. It is unnerving to say the least.

"I'm gonna need you to send me these," He extends my phone with a business card taken from his chest pocket. I nod and begin typing in the information.

"Are you the business owner?" he asks of Mrs. Jenkins. She nods with a croaking sob and tucks her head against Malcolm's shoulder. She shakes her head, indicating she cannot proceed.

"I'm Malcolm Deluca, this is my grandmother, Bernice Jenkins. She owns the bakery, but we run it together," he offers in her place. Officer Malloy jots down the names and the addresses Malcolm provides.

"Could you talk us through what happened this morning?" Officer Malloy asks, his tone is noticeably softer than when he first addressed me. Mrs. Jenkins looks at me wide-eyed and extends a hand for me to hold. A puzzled expression crosses Malloy's face, he glances to Chandra. She simply shakes her head and smiles, expecting no less. Malloy nods and looks back to the three of us. "Take your time, ma'am. There's no rush."

"I was behind the counter, using a break in customers to review a catering order we'd received by email. It was lengthy and I was ensuring we had enough stock, we bake daily to make sure it's fresh," returning to herself, she sits up straighter. "I was still looking down when I heard an awful bang. A tall man in a mask, kicked our door open. I screamed and turned to run. As I turned, the man reached for the register and attempted to lift it from the counter. You see, he didn't realize that Papa had bolted it to the counter decades ago after a break-in."

"From the kitchen, I heard the scream and bang, then ran to check on her. Mostly, I was afraid she'd fallen," Malcolm says looking slightly embarrassed. "Instead, there was a massive man yanking on the register. When he saw it wasn't budging, he began pounding on it with the gun in his hand. At that point, I shoved Nonna into the kitchen, shouting for her to call 911, and shut the door." His confidence now restored, he continues, "I grabbed the baseball bat we keep under the counter. Rushing toward him, I shouted for him to leave again and again. I took a risk that his gun wouldn't work after bashing like a hammer against the register. He didn't seem frightened at all, he kept the creepiest smile I've ever seen on his face, leaned forward grabbing cash from inside the open register. When he looked down to see what was left, I got one solid blow in, cracking him on the forearm. He screamed and made a break for the door. After he made it outside, he picked up one of the stones from the flower bed and threw it at the window. It shattered," he points to the gaping window. "A black car screeched to a halt in front, and he jumped in. Just before they roared away, he fired the gun into the bakery." Now he gestures up to the broken lights above us.

This was the first time I noticed the lights with broken globes. Sneaking my phone from my pocket, I take a few more photos. Not sure why, but something tells me they may be useful later.

Seb picks up the story here. "I heard the commotion and ran through the cafe, out onto the patio. Just in time to see the gun fire into the bakery. I didn't have my phone, or I would have called," he looks at Chandra apologetically. Instead of responding, she squeezes his hand and smiles. He describes the fleeing man, "taller than me, so a few inches over six feet. Very broad though, like a football player. I wasn't able to see his face or make out anything to describe him. He had one of those weird plastic masks, it was shaped like a lamb. He was dressed in all black and wearing gloves. The plastic kind that we wear in the kitchen. I wish I could tell you more, but nothing about him was familiar."

"You all have been very helpful!" Officer Malloy reassures us. "I'll need to get phone numbers for the Detective to have. There will be more questions, for now those can wait." He passes around his notepad for each to list our contact information next to our names. With a firm nod to our little group, he strides away, joining the group of officers near the register.

Released from questioning, Chandra pulls Seb and I aside. We step from the bakery and onto the sidewalk in front of the cafe. Away from the crowd, we huddle near a potted fern.

"That was a lot, huh?" she slowly begins, testing the waters of our emotions.

"Yeah, but you should have seen the way Seb launched himself over the coffee bar. It was Olympic level impressive," I can't help the mischievous grin forming.

"Hmmm...Olympic level?" she winks at Seb, curving her lips into a flirty smile, "Sorry to have missed all the action." He blushes a deep crimson and bumps her shoulder with his own. "Sexy athleticism aside, you two okay?"

Seb nods deeply, rocking his upper body back and forth with the motion, clearly embarrassed by the sudden attention.

His blush fades as he stares at the front of the bakery, "They've been a presence on this street for my whole life. I'd visit with my parents on weekends all through my childhood," his expression changes again, tenderly he says, "Mrs. Jenkins actually encouraged me to open the cafe next to her. She knew having my own business on this street was a dream." He gestures to the businesses surrounding us. The majority have been open for decades. A few newer spots, like Cafe Azúcar, have opened within the last decade. This street has a unique energy, so many similar neighborhoods are fading into history.

"It makes me sad more than anything. You know how I feel." Tightness in my throat pinches my words, tears of irritation threaten to spill over. "I can't stand for anyone hurting our friends and neighbors."

"I had an inkling you'd both be feeling it," she pauses and squeezes my shaking hands. "Shug, it may be best for you to head on home and wait for the detectives to call. They should be reaching out this afternoon." I nod somberly, going home to my empty house will make today even sadder. A smash and grab at the bakery next door was not on my bingo card for the day.

From the corner of my eye, I see Seb shaking his head. Chandra looks at him with a mix of confusion and concern. "Is that a no?"

"My people will need reassurance. If CiCi and I are this sad, imagine how they're feeling?" Seb's posture straightens, he's back in boss mode. "I'll go back to make sure everyone is safe and see if anyone needs to talk. We'll close early today anyway. The police on the street will cut our business down to nil." Chandra dips her head in agreement, reaching to hold his hand. I can see how proud she is. He's moving past this moment to make sure his team is okay, always thinking of others.

"If he's staying, so am I!" Chandra quirks an eyebrow at me and frowns. Her expression tells me she knows what I am up to. I clutch imaginary pearls and pretend to be offended. "Pardon me for wanting to support my employer!"

In lieu of a response, Chandra snorts and shoves me toward the restaurant. Guess our bonding moment is over?

4

Solace

Brad arrives about half an hour after Seb and I return to the cafe. Record time really. The front door flies open with a bang, and he fills the doorway. Without thinking, I run from behind the coffee counter into his arms. Burying my head in his chest, I murmur, "I'm fine, I'm fine." Through his shirt, I feel his pounding heart begin to slow.

"You scared the absolute daylights out of me!" he says, voice muffled. He's resting his face against the top of my head and breathing deeply. "I was in a new client meeting but told them I'd have to cut it short due to an urgent need. Telling them there was a shooting at my wife's work felt a little unnecessary." He chuckles with the last part. That's my man, finding humor in a stressful situation.

"Might have been too much sharing for the first meeting," I tease, continuing to clutch him tightly.

"Seriously babe," he whispers again and kisses my forehead.

"I know. I hated scaring you but *needed* you to be there with me." He nods against my head and I continue, "We heard the bang but had no idea what was going on. Seb ran from the cafe and I followed..." Brad leans back from me and frowns. "May not have been my best idea, but it felt right in the moment." At that, Brad sighs deeply and shakes his head. Relaxing his vise-like grip on me, he slides me under his arm, still holds me tightly but has clearly calmed down since his arrival. His breathing is no longer ragged and color has returned to his face.

"You got a taste for danger and there's no turning back," he laments, all while smiling warmly at me. I catch a hint of pride in his gaze.

"My man! You're here," Seb bellows and claps Brad on the back. A round of male greetings— fist bumps, back slaps— ensues. I slide from under Brad's arm and offer a coffee. He nods and grabs my hand, not quite ready to have me out of arms reach. I drag him toward the coffee bar with Seb in tow. Not an easy feat to pull a semi-distracted man across the cafe.

They rehash this afternoon's events. Seb shares his point of view and some of the history of the businesses on the street. As he talks, Linda pulls up a stool and listens in.

"The Jenkins have run the bakery for decades. It has been a neighborhood favorite since her parents opened shortly after World War II. They brought a mix of local and international flavors, creating a bakery unique to them and representative of the neighborhood. Italian, Cuban, Argentinian, a cultural mash-up that works. It tastes like the neighborhood feels— a melting pot that celebrates the homes of many." He bows his head, staring at the counter for a brief moment, and adds, "The best Cuban bread on this side of the state."

While they talk, I pour black coffee into a large lemon-yellow ceramic mug, topping it with steamed milk and a sprinkle of cinnamon. Sliding it to Brad, he takes a gulp of the hot coffee and gives me a wink and a thumbs up. He and Seb continue their conversation, and I get to work cleaning up the counter and machines. Now that Brad has arrived, I am feeling ready to go home. Soon I'll be in pajamas and an ugly bun on the porch with Brad and the dogs. Cleaning up as they chat will make it a faster process.

Surveying the restaurant, I notice only a handful of staff and the four of us remain. True to his word, Seb checked on the customers and staff, then closed the cafe for the afternoon. Through the window, I see the number of officers on the street has dwindled to a handful plus the crime scene team. Yellow and black police tape flaps in the breeze, a reminder that this far from over.

"Psst..." Linda hisses at me. She has moved away from Brad and Seb, leaning on the counter, she waves her hand for me to join her. I finish wiping out the steam pitcher and rest my elbows on the counter, inches from her. "So— I assume you took some notes?" I offer a shy smirk but don't respond. "And, I hope, maybe a few photos?" With this, I break into a wide grin.

"Now Linda, why would I have done that?" I tease, sliding my phone from the apron's front pocket.

"Because, my darling, you are nosier than I am." Linda's nose wrinkles and she taps it with a finger.

"I may have taken a few photos and jotted a couple of notes in my phone." I wag my phone in her direction. She gives me a satisfied smile and holds up her own phone.

"There might be a few in here as well," she says, eyes twinkling and cheeks flushing.

"Seems like we should probably compare notes?" a lilt of excitement on the last few words.

"Your porch or mine?" she grins and rests back on her barstool.

"Your snacks, my porch?"

"Deal!" she excitedly agrees.

"What are you two chickens chatting about?" Chandra calls out. I jump upright, startled that she'd come in unnoticed.

"Nothing," we say in unison.

"Sure. That feels legit," she retorts. "Will I be seeing you two later?"

"I mean, mi casa is always yours," I tell her, then get back to cleaning up. My vision of pj's on the porch is replaced by an evening of sleuthing with friends. As I scrub, Linda excuses herself with a generic, "I've got some baking to get to." Chandra eyes me suspiciously the whole time. After Linda vacates her stool, Chandra hops onto it.

"How many pics did you get?"

Feigning innocence, I stage whisper, "Who? Me?"

Rolling her eyes, she reaches for my phone. I snatch it from her before she has a good grip. "Rude...you could at least ask nicely." Unlocking the phone, I open to my photos. She scrolls through the images of the bakery, the car, all the way to my first coffee of the day.

"Nice latte art," spinning my phone back toward me, she shows the heart I'd successfully poured onto a coffee that morning.

"Thanks! I'm working my way up to palm trees. Very, very slowly." I drop my voice a few octaves for emphasis.

"You're doing great!" she reassures. "Seb sent me one you did earlier today and I was impressed." She continues to stare at the photo. I do a quick little shimmy of delight. How cool is it that he'd shared a pic of a coffee I'd made?

"Did you want a coffee? I can make you something and tell you about the break-in?"

"Whatever you've got left, don't start over just for me," she holds her hand over the pitcher still clutched in my hand.

"Hot or iced?" I say, picking up two carafes. She points to the iced. I grab a tall class tumbler, fill it with ice cubes, and pour in the thick dark cold brew. Feeling fancy, I top the cup with a cold foam cream I'd made this morning then sprinkle with chocolate shavings.

"Not bad for leftovers," she says after a long sip. Smacking her lips and widening her eyes to emphasize her delight. "Now— spill it sister."

With a dramatic sigh, I recount everything from the afternoon. Along the way, I share pictures that correlate with the events. A shiny black car, zooming in on the bumper stickers and outlines of the occupants. The shattered window, with the glittering gold lettering. Light fixtures with broken globes. The vintage cash register with the smashed screen and bent drawer. A baseball bat thrown to the floor inside the door, cast off as Malcolm ran after the thief.

Purposefully, I don't focus on the crushed pastries and damaged display cases. That feels especially senseless and hurts the most. I did sneak in a photo of Mrs. Jenkins and Malcolm. In that moment, it seemed so precious to see them talking with heads bent low. Each comforting the other. Again, it's the people that get me.

"I cannot understand why the bakery was targeted?" I muse. "Yes, they consistently do well. But, it's a Tuesday morning. Most businesses have limited cash on hand today. Picking this morning doesn't make sense..."

"Why does today make less sense than any other day?" Chandra asks, her curiosity is piqued.

"We drop the weekend profits off on Mondays," Seb answers. "All of the earnings from the weekend are deposited by lunch on Monday. By Tuesday, the only funds on site are leftover from the afternoon before."

"Do all the businesses around here follow that schedule?" she asks and opens the note app on her phone.

"It isn't a guarantee, but you will see most of us at the bank on Monday before lunch," he confirms and points to the bank down the street. "Mrs. Jenkins has mentored a lot of the owners around here."

"Which means that a lot mirror her process," Chandra agrees, tapping the details into the note.

"I can think of at least five that do," Seb confirms.

"Interesting. Right off the bat, that grabs my attention. It tells me the thieves were unfamiliar with the area businesses. Most would strike when there is the maximum amount of cash on scene."

"Could it be that money wasn't the goal?" I ponder.

"It could, but at this point, we don't know more than it was a robbery," she says, considering my point. "Unfortunately, they've not yet been apprehended. Until we get to dig deeper or find them, we won't know."

Seb stands and claps his hands loudly, startling all of us. "Let's wrap it up and head home everyone."

I anticipated groans, but surprisingly, everyone springs into action. Each remaining employee tackles their tasks quickly. The precision gives the impression; we're facing a health department inspection instead of closing for the day. In record time, Seb has ushered us out and is locking the door.

"Can I grab Darla and head over?" he asks, brow raised and smirk.

"I'll get the porch ready..." I say, grabbing Brad's hand with one hand and mocking a salute with the other. Giggling, Brad and I race for his truck.

5

Rallying the Troops

The doorbell rings and Brad glides down the hallway toward the door in his socks. He makes a whooping sound, in celebration of the arrival of dinner. On the way home, we threw out dinner options, settling on pizza, salad, and garlic knots. Not only a crowd pleaser all around, but it'll stretch. Knowing this group, the number of dinner guests will be a surprise.

He returns moments later with boxes and Linda. She's carrying a large white takeout bag with the salad. In lieu of a wave, she shimmies the bag in my direction, grinning proudly.

"Linda!" I shout and grab her in a hug. "Have you come to join our debrief?" I gesture to Seb and Chandra on the lanai. They wave in unison, also shouting, "Linda!" It's an entrance she's worthy of. We all dearly love Linda. She's been through so much in her lifetime, but remains a source of joy and comfort to many of us. Having her with us always adds to the fun.

"Only if you're okay with it?" she asks, a hint of hesitation in her words. Despite the entrance, she seems unsure if she's welcome.

"Of course! You were there and saw everything from a different angle. I'd love to hear what you say and your thoughts on it. You've been here almost as long as Seb." The smile on her face highlights her relief. From behind her back, she pulls a grocery store tote bag.

"I brought dessert, hope you don't mind," she unwraps a plastic container filled with a dozen cannoli stuffed with cream and decorated with chocolate shavings. Groaning, Brad snatches the container from her hands and sniffs the contents.

"You gotta let me taste those, cher!" Chandra bellows from out back, craning her neck to look through the open doorway, locked in on the container of cannoli.

In a burst of sound, three dogs race into the kitchen, jumping all over Linda. She bends and kisses each. They respond with grumbles and snorts, prancing in a circle. She deftly manages their frantic energy back outside. I always think about what an amazing teacher she must have been. Her skill in getting everyone to cooperate is legendary.

Settled around the table, pizza slices in hand, it's time to get this party started.

"Alright Linda, you're on deck. We've all heard Seb and I recount the day. But I'm dying to know what you saw..." I lean forward, gesturing with my pizza in her direction.

Resting the slice on her plate, Linda dabs her mouth daintily, then bends to reach for her tote bag. Freeing her phone, she opens the photos app and slides her phone across the glass top table toward me. Chandra beats me to it and grabs the phone. I harumph that she will get to see the pictures first. Gleefully she alternates swiping through and zooming in. Since I've got time, I open the notes app on my phone to jot down what Linda is about to share.

"I was at the coffee bar placing our orders, for my book club. All the ladies were with us today." Despite the seriousness, she smiles faintly at the mention of her beloved book club. "There was the crash that caught all of our attention. The next thing I knew, Seb had vaulted over the counter. Which was very impressive, my dear." Linda pats Seb's arm and he blushes slightly, nodding his head as a thanks. "CiCi was hot on his heels and sprinting through the cafe at a pretty good clip." Now it's my turn to blush a little. Maybe all those days running in the neighborhood are paying off?

"I made it to the door as CiCi started snapping photos of the fleeing car. I took a few myself. But I must say my favorite is this one," she reaches for the phone that Chandra has rested on the table. Swiping a few times, she brings up a photo of the street. Immediately, I latch onto the clear view of the license plate and attempt to zoom into the face in the side mirror. "No, this part..." Resetting the photo to the original scale, I murmur, "aww". I stand in the street, phone raised, snapping my own picture of the car. Brad's face is visible in the corner of my screen. Smiling, I turn to look at Linda. Gotta say, it is a pretty cool shot. "I think you look like Wonder Woman." Brad squeezes my knee under the table. He may not love that my curiosity takes me into unsafe situations, but he supports me regardless.

"You got some great images," Chandra interjects, clearly dialed in on the case and details. "I'd like to share a few of these with the Detectives. The lab should be able to enhance it enough for a possible identification." She has slipped out of friend mode and into cop mode. Despite the increasingly fierce look on her face, you can tell she's proud of Linda's quick thinking. Excusing herself from the table, she tells us, "Keep eating, I need to make a quick call." Unfazed by what we consider her normal behavior, we chow down on pizza while Linda finishes her story.

There aren't many additional details beyond the incredible photo Linda got. Our retellings all have similar timelines and highlights. But it's still nice to hear her perspective.

"How long have you known the Jenkins?" Brad mumbles around a steaming garlic knot that is dripping with marinara.

"Oh gosh, let me think. When I first moved here, I was thirty-one. That would have been in the late seventies— maybe 1978? I met the Russo's at a community night at the school. Once we were introduced, I started visiting their bakery. Mr. and Mrs. Jenkins took over the bakery from her parents in the mid-eighties. Their health was failing, and it was time to pass the torch. They've worked for decades to build the business from scratch. It has become a landmark, for locals and tourists." Her tone changes from fond to a little sad. "You know who really knows them?"

"I'm going to hazard a guess— Desmond and Karen?" I say, a smile twists the corners of my lips.

"How did you ever guess?" Linda grins at me, a twinkle in her eye. "If you wanted, I could call Des..." A unanimous "YES" echoes through the lanai before she can finish his name. "Well, in that case..." she giggles and picks up her phone.

"Des? It's a go." Linda says mysteriously. "Come on over, there's pizza and cannoli."

"I see how it is," I tease. "You two obviously worked this out before you got here." I can't help but laugh, I should have known.

A few minutes later, Chandra and Desmond Canistel appear in the door. He's carrying a six-pack of beer and a pitcher of Karen's famous frozen mango margaritas. Even though Karen is still recovering from her stroke in the nursing home, Desmond finds ways to include her. Brad and Seb cheer loudly as he steps onto the lanai.

"I must have missed something," Chandra begins, her brow furrowed and a frown forming.

"Grab some glasses and we'll fill you in," I tell her. The perk of having a best friend who's at your house all the time, is that it becomes their house too. I know she'll even grab the cute ones with gators on the stems. We bought them last month on one of our shopping excursions after brunch.

As anticipated, Chandra reappears with woven sea grass tray and six curvy margarita glasses. The blown glass gators on the stems are each in a different position. They were just too cute to pass up. Chandra got a set with seashells on the stems. It may be my imagination, but some of her recent purchases have a planning for the future vibe. Could that be wedding bells I hear?

"Now, pour me a drink and catch me up," she insists. I pour to the rims and pass out them around the table.

"Should I start with how long I've known the family?" Desmond asks after a long sip from his frosty glass. We resemble a bobble-head collection, aggressively nodding. "I guess it goes beyond how long I've known the family. My parents met the Russo's, Gerardo, and Juanita, in 1939. They'd arrived the year before and did their best to put down roots right away. At the big church in town, which really wasn't that big during those years, there was a group who formed friendships. The Russo's and my parents became friends. While they didn't share the same immigrant experience, they did understand trying to find community when the world was on the cusp of war."

"How long had your family been here?" Seb interjects.

"As best as I can tell and from old family lore, my father's family were descendants of Spanish soldiers that arrived in the late 1780's," a collective gasp from our little group, then he continues, "My mother's family moved down from the Carolina's in the early

1830's. The years have become unclear over time, but I do know we go back many generations." Pausing momentarily, he grows quiet and sips his drink. I picture the hundreds of years his family has lived in Florida, finding it impossible to grasp. "I have some old pictures if anyone ever wants to see them?" I make a pleading hand motion and he nods, delighted that I am so interested. "Anyway, back to the Russo's. Their son, Giovanni, is the same age as my eldest sister Ana Mae. For a while, the parents thought they may marry but he joined the military at seventeen, leaving Florida, and Ana Mae, behind. He came back every now and then but had settled in Oregon the last I knew. Don't think he was too big a' fan of the heat," Desmond chuckles, "A couple of summers in my teen years, I worked at the bakery with the family. My brothers did too. It was heavy work, lifting flower sacks and loading the ovens. Taught me a lot in those years. Mostly, that I didn't want to work in a bakery." We all laugh at his confession, it's more than relatable.

"In the late 1970's, Juanita had a small stroke. It affected her until her death. She had limited strength on her right side, which prevented her from working in the bakery. By then, their children were adults and able to help. All but Bernice eventually moved on. She and her husband, Leonard took over the bakery in the 80's. Gerardo and Juanita didn't live to see the 1990's. Once she died, he followed within a few months." We're all listening with rapt attention. The opportunity to hear someone like Desmond recite the history of families and the area is fascinating and such a rarity.

"Bernice and Leonard had two children, Serena and James. Sadly, James was killed in Dessert Storm. He'd been in the Reserves for years and was called back to active duty. Shortly after arrival, he died. His wife moved how to be with her family. Which left Serena and her family to carry on the tradition. Her husband, Eddie, dove right in without a second thought. They've helped for the last twenty years or so. Now their son, Malcolm, does a lot of work. Impressive to have four generations involved, right?" Desmond raises his glass and gulps his rapidly melting margarita.

"Sheesh— Linda said you'd know more about the family, but I wasn't prepared for all that," my eyes bug and I am in awe of all that he's shared. I'd expected some sort of general overview, this far exceeded expectations.

"The history is part of why this is so heartbreaking," Seb offers, the sadness thick in his voice. Chandra leans over and presses her head to his. He pulls her into him and rests his chin on her head.

"The biggest question I have after all this, is how can we help?" Linda asks, swirling the remnants of her margarita.

"Oh Lord...I was afraid of this..." Chandra grumbles.

"I mean, we were mostly all there when it happened. You can't get more involved than that!" I argue.

"Brad wasn't," she retorts.

"I beg to differ Officer Boudreaux, I was on a video call," he says with a boyish grin. Those dang dimples get me and I smooch him on the cheek.

"See?" I echo. "I wish I had a whiteboard like a real true crime sleuth." Flopping my chin into my hand, I survey my itty-bitty house and wonder where I can fit one.

"The community center does," Linda offers, her expression revealing that she's already confirmed.

"Anyone want to go for a walk?" Chandra asks, which prompts a barking frenzy. "Guess that's my answer."

6

Outlines

With a satisfying snap, the overhead fluorescent lights come to life. I breathe in the cool, dry air of the Mint Flamingo Bungalows Community Center and cough slightly.

Instead of refreshing, the air is tainted with a faint tang of leftover brussels sprouts, fish, and hot glue. Flecks of leftover glitter sparkle in the bright light. I assume yesterday's luncheon to raise funds for the local elementary school went well. Normally, I'd have been in the thick of it. But adulthood called and instead I had a day full of appointments. Maybe I can sneak a look at the posters when we're done?

A harsh squeak brings me back to the moment, Brad has stopped short to avoid crashing into me, his sneakers gripping onto the linoleum floor. Startled he mutters my name under his breath and grabs me around the waist to steady us.

"Sorry— I was thinking about the fundraiser prep," I offer as an apology and explanation. Brad kisses the back of my head and walks around me, a knowing smile on his face. This is nothing that he isn't used to.

"Girl, you better thank your stars with that one," Chandra tells me, nodding at Brad and smirking. Linda and Desmond chuckle and walk around us, on a mission to set up the conference room.

"Every day since my sophomore year," grinning and remembering the day Brad asked me out, my cheeks flush. I thought he was joking when he asked me to a bonfire on the beach. We'd been friends for a year but I'd had the biggest crush on him from day one. The cute surfer boy I met in my freshman social studies class, has turned into the man of my dreams over the last thirteen years. My cheeks warm and I know it's time to get back to our task. Clearing my throat, I gesture to a door on the opposite wall. "The conference room is this way..." Cackling at my embarrassment, Chandra steps in front of me.

Brad and Seb beat us into the room. The door is propped open and the lights on. At the door, Chandra and I gasp in unison. The small room is musty, cluttered, and about ten degrees warmer than the main community room. The scent of brussels sprouts and fish clings to the air and is no longer mildly unpleasant. It's downright foul.

"Stanky!" Chandra exclaims while pulling her t-shirt over her nose and mouth.

"I have to say, this is very unpleasant," Linda says, obviously appalled. "Adding airing the place out to our standards for use." She looks at Desmond, he is already making a note on a cast-off legal pad. Seemingly pleased, she leaves the room. I assume she needs a breathe of semi-fresher air.

Wincing, I pinch my nose. Surveying the room, I spot an ancient metal box fan in the corner and point to it. Brad lifts the fan and strides quickly to the window. A few tugs on the sash reveal it is fairly stuck. Humidity has swollen the frame, and it screeches as he fights to open it wide enough to wedge the opening enough to place the fan. A small eternity later and the warm, funky air is being sucked out.

With a screeching hiss, the faint sweetness of orange blossoms overtakes the room, Linda is aggressively spraying air freshener. Through the hazy, cloud of spray, she says, "Found it in the bathroom." In a moment, we're all able to breathe through our noses, the sounds of mouth breathing has dissipated with the fug of fish.

Satisfied with our efforts, we clear space at the table and empty Chandra's overstuffed tote bag. Desmond wheels a large whiteboard from the back of the room over to the edge of the table. Squealing with delight, I grab the new pack of markers. Grateful that we'll be able to get to work without a trip to the store.

"Shall we?" Chandra asks, tapping her fingers against the board, her bright red nails clack loudly. Heads nod all around the room. Part of me is in shock that she's is up for this. I figured she would tell me to mind my own business and let the police handle the incident. Who knows? Maybe Chandra is carried away by our excitement.

"Let's split the board into sections." Grabbing a thick black marker, she sketches columns onto the bright white surface. Letting the expert get to work, we plop into chairs and watch Chandra organize the board.

In a few strokes, she outlines areas for case details, first responders, witnesses, reports, evidence, suspects, and notes. Quickly she lists the location, date and times in the case details column, the names of those of use on scene in the witness category, then the names of the responding officers.

"It will get us started for now. We can add to it as we go." Standing back to survey her work, she chews lightly on the marker cap. Nodding briskly, she pops the marker out of her mouth and whirls to face us. "Who wants to go first?"

Seb politely raises his hand, mimicking a student in a classroom, "Since I was the first to arrive, should I start?" Chandra extends the marker like a queen with a scepter. He bows and gracefully slides the marker from her outstretched hand, wiping the wet cap on the leg of his shorts. Took one for the team with that move. He begins with the case details column, writing in all the information he can remember. Then in witnesses he adds Mrs. Jenkins and Malcolm. Turning to me, he passes over the marker.

I'm wracking my brain trying to come up with additional thoughts. The only things springing to mind are images of the damage to the bakery. Staring at the board, I am lost in the scene. Until a throat clears behind me. Looking over my shoulder, Linda flips her hand in a quick, tight circle, indicating I should go ahead or maybe hurry up. I'm not sure but do realize that it's taking me way too long. Blushing slightly, I step to the board. Assuming we can make changes if I pick the wrong spot, I head to case details. Calling up the images, intentionally this time, I make quick notes of the items damaged. In the notes column, I add "see photos". Mentally, setting a reminder to print them. Satisfied, I smile and pass the marker to Linda.

Walking back to the table, my watch dings. A reminder note from Brad, "Print Photos" set for tomorrow at 10 a.m. With a giggle, I take my seat and whisper, "Thanks, babe!" He smiles and winks at me, melting my heart. He knows there was a zero chance I'd remember to print the photos.

Linda adds in her details, including quite a few on the suspects and their vehicle. I am in awe of her recall. She too leaves a note that she'll print photos. But in her case, it is a guarantee she remembers to ASAP. As she slides her chair out, I whisper, "How in the world did you remember all that?" I motion to her notes and a small drawing showing the positions of everyone on the scene.

"I was a teacher for over thirty years," she sweetly responds. "Highly detailed incident reports were more common than you'd imagine. Committing events to memory is a necessary skill." With a sage nod of her head, she hands the marker to Brad.

"What's this for?" he says, his brows furrow in confusion.

"Bradley, as you reminded us earlier, you were there as well. Even if only virtually, it still counts," Linda says with a mix of light reprimand and humor.

"Ahh…yes, I sure was. Let me think for one sec," Brad stands with a salute and walks the handful of steps to the board. He paces back and forth a few times. Approaching the board, he starts to draw instead of write. Murmurs of understanding bubble up. He's drawing the bumper sticker from the car. Shrugging his shoulders with a sheepish grin, he drops into the seat beside me.

"I was worried it wouldn't be clear in the pictures. And I could swear I've seen it before, but can't come up with where," he explains. I pat his knee and smile at him, pleased with his contribution. He may think it's insignificant, but at this stage, nothing is too small to ignore.

Chandra approaches the board and takes a series of photos. Which is brilliant and I wish I'd thought of it. There's always a chance someone could erase the notes in the spirit of tidying up. Satisfied, she slides her phone into her pocket. I know what's coming next.

"You got any pie?" she asks and bats her lashes at me. Laughter erupts throughout the room.

"You know I do. You were in the fridge earlier," I say, still laughing. "Y'all head to the house, I'll lock up and meet you there." They leave the room single-file and I find myself giggling again. They're led by Linda, and look like students dismissed for lunch.

Slowly, I close up the community center and give one last spritz of air freshener for good measure. It still smells a little funky in here. But that's a tomorrow problem.

7

Edna

A tinny horn beeping relentlessly startles me while I am locking the door to the community center. Without turning, I can guess who it is. Before I have the key out of the lock, a piercing nasal voice rings across the empty lot.

"CiCi Larkin!"

My heart sinks a little. Edna Sparks, my octogenarian nemesis is home from her cruise. Sighing loudly, I plaster the biggest smile I can muster onto my face and force my shoulders off my earlobes. Slowly turning, I face Edna.

"Welcome back!" I trill, waving enthusiastically in her direction. My voice feels tight, and the words squeak at the ending. Classy CiCi, classy. She won't know she intimidates me at all.

Edna simply stares at me from the driver's seat of a shiny, new golf cart. I wonder if glowers is a better word. Doesn't matter, she's got me locked in her sights. My palms are slick with nervous sweat, and I shift the keys to avoid dropping them. No need for her to see how she gets to me. Stuffing the keys in my front pocket, I clasp my hands tightly in front of my waist.

"Everything, okay?" I ask. Unconsciously, I lick my suddenly bone-dry lips.

"I thought there was intruder," she barks, "instead it's only you." Pursing her lips and frowning, she doesn't hide her disappoint and that *you* feels like a kick to the shin. I catch a glimpse of a hefty nine-iron golf club in the front seat. My mouth drops open, and I whisper, "Oh my..." Edna follows my gaze and breaks into a surprisingly mischievous grin. My shock clearly delights her.

"Did you think I'd come unprepared?" With a cackle, she slams down the accelerator and tears away from the curb. Stunned, I watch her taillights quickly dim as she speeds down the street. I honestly had no idea that those little carts could move so fast. That woman is one surprise after another and rarely ever is it a good surprise. Shaking my head, I return to the task of locking the door. I may forget to lock my own house but never the community center.

Jogging into the darkness toward home, I relax, acknowledging that the night feels safer knowing Edna is patrolling with a golf club and a bad attitude. No one in their right mind would take her on.

***

Huffing and puffing, I fling open the front door and savor the cool air. Voices carry through the house from the lanai out back. Smiling, picturing everyone gathered around a perfectly chilled key lime pie. Cooking my not be my forte, but key lime pies are. Over the years, I've nailed down the recipe and it is consistently delicious.

Running feet herald the arrival of the dogs. I'm met with slobbery kisses by all three as I drop to floor to untie my shoes. Scooping up the smaller dogs, I head for the porch. Darla runs behind us, bumping me with her head hinting that she wanted to be carried as well. Giving in, I struggle to add her to my arms. She wraps her paws around my neck and clings to me as we make our way through the house. Teetering onto the porch, I clumsily walk down the stairs. Walking while three dogs is far from graceful.

The group has expanded to include Moshe and Francine Cohen. They've lived across the street from us for nearly a year, having relocated from Philadelphia. We bonded together over Francine's stolen wallet and are more like family than friends. Brad had grabbed a second pie from the freezer and there is plenty to go around. A bottle of Cuban rum has made its way onto the table as well. Small tulip-shaped tumblers sit in front of each person. Seeing me, Brad lifts a glass in my direction and waves me to sit with him on the chaise lounge. A chorus of "CiCi" erupts and I curtsy before setting down my canine cargo and dropping onto the chair.

"Guess who I ran into?" cocking an eyebrow and looking point-edly around the table, I wait for them to guess.

"The queen of the bungalows?" Desmond asks with a grimace.

"Nailed it!" I shoot finger guns in his direction, "She got me at the community center. Apparently, she was concerned I was an intruder and came armed with a massive golf club to bludgeon me with."

"Doggone!" Chandra exclaims. "I suppose if anyone could intim-idate a thief with a golf club, it'd be her." Heads nod around the table. I can imagine her swinging it like a samurai in a battle. There's no doubt in my mind she'd be the victor.

"Weirdly, I felt safe knowing she's terrorizing potential thieves, chasing them around in that canary yellow golf cart with a club," I reflect.

"I would too. Between her and the network of neighborhood gremlins she's accumulated, we're all under continual surveillance," Moshe chimes in. "She got me last week for my trashcan and recy-cling on the street. Telling me that I've lived here long enough to know recycling is every other Monday."

"We're frequent victims of the trashcan police," Brad says with a chuckle.

Around the table, recent offenses are shared— lawn clippings in the street, packages on porches, leaving outdoor lights on overnight. The list could go on for days. We laugh about it, all aware of the undercurrent of stress Edna creates in the neighborhood. Linda once referred to her as a "boil" which sounds mean, until you've interacted with her for more than a moment. After the thefts last summer, I'd genuinely and naively thought we were turning a corner and may become friends. Then she threw a bag of trash on our porch with a note that she knew I'd been littering. The brief respite ended in that one encounter. Following that day, an all-out war began for a few months. Until she went on a month-long cruise with her sister, Evelyn. It had been a peaceful month. Her lead cronies, Fredrick and Dina Avalon and Hubert Walters, were reasonably pleasant. They'd call out a hello, instead of a made-up infraction, when walking in the evenings. It will be interesting to see how they'll act now that she's back.

The night slowly winds down with Seb and Chandra as the last to leave as usual. Brad and I fall into bed around midnight, exhausted beyond words. While today had not gone as planned, it ended on a high note. Curling against my husband's warm body, I am asleep in seconds.

8

Picture This

Azúcar doesn't stay closed for long. Seb opens early the next morning, greeted by a group of undercaffeinated and hungry locals.

Grateful for two days off, I plan to use them wisely. By 9 a.m. I am tucked in at the community center with a jumbo iced coffee, my laptop, and our crime board. Leaving the window cracked overnight gave the room a chance to air out and the smell is a mere whisper of what it was. Totally bearable now.

Sliding the whiteboard over to the table, I lean back to survey our progress from last night. The majority of information is listed in the case details and notes sections. Thanks to Brad's quick thinking and reminder note, I remembered to print a selection of photos. By some miracle, we even had a new roll of tape in the junk drawer to put the pictures up on the board.

Laying the photos out on the table, I toy with different layouts. None of it looks right or makes sense the way I need it to. Shuffling the stacks around, I shriek when the door opens. A grinning Linda enters with a container of cookies. Trailing behind her are Desmond and Mirabel Hernandez. Without fail, Mirabel lights up the room—part her personality and part her outfits. At ninety-three, she's as spry as many in their seventies. Today she is wearing turquoise gauchos, a gauzy tunic in a Picasso inspired print, and white slip-on sneakers. As usual, her glasses coordinate. She sports chic tangerine, square-framed amber tinted glasses. On me, they'd look like I was prepping for a snorkeling session. On Mirabel, they're adorable.

"Want some company?" Linda calls out cheerily and passes me the cookies. Nodding, I greedily crack open the lid and am delighted to see the powdery white balls. Mexican Wedding cookies are hands-down my favorite.

"What have we got going on this time?" Mirabel asks while I stuff a cookie into my mouth. Holding up a finger, I chew as quickly as possible.

"Don't choke my dear, we'll fill her in," Linda says and pats my hand for me to settle down. Trying to power through the powdery cookie would be the end of me. I throw a thumbs up in her direction and slow my chewing to a reasonable pace. No need to choke in front of everyone. Death by cookie would be mortifying but very true to who I am.

While I munch through a few more cookies and sip my coffee, Linda and Desmond describe the events to Mirabel with the aid of the crime board. She offers appropriately timed 'ooh' and 'oh my' commentary. As I listen in, it dawns on me that none of the details shared by Mrs. Jenkins and Malcolm have made it onto the board. Dusting off my fingers, I reach for the cup of markers in the center of the table and bound over to the whiteboard. Wordlessly, the three step back to the row of chairs. Desmond swipes a couple of cookies while he watches me. Listing their names first, I jot down the timelines and information they provided. Taking time to riffle through my photos, I describe the struggle for the register and the baseball bat Malcolm had grabbed when chasing the thief. With the screenshots from my video call with Brad, I mark timestamps with the photos. When I move to the notes column, I pause, drumming my nails rhythmically on the edge of the board. There are scattered images in my mind of the damage to the shop.

Returning to the table, I begin sorting photos again. But, I remain stuck on how to order them on the board. The trio joins me and watches for a moment. The right sequence continues to elude me, I groan in frustration and scatter the printouts.

"Might I give it a try?" Mirabel asks. I forget that she was a librarian for many years, sorting and cataloging come naturally to her. Gesturing for her to continue, I step to the side. She walks to the other side of the table to give her a better view of the whiteboard. After studying it quietly for a moment, Mirabel begins to move the photos into columns, occasionally changing the position of one or two. Moments later, she steps back and says, "Try this my dear."

"Whoa!" I murmur, surveying the now organized images. "This is amazing!" I whisper, and slowly stretch for the tape Desmond is holding. My hands feel shaky, as silly as it is, I am suddenly afraid to move too quickly and mess this up. Is it nerves or the massive intake of sugar and caffeine? One never can tell.

One by one, the photos are taped to the board in the order Mirabel suggested. They paint the scene perfectly. Somehow after a brief overview of the case, she's organized not only by category but in chronological order. The flow has brought the crime board to life.

"That makes it a little easier, doesn't it?" Desmond says softly. I nod, immersed once again in yesterday's events.

"Do you think Mrs. Jenkins would be up for chatting with us?" I ask him, assuming since they've been friends since childhood, he would have a better idea.

"I can always call to find out," he responds with a smile.

***

My cell phone rings loudly with an unfamiliar techno beat. I stare at it briefly, debating if I'll answer. Surprise phone calls are usually scams or a bill I've forgotten to pay. Considering that it is a local number, I risk it and answer.

"CiCi?" a quavering, female voice asks after my brief hello. It sounds familiar but I can't place it.

"This is her," I respond, my tone is clipped and tight. In the split second of waiting for her reply, I regret answering.

"Oh good, this is Bernice Jenkins. Desmond shared your telephone number and said I should call when I feel up to it." Her words soothe my indecision, replacing it with a stab of guilt.

"Mrs. Jenkins!" I exclaim, "Thank you for the call."

"I'm sorry that it took me a few days to call. This has been…a lot to take in," she haltingly says. Her voice is thick with emotion, and I hear her sniffle when she pauses. A scratching noise crosses the line and I can picture Mrs. Jenkins wiping her face with a handkerchief.

"Please don't apologize!" I rush to reassure her. "Mostly, I wanted to see how you are and if there's anything I can do to help." More sniffling and scratching come through. Giving her time, I wait for her to continue. She calms after a moment.

"Malcolm and his sister have been in touch with the insurance company. Sadly, we can't have them in to begin assessing the damage until the police allow it. The police have spoken with us several times, but I am not sure how much progress is being made. So, we wait," a heavy sigh follows. "I know it's too early to feel like giving up. Yet, I can't help it."

"I'm sorry to hear it's moving slowly. It can take time to kick off an investigation." There isn't much I can say to reassure her. It probably does, there is so much red tape when it come to the start of an investigation. "Is there anything I can do to help?"

"Well…I'm glad you asked," she begins, "I remember hearing how you helped Francine a few months ago. Is there anything you can do?" Her tone belies her nerves, shaking slightly and ending on a breathless note. Despite having started to investigate on my own and asking Desmond if she'd be willing to talk with me, I am still caught slightly off guard, which causes me to hesitate momentarily. This is what I wanted, right? Then why am I not answering?

Taking a deep breath, I speak slowly, "I'd be happy to help," adding noncommittally, "however I can. Was there something you had in mind?"

"I don't know dear, but I do know you helped Francine. I don't want this to drag on forever with no resolution. We've got a business to run after all."

Her response makes me giggle softly. I can picture Mrs. Jenkins standing proudly at the door of the bakery, welcoming in her regular customers. She's an institution in the neighborhood and local business community. Getting her back up and running is a priority. Suddenly, I feel itchy to get down to work.

"Well, let's get you back to it!" I agree. We need to get her bakery open as soon as possible. Guiltily, I add, "I may or may not have already started."

"I suspected as much when Desmond called me," she admits. "Have you made much progress?"

"Not as much as I'd like. There are some things I'd like to run past you and get some of your insights."

"Of course, anything you need!"

"I appreciate it. Hearing from you will help me put the pieces together."

"Would you like to come over for some coffee? I just pulled a fresh pan of cinnamon rolls out of the oven."

"You're speaking my language!" I exclaim, my mouth watering at the thought of fresh pastries. Gerardo's is not only a local favorite but a family favorite. When my parents and aunt are in town, they snap up dozens of baked goods and take them home to freeze. They cannot get enough. "I can get your address and head your way in about fifteen minutes."

9

Roll the Tape

Thankfully Mrs. Jenkins doesn't live far from me. Enroute, I stop at the store to get her flowers. Something about those sunny colors and fresh blooms that is a mood booster no matter what is going on. After all she's had going on, this is definitely the time for flowers. Sunflowers and fluffy greenery fit the bill, bringing some extra warmth to the day.

Taking full advantage of the slightly cooler weather (mid-80s= hello Florida fall!), Mrs. Jenkins and I sit in the shade out by the pool. Oversized banana plants and palms tower around the edges of the yard, creating a little oasis from the golden, mid-morning sun. Despite the heat, we each have a steaming of coffee and fresh from the oven cinnamon roll. It's the perfect cinnamon filling to icing ratio and I end up burning my tongue in my haste to get to the first bite. Exhaling harshly through my open mouth, I attempt to cool the burn. Not as effective as I'd hoped, but it helps slightly. A delighted groan escapes unexpectedly. This is in the top five cinnamon rolls I've had. And I eat *a lot* of pastries.

"Shall we get to it?" Mrs. Jenkins asks when I'm popping my second bite into my mouth. I nod vigorously, my mouth too full to speak. "Well, let me think. My granddaughter-in-law, Melody, saw some strange things on our security cameras."

I gulp down the hot coffee and ask, "Can you define strange?"

"At the time it didn't seem like much, motion she couldn't quite capture, sound alerts, one of the cameras actually went offline two weeks ago."

"Did you let the police know?"

"I honestly didn't think of it until after I spoke with you. The events were all so small. When I told the kids about it, they suggested I let you know and then we can decide what to do." My eyes bulge slightly that she considered talking to me first as the better choice. Never in my life would I have thought that. Now that I'm here, imposter syndrome rears its head aggressively. A sweat breaks out on my forehead and lower back, shuffling slightly in my seat, I make an effort to appear professional. Hard to do in my current state but I'll at least try.

"To start, can I take a few notes?" Reaching for my bag, I slide out a small colorful notebook and pen.

"Of course, I would love it if you could help me in anyway." She smiles so sweetly that I feel myself relax a little. My focus shifts from worry to my genuine desire to help one of my neighbors through a tough time.

"Thanks!" I chirp, mood boosted suddenly. "Can you tell me what was the first in the strange events y'all noticed?"

"From what I remember, it was the motion lights out back. Malcolm and Melody were at the bakery early two weeks ago. It must have been around 4 a.m. They like to get a much earlier start than I do these days," chuckling softly, she points to the quad cane next to her chair, indicating her age. "Melody gets the security system alerts sent to her phone and watch. When she was preparing to remove some dough from the proofing cabinet, the buzzing caught her attention. If it had been a few minutes later, she would have already removed her watch and most likely wouldn't have noticed."

"What did the alert say?"

"It was a generic alert of motion captured on the camera above the rear door. To silence the persistent alert, Melody opened the app on her phone to acknowledge it. When she opened it, there were a series of alerts. She couldn't see more than an outline, but it was a bulky figure in a dark sweatshirt. It struck her as so odd because of the temperature that morning. The humidity was so high, her glasses fogged up while walking to the car. A sweatshirt was not appropriate for the weather." Mrs. Jenkins appears slightly offended that the person on camera was wearing an outfit she deemed unsuitable for an early-autumn morning in Florida.

"Was she able to get any details on the person? How tall they were? Male or female?"

Mrs. Jenkins stops for a moment, slicing a bite from her cinnamon roll while she thinks. "Malcolm went out to check, despite Melody's protests, I would like to add. By the time he got out the door, the person was gone. No one even in the alley behind the building." My excitement dims with this revelation. "From the video clips and picture, we guess it was a man. He was broad, like a football player." Her description brings to mind the people in the getaway car, the passenger filling most of the front seat. Realizing I've not written any of this down, I pause my questions for a moment to make a few notes.

"You mentioned there were strange things, was it all on the same day or different?'

"All different and nothing similar between them."

"Can you share the next time the cameras alerted?" I sit with my pen poised in the air.

"Well, let me think for a second," I drink my coffee, giving her time to recall the events, "I believe it was a few days later but the exact date escapes me. I wish I'd thought to invite Malcolm or Melody," she muses aloud.

"It's okay to give me the basics and maybe they can provide more details later?" I suggest. This is too good to derail by calling or waiting for them to arrive.

"I'll do my best," she reassures and once again goes quiet while remembering the details. "It must have been sometime between midnight and when they arrived at four o'clock." The suspense of waiting is killing me. A blend of anxiety from wanting to hurry her along mixed with the knowledge that I need to wait it out makes my leg bounce, like I'm prepping for a race. "The camera kept sending alerts to Melody, but the screen was black. She'd shown Malcolm and they assumed it was some sort of malfunction or the batteries had died." She pauses again and I softly drum my nails on the open page of my notebook. "I'm trying to think of what was wrong with the camera, at the moment, I can't get exactly what it was."

"Had the battery died?" I prompt, unable to restrain myself any further.

"No. Malcolm checked the camera. It was recording and the batteries were nearly full. But there was something over the lens. Whatever it was had blocked the view." This spikes my interest once again and my mind begins a visual slide show of all the common things it could be. Tape? Gum? Paint? The images are disrupted by a very loudly ringing phone. Startled, the pen flies from my hand and falls to the ground. As I bend to pick it up, Mrs. Jenkins pulls a cordless landline phone from her dress pocket. I do my best to distract myself while she takes the call, I may be nosy but I do respect other people's privacy when possible She answers with a loud, "Jenkins' residence." Muffled voices and laughter come through the call.

"Of course you can! Come on over, CiCi is here and I want you to meet her," she responds to whomever is on the line. With a brief goodbye, she disconnects. By that point, I've given up the pretense of minding my business. "My daughter was on her way to the store and thought about stopping by. But, she saw a car in the driveway and kept going. She always worries about me, so she called to check in. Never can be too careful, you know. She said she felt a little silly when I answered, but, I think Serena will be able to help with details. She's much sharper than I am." Her affection for her daughter shows in her tone. "It will only be a few minutes, she was at the stop sign right up the street."

"Great! I'd love to meet her and the more the merrier in these instances." Using the gap in conversation, I grab my fork and spear an enormous chunk of cinnamon roll, then shove it into my mouth. As I am attempting to chew without choking, a voice calls out from inside the house.

"We're here," Mrs. Jenkins responds. A petite woman with silver-streaked dark hair, wearing oversized sunglasses and running gear hops out the backdoor. I immediately regret the tank and jean shorts thrown on after Bernice's call. In her hands is a plate with a cinnamon roll and an empty coffee mug.

"Hey Mama!" she chirps. Before plopping into one of the open chairs, she kisses her mother on the top of her head and reaches for the coffee carafe. While pouring, she makes eye contact and introduces herself. "I'm Serena DeLuca, Bernice's daughter. You must be the CiCi I keep hearing about." A broad smile creases her face. She radiates the kind of warmth that makes strangers feel comfortable. The self-consciousness disappears in an instant.

"It's nice to meet you! I was hoping we'd meet," I respond pleasantly.

"Yes! Mama and Malcolm were all abuzz the day of the robbery. They couldn't believe you ran over to help. Most people wouldn't have run to their rescue."

"It was nothing! Just checking on my neighbors," I say in an attempt to deflect as my face warms.

"Don't you do that," Mrs. Jenkins chastises. "What you did was remarkable, and you should accept that praise with pride."

I bow my head slightly and nod, desperate for her not to see the tears stinging my eyes. Furthering my distraction technique, I reposition my pen and notebook. Lining them up in a very organized, and not-very-CiCi way. There's a moment of awkwardness, almost a silent acknowledgement of my discomfort.

"Would you like to get back to it?" Mrs. Jenkins asks. My sunglasses bounce up and down as I aggressively agree. "Serena, do you remember when the camera wasn't working behind the bakery a few weeks ago?"

"I do. That was a weird morning. The whole family kept getting repeat alerts from the camera, but we couldn't see anything. When the kids got to the bakery, Malcolm got the ladder out to check it," Serena adds. She shares many of the same details, assumptions about batteries, but then gives some new details. "The camera had a sticker over the lens. It was one of those big smiley face stickers that the corner market gives out to kids. Malcolm remembers seeing their logo on the bottom edge. Isn't that goofy? I can't figure out how that would have made it onto the camera." She shakes her head and drinks from her coffee. Clearly, the sticker on the camera doesn't connect to anything for her.

I hedge my bets and ask, "Did Malcolm take a picture of the sticker by any chance?"

Shaking her head, Serena says, "Not that I know of. He did hold it up for the camera for the family to see. I'd guess he threw it away in the cans in the alley. Knowing my son, he wouldn't bring a grimy sticker into the bakery, even if it was just to trash it." She and Mrs. Jenkins share a knowing glance and chuckle. In my mental notes, I catalogue Malcolm as germ conscious.

"What are the changes the video clips are still in the app?"

"Pretty good I'd say. After those two incidents, Melody started to get a weird inkling that something was going on behind the bakery. I'm embarrassed to admit, I brushed it off and figured it was kids up to no good," Serena tells me as she picks up her phone. Tapping a few times, she whispers, "Success!" and turns her phone for me to see. On the screen, the image goes from all black to smudging and finally a sticker fills the screen followed by Malcolm mugging a face and sticking out his tongue. The moment makes all three of us laugh momentarily.

"Is there any way you could send me the video from that day and any of the images from the first incident?"

"What first incident?" Serena asks with a hint of alarm. Caught off guard, I freeze thinking of how to answer. Before I can speak, Mrs. Jenkins takes the lead.

"We didn't think much of it at the time. A few days before the sticker, there were several alerts for motion on the camera when Malcolm and Melody were at the bakery early one morning. It captured someone out in the alley, but the images didn't have much detail."

"You mean, there might have been someone watching the bakery?" Serena nearly shouts, her eyes bulge as she stares at me.

"It sounds like that might be the case. One set of alerts could be a coincidence, but add in the sticker and it seems to be more of a pattern." I respond cautiously, careful not to give the impression of certainty. "Best course of action would be to share the images and videos with the detective handling the case. And...me too." A sly smile crosses my face.

"Here, put your number in," Serena passes her phone to me once again. "Can you remind me who the detective is?"

10

Spotted

"**N**ora!" I call out while pressing the plastic lid firmly in place. The snap is so satisfying. Every single time. It is a little celebration of a completed order. I can't revel too long and turn to prep the next order. This morning has been non-stop, which still surprises me considering the recent events on this street. All of the local customers seem unfazed and the dwindling tourists seem unaware. A high-pitched "thanks" and the iced latte with cinnamon cold foam is swiped off the counter before I can turn back around.

The squelch of the frother finishing mostly drowns out sound around me briefly. But as I am pouring the milk onto a steaming coffee, I hear, "Uh...CiCi?" Assuming it to be an order issue, I spin and slosh the hot milk all across the worksurface.

"Oh geez, I'm so sorry," the woman at the counter says. She looks vaguely familiar but I cannot place her. "I didn't mean to startle you, just wanted to say hello and thank you before I head out." Wracking my brain, I have no clue who she is.

"No worries at all..."I trail off, regretting thinking her name would pop up spontaneously.

"Gah! I'm not doing so great with this," she admits with a blush, "I'm Melody Deluca, Malcolm's wife. We've never actually met, so please, don't be embarrassed."

Relief washes over me and my furrowed brows are replaced with a genuine smile. Wiping my hands on a bar towel, I extend one in her direction across the counter. "So nice to meet you!" She pumps my still damp hand firmly, both of us pretending not to notice.

"I wanted to say hello and tell you how much I appreciate you helping Malcolm and Granny Bernice. It means so much to the whole family!"

"More than happy to help, it's what neighbors do," again deflecting my discomfort at the recognition.

"Yeah, I hear you keep saying that. But, I doubt most would," she says. Her face remains pleasant but now has a firm set to her jaw. Gulping slightly, I simply nod in thanks. She's vaguely threatening despite her friendliness, completely opposite of her mother-in-law.

"Well, I like to help whenever I can," I say instead.

"Glad to hear it," she begins. "I have some other information that I'd like to make sure you have. Honestly, it may be nothing, but I'd rather you have it." If I could see my expression, I'd assume it would be like one of those cartoon characters with stars shining in their eyes.

"Oh my goodness— of course! At this point, every little observation matters. I'll be working until two, so maybe we could chat after that?" I suggest. She tells me her number and I promise to call on my way home. Could her info be what we need to move the case forward?

***

"Can you talk?" I ask in an over-the-top whisper. Not sure why I am compelled to whisper, I'm done with work for the day.

"Why are you being so weird?" Chandra responds. Definitely not whispering. Apparently, I always picture her mid-crime scene investigation. But, more likely she's in her cubicle at the station.

"Oh, I thought maybe you were at work," I say, chuckling at myself.

"I am but I'm stuck cleaning out the car at the moment, so I've got all the time in the world to chat." Her voice becomes muffled, followed by scratching. She's tucked in the phone between her shoulder and chin, freeing up her hands. Chandra isn't a fan of earphones, according to her they 'decrease situational awareness'. She does have a point— I had mine in during a run-in with Edna, didn't hear her coming, resulting in a plant being thrown at me.

"Goodie! A captive audience," I say cheerily. Chandra sighs loudly, but doesn't object. "Guess who I met with?"

"I have some guesses..." Wariness in her voice.

"Mrs. Jenkins, her daughter, AND granddaughter-in-law," dramatically drawing out the last part and twirling in a circle, deranged ballerina style. Taking her silence as a positive, I continue, "They had some enlightening moments to share."

Suddenly, a roaring wind blares through the line and a muttered, "Daggone it!" Chandra argues with herself and the vacuum cleaner for a few seconds. "You still there?"

"Yep! I didn't want to disturb your verbal assault on the vacuum," I tease.

"I couldn't find the off switch and had my end muted, or so I thought," she grumbles. "Tell me more about these moments. I'm sure I'll have questions."

"There has been some sketchy stuff happening for weeks around the bakery. Cameras catching movement, stickers over the le—"

"Did you say stickers?" Chandra interrupts.

"Sure did, they'd thought the camera was offline but instead there was one of those smiley face stickers from the market over the lens."

"Which camera? When? Do they still have it?" she flings out the questions rapidly.

"Ummm... it was two-ish weeks before the break-in and over the camera facing the alley, the one above the door. Don't get your hopes too high, he threw the sticker out right after peeling it from the camera. It didn't seem ominous at the time."

"Shoot— any pictures?"

"Actually, yes. There are screen grabs of the lurker and of the sticker. But, if you'd have an ounce of patience, I'll answer your questions before you can interrupt." Chandra snorts but stays quiet for a second. Scrolling through my photos, I select the blurred camera images and send them to her phone.

"I assume you've sent them in?"

"I asked Mrs. Jenkins daughter to send to me and Detective Cassidy,"

"So, that means you got'em?" she asks, her tone conspiratorial. I notice a change as we've chatted. Her speech slows and her Louisiana-drawl thicker, meaning she's dialed into the conversation. The slower she talks, the more she focuses.

"Already sent them to you while we've been talking. " Excitement prickles the back of my neck. She's in! "It gets better though..."

"Spill it!"

"Malcolm's wife and I are meeting for coffee at four. Are you free?" The loud groan tells me that she isn't.

"Ugh! I wish, but I'm on until seven. Catch me up after, cher?" Promising to chat after she's done, I leave her to get back to cleaning.

***

Four o'clock sneaks up on me and I find myself jogging from the parking lot at five after. From the last stop sign, I shot off a text that I was running late. It's not like I was doing anything important either, simply puttering around in the yard. The next thing I knew it was 3:48, leaving not enough time to make the drive and be on time.

Almost there.

Bouncing on my heels at the crosswalk, a half dozen or so cars crawl past. When the road clears, I step out into street. My phone begins to chime, with the 4 p.m. alarm I'd set after chatting with Melody, earlier in the day. That's how committed I was to being on time, not that it's done me much good. Nothing like leaving a bad impression for our first meet up.

Distracted with fishing for the phone in the bottom of my tote, I am not paying attention while crossing the street. Triumphantly cheering for myself, I wrap my fingers around the phone. As I pull it from my bag, I open the screen to silence the alarm. In that moment, tires squeal and a force topples me to the ground.

Stunned, I lie in silence on the ground.

The blow has knocked the wind out of me and I struggle to take in a breath. Writhing on the pavement, a searing pain in my right knee worsens my inability to draw a breath. Distant voices shout, but the words are unintelligible. Trying to catch my breath is the only thing I can focus on.

Until a person drops to the ground next to me.

"CiCi!! Can you hear me? CiCi!" the male voice shouts. I can hear, but can't speak. Continuing to gasp, I frantically grab onto their arm as my vision swims. "Someone call 911!" he shouts, now holding both of my hands.

"Breathe with me, hun, you'll be okay," a soft female voice murmurs to me. She places a warm hand on my shoulder and gently pats me. The pain in my chest eases slightly and I guppy breathe sips of air. Freeing one of my hands, I reach for her. She coos and repetitively whispers, "You're alright, darlin', you're alright." It reminds me of a mother soothing an injured baby and tears slide down the sides of my cheeks. Suddenly, I miss my mother, aching for her to be with me.

"Call," gasp, "Brad," gasp. Both heads nod in unison and I see them looking around for my phone. Grimacing, I realize the phone is under my backside. Is it safe them to move me? Having never been in this situation, I have no clue. But, I point underneath my back. Seeming to understand what I am saying, the woman gingerly slides a hand beneath me. The cracked edges of the screen are sharp against my skin as the phone grinds between me and the pavement. Pleased with herself, she holds up the lit up but shattered phone to my face. Thankfully it unlocks without further intervention.

"Do you know her?" she asks the man at my side.

Bobbing his head vigorously, he tells her, "Si, I mean yes, we work together in the cafe." Recognition dawns and I whisper, "Tev." He shifts his focus to me once again, and reassures me, smoothing my hair away from my face. "I'll call Seb, he'll know what to do."

Never once have either of these kind souls fully released my hands. They alternately pat me and squeeze my hands. Each doing their best to comfort me while also keeping me awake. Slowly, my breaths are becoming easier. Pain shoots through my right knee and now my shoulder, but otherwise I feel generally intact. It seems that way anyhow.

"The ambulance is coming, ma'am," a third voice calls out. Afraid to move too much, I smile weakly in their general direction.

"Brad? Is this Brad?" the woman calmly says into the phone. "My name is Dottie. I don't want you to panic, darlin', but I'm with your wife. She's been hurt in an accident." Mumbled responses that I can't make out follow. Knowing Brad, he has a flood of questions for her and justifiably. "She's banged up, but awake. I'll stay with her until the ambulance or you are here, whichever is fast— no, no, she's awake... okay, one second..." She tapers off and holds the phone away from her face. By the distinct tone, she's starting a video call. Seconds later, my husband's terrified face fills the screen.

"Hi baby," he says quietly, voice catching. Tears pool in his eyes. Seeming him the dam breaks and I cry out loud, sobs wrack my body and I wince with the pain as it vibrates through me. "You're alright, I want you to take some slow deep breaths. Remember how we practiced with your sister before the baby?" He imitates the Lamaze breathing we'd spent hours learning. Calmly, I watch him through the screen but realize, deep breaths are beyond me in the moment. Still, I give it my best shot. "Can one of you tell me where you are? I'm on my way to my car now." He pauses for the answer, but continues the organized breathing pattern. Rolling his hand, he gestures for me to keep pace with him.

"We're at the corner of West 7th and Calendula. Right in front of the florist," Trev answers quickly. "I called Seb already, he said he's calling Chandra.

Brad mumbles, "Thanks, man!" and continues the breathing exercise. A wave of dizziness washes over me and I can't tell if it is from the deep breaths or the accident. In a moment of unspoken kindness, Dottie rests the phone of my chest, I can still hear Brad as he talks to me, but don't have the energy to watch the screen. "Baby, can you hear me?" he says softly. A whispered, "Yep", is all that I have. "I'll say a prayer with you— you rest until the ambulance comes." His deep, soothing voice begins as his truck door slams closed and the engine roars to life. My eyes close and the dizziness begins to lessen.

Sirens wail in the distance yanking me back to the reality of the moment and away from Brad's voice. Those sirens are for me.

11

911- What's Your Emergency?

Silence surrounds us in the absence of the sirens. For a split second, I consider that maybe I've gone deaf.

"Hey cher, you holding up?" Chandra asks, dropping to her knees beside me. Dottie and Tev stay with me but shuffle to create space.

"I'm not dead...but I don't feel so hot," I admit.

"Humor intact," she says and smiles at me. Reaching for my phone, she holds it up for Brad. "Our gal is coming around." He grins at us through the phone and he thanks her for getting there so quickly.

"I should be to town in about thirty-five minutes," he laments. Sirens again sound in the background.

"My chariot awaits," I murmur, prompting tense laughter from those around me.

In another moment, three burly men race through the path cleared in the growing crowd. The clatter of a stretcher accompanies them. Some hands reach out and clap them on their passing backs as a thanks.

"There's our VIP!" a booming voice with a thick old Florida accent calls on approach. He squats on the ground next to me as the two others begin lowering the stretcher and opening bags. Seamlessly, the team gets to work. "My name is Howie, these knuckleheads are Tommy and Gus." Pausing to do a quick look at my eyes, he shines a bright light, forcing me to squint. "Can you tell me how you got into this pickle?" His tone is calm and steady, he smiles but it doesn't reach his eyes. As I begin telling him what I recall, he gently places a stiff plastic collar around my neck. A whispered, "Small poke," followed by pinch in my arm surprises me and I squeak, another of the team has started an IV.

"I don't really know. The street was clear when I started to cross, but my alarm was going off—oh God! Chandra! I forgot that I am supposed to be meeting Melody!" I wail.

"Calm yourself, girly. I'll get hold of her," she soothes. "Go ahead and finish with these fellas first." Nodding with the stiff collar on is impossible, instead I roll my eyes toward her. Turning things over to Chandra is my only option, she can deal with it.

The paramedics continue talking with me, asking a million questions, and then Howie tells me it's time to move. Based on the pain in my leg and now my head, this holds zero appeal. Grimacing, I stare at Howie, moving onto the stretcher sounds like it's going to be awful.

"We've given you a little double margarita in that IV, so this shouldn't be too bad. I just need you to do your best to stay stiff like a statue. I've gotta get a real hard board under your back. Fair warning, I am not going to be your favorite person..." he says with a strained smile. Bless him for attempting to add some humor.

As promised, being rolled on the hard board and taped into place was horrid. My leg screamed with pain and a tsunami of dizziness hit me. To add further indignity, I was strapped down and my head taped between two foam blocks. Briefly, I considered how I would get into the ambulance. Suddenly, I am hoisted into the air in a stomach-churning swoop. Without meaning to, I screech out loud. Startling Chandra, she fumbles my phone, nearly dropping it. Scrambling and terrified, I reach for her. She threads her hand through the straps and grips me tightly. I hear her murmuring into my phone, "She's okay, just scared." I appreciate her more in this moment than ever before.

"Cees— I gotta talk to the officer for a minute. They're taking photos and statements from the crowd. I'm letting him know that

I'm riding with you in the bus." She gestures up and over my face so I can see her hand. I squeeze tighter, dreading her leaving me. Tucking my phone onto my chest, she says, "Give me a sec?" to Howie and the crew. He nods tightly and they continue escorting me to the waiting ambulance.

"Can you hear me, baby?" I hear Brad's muffled voice.

"I'm with ya, babe." I do my best to speak loudly and clearly. The plastic collar makes it difficult to fully open my mouth. It comes out garbled and frustration builds. Tears again flood down he sides of my face, pooling in my ears. "How much longer?" I mumble.

"Almost there my sweet, I'll beat you to the hospital and won't leave you for a second," he promises in a thick voice, clearing his throat repeatedly. Brad is always in control of his emotions, it hurts my heart to hear the pain and stress in his tone.

"She's smiling for ya, my man. We're taking good care of her," Howie reassures Brad. I am so thankful for the effort he's making. "Alright ma'am, time to load up. There are gonna be a couple of bumps, so hold onto that phone."

In a jumble of wheels hitting the metal track, the gurney snaps into place in the back of the ambulance. Within seconds, I am clicked in and hooked up to a small machine. Chandra launches into the back door, or at least I assume she does. All I hear is stomping boots, rustling clothes, and a squeaking gun belt before I hear her voice beside me. She speaks quietly into her phone, the words entirely unintelligible.

***

Our arrival meant a flood of nurses and doctors in fluttering paper gowns and googles. Chandra was whisked from my side and into the hallway for all the initial activity. When the staff began checking me in, the nurse mentioned I already had company and it made the process less stressful. Relief flooded me with the realization that Brad was in the building and would be with me soon. Sadly, I wasn't immediately sprung from my plastic fortress despite my insistence that nothing in my neck hurt. I did try to plead my case, but wouldn't win until a few the X-rays prove it. Pretty sure, they took snapped images of me from head to toe. I am wheeled back to my room through the blindingly white hallways. The glaring overhead lights give the sensation of traveling at supersonic speed in space. It reminds me of all the Sci-Fi movies Brad has forced me to watch over the years.

"See, I promised I'd be here before you," Brad bends and gently kisses me. He's tall enough that leaning over the added bulk of the collar is no issue. "You know, you could have just called and asked me to come home early?" he says with a twinkle in his eye.

"Where would the fun be in that?"

"Seriously, this is enough close calls, honey. First the break-in and now this. I'm a little nervous to leave you home alone." Despite the teasing tone, I see the genuine fear for me in his eyes.

"Completely unrelated! Don't worry, no one is out to get me—," I begin, but before I can finish, Chandra cuts me off.

"Not so fast." Brad and I stare at her in shocked silence. I mean, he looks at her. My version is a whale-eyed stare from the corner of my eye, which I'm certain is precious to observe.

"There was a report that it was a small car. Passengers unknown. I'm not saying it was the same guys, just that something feels off about all of this. It's too soon to make a connection, but—-"

"At this point, everything matters," Brad and I say in unison. Chandra attempts to glower at us, the smile makes it hard and she ends up smirking.

"Move over this way, you're giving me eye strain and I don't need more problems," I beg and use a free hand to swoop her closer to the bed. "Tell me more about what the witnesses said." She shuffles over to lean on the back of Brad's chair.

"Nope. Not tainting you with that. You'll need to speak with the Detective first. Then I'll give you the scoop." This is not what I was hoping for but she does have a point. I am a little fuzzy on exactly what happened. Hearing what everyone else says isn't going to sharpen my memories. It likely would shape them into something inaccurate though.

"Was I summoned?" a female voice with a hefty Boston accent calls out from the doorway. Chandra and Brad turn to greet Detective Blair Cassidy. We'd met Blair and her husband Alan at a barbecue a few months ago.

"Hey, funny meeting you here," I mumble lamely from the stretcher.

"Girlfriend, I can't tell if trouble finds you or you find trouble," she teases.

"To be fair, neither can I," Brad responds and squeezes my shoulder.

"Can you tell me what you recall?" Blair asks, her tone shifting into business mode.

"I was rushing to meet Melody Deluca. She'd come into the coffee shop earlier in the day and asked if we could meet up. There were some weird events in the weeks before the break-in. Her family has asked me to help get it put together to share with the police." Which is mostly the truth, but I don't want to tell a Detective that I've launched an unsanctioned investigation. "I left the house late and was jogging from the parking lot down the street to the cafe. I was almost there when the light changed. Catching my breath for a second, I waited for the walk signal, I'm sure that I did. Just as I stepped into the street, my alarm started ringing. Instead of paying attention, I started rooting around for it. The phone was all the way in the bottom of my purse. In the moment, that felt more of a priority than getting across the street," stopping to get my fuzzy thoughts together, they're starting to scatter with the effort, "but, I swear, there were no cars coming. The next thing I knew, there were screeching tires and then something knocked me to the ground. That's all I know. No one with me shared anything they saw or heard. My guess is they would have at least seen it, there were so many people waiting with me." I rush through the story, not from anxiety. Simply from a lack of details to provide. I am antsy for Chandra and Blair to share what they know.

"Mrs. Larkin?" the doctor asks as he approaches my bed. He's accompanied by Freddy, my nurse from earlier, and someone I haven't met yet. "Time to break you out!" he says cheerily. Working as a team, they cut through the tape and undo the Velcro straps. Freeing my head, sound rushes in and in that moment I realize how muffled everything has sounded for the last hour or more.

"Ma'am, we're going to roll you onto your side. I can guarantee it ain't gonna feel great, but we'll be as gentle as we can," the nurse explains. "You're going to roll right up against me, Doc is going to give you another once over and Max is going to hold your leg still." In an expertly executed move, I am tipped up onto my left side, cradled by the nurse. Cold hands run down my back and legs. Wincing, my entire body tenses as he nears my knee.

"It appears the vehicle struck the right side of your body, and your knee took most of the impact. From the initial x-ray, there isn't a visible break. You're pretty bruised and swollen. I suspect there are additional injuries that aren't showing on the simple X-ray. I'd like to do more testing on your knee and this hip," the doctor advises. As he speaks, Freddy gently rests me back onto the much softer bed. Not having the hard board behind me makes this mattress feel heaven sent. Max begins strapping a soft brace around my knee, it stretches from mid-thigh to right above my ankle. "Sit tight and we'll get you finished up and home in the next couple of hours." My stomach growls loudly at the mention of going home. I regret skipping lunch, the day had become so busy and I kept meaning to grab a snack.

"Brad!" I squeak, and he rushes toward me in a near panic, "The dogs!"

"They're fine. I called Linda and she took them to her house," he smiles and reaches to touch my face. It feels good to smile and move without the plastic armor.

"We're going to chat in the hall for a minute," Blair announces, gesturing between herself and Chandra. Frowning, I stare pointedly at them. I'd much rather they talk in here.

"You'll be fine, nibby," Chandra jokes as they leave the room. Doggone her. Now I have to hope she tells me everything later.

"It's better if you rest for a little while anyway," Brad tells me. He pulls the covers tighter around me and sits on the edge of the bed, leaning forward to caress my face again. I lean into his touch and nod, smiling. This is better. Plus, we haven't had a moment alone since we got here.

"Sorry, babe," I whisper, tears stinging my eyes.

"You've got nothing to be sorry for. It was an accident. I'm just glad you're all in one piece."

Our peace is short-lived. An orderly arrives to take me for more testing, promising to have me back "in a jiff." Off we go ahead, through the white halls and bright lights.

True to his word, the testing doesn't take long and I am back in the room within fifteen minutes. Entering, we disrupt a conversation between Brad, Chandra, and Blair. All three are tense, brows furrowed, shoulders hunched. Chandra and Blair each hold small notebooks and pens.

"Huh, seems like I might have missed something…"

"There have been a couple of updates, but let's get you situated first," Brad says, turning toward my bed and forcing a pleasant expression. Chandra and Blair don't make the same effort.

"Oh geez. This wasn't an accident, was it?"

12

Brace Yourself

T he tension in the room escalates as Blair and Chandra check in with one another silently. This won't be good news based on the expressions on their faces.

Chandra steps forward and sits on the edge of my bed. Her hands are clasped tightly in her lap, knuckles whitening with the strain. She takes a few breaths and pulls her notebook from under her leg.

"Do you remember anything about the car that struck you?"

"No, I didn't even know I'd been hit by vehicle," I say then pause to really consider what I remember from this afternoon, it's the same as an hour ago. But, maybe a little clearer? "I *swear* I looked both ways first, there were no cars in either direction. When my alarm was going off, I did get distracted and focused on finding the phone. As always, it was buried deep. Just as I silenced the alarm, there was a squeal from tires. I can't recall if it was speeding up or coming to a rapid stop. Then there was something hard that smacked into the backs of my legs and I fell onto the pavement. The next thing I knew, Tev was on the ground with me."

"From the best we can tell at this point, there were no cars on the street when you stepped out. Chief Mercer has the tech team working on pulling footage from the traffic cameras and canvasing the businesses nearby. There have been several that have already volunteered footage that may help. It will likely be a few days before it is ready. In the meantime, we've been talking with witnesses that were on scene. Unfortunately, many came out when they heard the commotion but were not witnesses to you being struck by the vehicle," Blair's no-nonsense tone makes more nervous.

Chandra picks up here. "Tev was the first to recall the color of the vehicle. Would you like to guess what it was?"

"Uh... I'm pretty sure you're about to tell me it was a black, two-door car."

"Nailed it. Black, two-door car, loud muffler, white sticker on the back end. Can't confirm from interviews if the sticker or plate are the same but we'll get that from the cameras," Chandra's tone matches Blair's, which heightens the anxiety. My chest tightens, and my throat begins to burn. Tears are stinging my eyes and I bite the inside of my cheek to keep them in check. Could it be the same guys? It doesn't seem possible. They wouldn't have intentionally targeted me, would they? "Steady your breathing, cher." Chandra encourages me to take breaths with her. I flash back to the Lamaze style breathing Brad had me practice on the way into the hospital. Mimicking them, I inhale deeply and purse my lips to breathe out. After a few breaths, the tightness begins to ease and I can focus again on the conversation.

"It's too early to tell if this was incidental or intentional. Due to the similarities in the vehicle description, I'd like to encourage you to exercise extreme caution for the next few days until we've gathered more information and reviewed the video footage," Blair advises. "I do not believe at this time there is a reason to panic." Easy for her to say, no one tried to run her over this afternoon.

Brad has stayed quiet for most of the conversation, but during this last part, his grip on my hands tightens. His breathing quickens, and suddenly I'm entirely overwhelmed, collapsing back onto the lumpy pillow. He clears his throat and announces, "I think that's good for today. CiCi has had a really rough afternoon and a good bit of medication. She'll be laid up for the next couple of weeks and I'll keep a close eye on her." Blair and Chandra nod in unison. Blair takes the opportunity to say her goodbyes and promises to check-in with us in the next day or so. Chandra opts to stay but changes the subject.

"How about I pull some downhome Cajun goodness from the freezer and drop it by y'all's tonight?" she asks, genuine concern in her eyes.

"That'd be lovely. I'm hoping to stay awake long enough to make it home. I don't know if I have energy to even order a pizza." The surge of adrenaline has completely evaporated and I feel like a wrung out dishcloth.

"Perfect, I'll head out to grab it and leave it on the table for you at the house. You work on feeling better!" She bends to hug me in a very non-Chandra move. Brad walks her to the door and I hear their murmuring voices on the other side. Exhaustion overtakes me and I am asleep before he returns to my bedside.

***

When Linda offered to keep the dogs for the night, I readily accepted. At that moment, we had no idea what time we'd be home and it was too much to ask for her to make a midnight drop-off. She's already going above and beyond for us. Driving past, the lights were off and her house was quiet. Confident in having made the right call, we're ready for some rest. Brad makes plans to bring pastries for Linda when we pick up the dogs in the morning. At the mention of pastries, our stomachs growl in sync. I can picture a warm flaky crust, stuffed with guava and cheese.

Parking in the driveway, I stare at the distance to our front steps and burst into sobs. How in the world will I get all the way there? Brad offers to carry me, but I refuse. I'll walk it or sleep in the truck. As appealing as staying put is, our bed sounds way better. I do accept Brad lifting me from the truck and helping me stand on the sidewalk. Determined to prove I can use the crutches, I hobble to the steps, the trek equivalent to a mile-long, uphill hike. Grumpy, sweaty, and fatigued— I am an absolute mess and tears are flowing like river down my puffy face. Brad parked me on the couch with pillows surrounding me. A cool cloth soothes my tired eyes and pounding head while dinner is warmed in the microwave.

The turkey sandwich we'd shared around 8 p.m. was long gone and both of us are starving. A bowl of Chandra's gumbo, thickly sliced cornbread, and lemonade on the lanai hits the spot. Now nearly midnight, it has been far too many hours since I left home to meet Melody. A playlist of classical cello pours from a Bluetooth speaker on the side table, combined with the twinkling porch lights and symphony of nighttime bugs, it gives us the peace we need. Despite my earlier exhaustion, restlessness has taken hold. My brain is buzzing with the events of the afternoon, including the potential of this being intentional. The temptation to add to the crime board at the community center makes me twitchy.

"It can wait until tomorrow, sleeping on it will help you feel clearer," Brad's ability to read my mind never ceases to amaze him. I stare at him slack jawed. He has a point though, nothing productive will come from making notes this evening. Chandra and Brad can always help assemble the pieces when we're better rested.

"Meds and bed?" I suggest. Brad nods dramatically before rocking from his chair.

"Wait here. I'll help you up the steps. No need to revisit the ER tonight. "He smirks and sidesteps away from my attempted swat. Again, the man has a point. I'd fully intended to attempt to get in the house on my own. How I would swing this brace and manage crutches is beyond me, but I was willing to try. Instead, I raise my arms to him. He lifts me easily, pressing me against his chest, and carries me to bed.

13

Sourdough Sympathy

urching down our short hallway, I finally make it to the front door. You'd think after nearly a week on crutches, I'd be more adept and a little quicker. Sadly, I am not. Walking around in the house, I've adopted a hopping and clinging to furniture method to avoid using the crutches. Plus they hurt my armpits and I can't take it anymore. Without any sort of medical advice or opinion, I've decided to end my relationship with them.

Sweaty, disheveled, and slightly out of breath, I wrench the door open. The unexpected force nearly topples me. Listing to the side, I make eye contact with the startled woman on my porch.

"Oh my gosh, I knew I should have called," she says meekly, in a high-pitched but soft voice. Face reddening, she stares wide-eyed at the brace on my leg. When she looks back up, I place her right away.

"Melody, right?"

"Yes! I'm so glad you remember me. Makes this a little less awkward," she squeaks. In her hands, a paper sack crunches as she works it back and forth.

"Would you like to come in? It'll take me a sec, but we can sit out back and chat," I lean away from the open door and gesture through to the lanai. She grins eagerly at me and steps in from the porch.

"I brought a loaf of my new fall sourdough. If you want to try it, I can slice it for us?" Melody suggests, holding the paper package out in front of her body. She doesn't think she needs to bring a peace offering, does she?

"Definitely! Help me hobble to the kitchen and I'll make coffee while you get the bread ready." She extends an arm, like a gentleman in a regency movie and I happily accept. Together, we limp down the narrow hall to the kitchen. "Knifes are by the sink." Pointing for her, I reach for the moka pot on the stovetop. All afternoon, I'd craved a sweet treat and coffee. So my afternoon is most certainly looking up. "Tell me more about this sourdough."

"I'd love to! A few years ago, we decided to add seasonally flavored breads to our rotation at the bakery. There were a few flops before I got this one right. It all begins with Malcolm's great-grandparents sourdough starter that's been around since the 1960s," I must have grimaced at this. She giggles and continues, "Sounds disgusting, I know, but it really it isn't. If properly taken care of, sourdough starter won't go bad and can last forever." Nodding slowly, I remain doubtful but will give her the benefit of her expertise in baking. "As part of the baking prep, we layer fall spices like cinnamon, nutmeg, and cardamom into the dough. A little orange zest and chopped currants are folded in once the spices are fully mixed in. The bread ends up with layers of different flavors in each bite."

Throughout her explanation, she's calmed and speaks with confidence and pride. In the space of a few sentences her entire demeanor changed. She's no longer shy and beams as she hands me a slice of bread with creamy butter thickly spread across the top. The aroma hits me first, a citrusy sweetness combined with an earthy spice blend gives all the scents you'd dream up for autumn. I do a stilted happy dance with the first bite. Chewy, buttery, and loaded with flavor.

I'd become so engrossed in her description that the coffee has gone untouched. The only progress made was opening the moka and the canister of beans I'd ground this morning. Pivoting slowly, I flip on the electric kettle and prep for a pour-over pot. We're going to need more than a cup each.

"Why don't you have a seat outside and I'll carry everything?" Melody suggests. Part of me wants to assure her that I'm fine and can help. Then I remember my hunched over hobble.

"That would be... amazing!" I say instead. Melody smiles pleasantly and slides off her stool to help me.

Dropping like a cannon ball onto the wicker chaise lounge, it creaks in protest. Silently, I tell myself we inherited this set from Brad's grandma and should probably take it easy on them before it ends up broken. In an attempted apology, I pat the knobby armrest after swinging my legs up as gently as possible. Wincing and sliding a pillow under my knee, it's a reminder that at the moment, I can't do everything I usually would. Which includes standing in the kitchen while waiting for the coffee to finish. Yet another thought that I don't want but can't avoid.

Yipping and scrabbling toenails erupt through the house in an explosion of sound. CoCo, Aggie, and Darla bolt from the patio door, bypassing me and charge into the yard. Their afternoon at the dog park has clearly wrapped up and they're still filled with energy. Chandra swings out the door and plops into one of the rocking chairs. Without speaking, she tips her head toward the kitchen and raises an eyebrow.

"Isn't it nice that Melody stopped over?" I loudly say, extending my bread and butter, "You've got to try this, you'll love it."

She snatches my plate and takes a big bite. Her eyes bulge as the flavor hits and she murmurs, "Yummmmm..." before scarfing down the last of it. Scowling, I tell her, "You better refill that plate!" She salutes and jumps up for the kitchen.

Chandra and Melody have met a few times, so there's no guilt over the lack of introduction. Moments later the duo appears carrying snacks and coffees for all of us. I'm so glad I opted for a pot of pour-over. Melody has returned to her shy posture. She silently sits in a rocking chair and stares down at the floor. Giving Chandra a silent, "What did you do?" face, she frowns and shrugs. Melody sighs so deeply that I wonder if she's seen us.

"I'm going to take a stab here, is something is on your mind?" I cautiously begin, trying not to pry but she did show up unannounced at my house. And is acting a bit odd. Although in fairness, neither of us know her and her behavior is a mystery.

"I...I guess I'm feeling guilty," she confesses, slowly at first, then her words tumble out. "You were on the way to meet me. I'd told you I had more information but it really is more of a hunch. If I hadn't insisted you come back downtown that evening, you wouldn't have been hit by the car." Tear spill from her eyes, flowing down her cheeks. The rush of emotion catches me off guard.

"Oh hun— you didn't cause any of this. Those boneheads blasting through a red light did. And anyone who knows CiCi is aware that she can't be trusted crossing streets solo." Chandra's words make me guffaw in a super un-ladylike manner. "You ever watch Brad cross a street with her? That man has a grip on her like she's a felon in custody." Laughing, I toss a balled-up napkin in her direction, which she catches before impact. I laugh because it's true, I get distracted easily and Brad has a viselike grip on me. Part of me thinks it's his protective nature but more of me knows it's fear for my safety.

"She has a point," I concede. "This is in no way your fault. My phone distracted me and that's when the car got me. Now, I'm not saying I could have stopped it by paying attention, but it certainly would have helped." While Chandra and I talk, Melody sniffles into the sleeve of her sweatshirt. She shakes her head and attempts to rally herself.

"Rationally, I know that it wasn't my fault. But, why couldn't I have just waited around for when you had a break and showed you the photos then. It's not like I'm a CIA operative. It would have taken ten minutes."

"Meh! This is all part of the fun. Embrace it. When else will we get to act like secret agents? Chandra always says at this stage, every detail is important. Do you feel up to sharing?" Melody wipes her face with a napkin, takes a gulp of hot coffee and tightly nods. She slides her phone from her pocket and swipes the screen a few times, then holds it in my direction. I gratefully accept it and wave Chandra over to sit closer and check the images with me.

"Nonna told you that I've seen a few things that didn't make sense. It began almost three weeks before the break-in. Check out this image— tell me what you see," pointing to the grainy screenshot. Zooming in, Chandra and I study it silently. At first glance, there's a hulking figure with little details. Staring intently, Chandra moves to all corners of the phone. Her lips move wordlessly. The swiping and zooming speeds up and then stops in the bottom right corner.

"There it is!" she whispers and points at the screen.

I shift my focus to the area Chandra is locked into and see...absolutely nothing.

"As much as I'd love to know what you're seeing, I'm not," I groan, wishing my investigative skills were even close to hers. What spectacular clue has she uncovered? And why do I have no idea what it is?

"It's not *what* I'm seeing. It's what I'm *not* seeing," she says cryptically and points to the lower right corner again. I shake my head. "What about his hand stands out to you?" Squinting, I stare even harder, my eyes nearly cross with the effort.

"What about it? I can't even see his hand."

"My point exactly. Look again."

I pull the phone right up to my face. I've zoomed until the phone won't anymore. Vague connections start forming. "What's he holding in his hand? Or is he missing a hand?"

"My vote is, he has something in his hand. A dark, oblong object. It's covering his palm." The void in the image begins to make sense. His hand isn't visible because of what he's holding. Unfortunately, the picture is at the limit, the grainy image provides further details. This guy knew what he was doing— face obscured, hoodie to hide shape and hair color, dark clothes and glasses. It's like he appeared from nowhere.

"That's not the only image, keep swiping," Melody prompts. Without speaking, Chandra releases the image and swipes to the next. Following her same process, she zooms into every corner of the image multiple times. There are five in this collection plus a clip of the man walking toward the door. The camera didn't pick up his initial approach, but does capture him looking straight into the lens. After several seconds, he disappears off screen. A shiver runs through me. Despite not being able to see his face, I am completely creeped out.

"Ick," I sputter and run my hands up and down my arms. Goosebumps prickle my skin.

"Yeah, that was my reaction too," Melody says, "I cried when I saw it. Took Malcolm a while to calm me down." She gazes down at her hands and twirls her wedding ring set. "In the span of watching the clip, I'd convinced myself that he knew who we are, where we lived, and was laying in wait somewhere for us. I was an absolute mess."

"I would have been too! The way he stared at the camera was menacing. He knew you were going to see him and he didn't care."

"It definitely shows a lack of fear. He does not appear to be concerned that he'll be identified. Can you send me these? To my work email?" Chandra asks, her tone has gone from curious to business. Melody nods and takes her phone from Chandra's outstretched hand.

"There are more," she begins, then Chandra pulls the phone back. Gesturing with her finger, she pantomimes swiping. Melody smiles and nods her head. "Skip through the rest of that week and look for

Saturday." Eagerly, Chandra swipes quickly. Her eyes widen when she starts a video. Scooting to me, she holds the phone between us.

Another grainy video begins. The night vision on this camera is not great, I have to admit. Anyway, the screen is mostly dark but there is what appears to be pinholes of light, almost kaleidoscopic. The pinholes shift back and forth. Seconds into the video, I realize there is something over the camera. It pulls away and the camera goes completely dark. The next video has light slowly reappearing. A finger passes over the lens and a nail scratches. Malcolm's face fills the screen, he's sticking out his tongue and holding up a smiley face sticker with the phrase, "Next Time!" written along the bottom edge. I can't help but to chuckle. His silliness is endearing.

"I know that sticker!" Chandra exclaims, "Magpie's puts them on every carry out order. You know the ones from the lunch counter?" I slowly nod. Magpie's is a small sandwich shop inside Delman's market. The vintage corner store has been in operation since the late 1940's. It's had many owners, yet manages to keep the old-timey, small-town store feel.

"They have an amazing corned beef on rye," I murmur. My stomach growls, even though I'm on my third slice of sourdough. Chandra pokes my side and raises an eyebrow. "Listen, I haven't eaten there in months. My stomach is just reminding me how good it was." She and Melody look at one another and shake their heads. I cannot tell if they're impressed or disappointed.

14

Community Ties

If I spend any more time in the house, I'll go bonkers. Hanging out at home because I want to is a VERY different story than staying home because I'm forced to. By the next morning, I've convinced Brad that spending time at the community center will be good for me. He reluctantly agrees to drop me off if I promise to rest and give my leg a break.

"Pinky promise," I say, then fling my arms around his neck as he helps me from the truck. I cover his face with kisses in the moment it takes to settle me on the ground. He laughs and spins me toward the door.

"Behave yourself and stay off that leg," he scolds while smiling, "I've got spies everywhere..." He trails off, moving around the side of the truck. Blowing him another kiss, I straighten up and barely lean on my crutches, waiting as he climbs into the truck.

"Do you think he really believes you'll listen?" Desmond asks, he's appeared from nowhere. I crank my head to look at him wide-eyed.

"Not a chance," Linda pipes up from my other side. "But, we'll keep an eye on you for him. We've got a crime to solve and can't have you laid up much longer." She turns and offers me a wheeled walker with a seat. "Park it, CiCi." She points to the small bench. "Des and I will wheel you in."

Standing my ground, I stare at her. It's not that I'm unappreciative, the whole thing just feels a little ridiculous. Tooting the horn, Brad waves as he drives off. In that moment, reality hits that I'm not winning. Sighing loudly and doing a modified pivot, I land with a thunk onto the seat. Linda smiles and pats me on the cheek. She's triumphed and is trying not to gloat.

"Onward!" Desmond says, grasping the handles to release the brakes. He begins easing the walker forward, as Linda takes my crutches and gestures me to lift my feet off the ground. Supporting my bad leg, I cross my good leg underneath and roll my eyes. A clicking sound catches my attention, a grinning Linda is holding her phone up, snapping pictures rapidly. "For Brad. He wants to make sure we're taking care of you," Desmond tells me. That explains my husband's willingness to help me get out and about.

***

From the walker, I call two rounds of Bingo for the group before we break for coffee and pastries. Mirabel, Alfie, and Elena appointed themselves the snack committee for the day. A spread of bagels, empanadas, and cookies fills nearly half the table. Linda insists that she bring me a plate instead of letting me help myself. The plate she brings me is piled with two empanadas and a handful of cookies.

"You're healing, eat up," she admonishes while refilling my coffee.

"Yeah and I'm also sitting all the time. At this rate, none of my pants will fit in a month," I complain. This whole episode has not only been painful, but also wrecked the progress I'd made in my workouts over the last year.

"The faster you heal, the faster you'll be up and running." I grudgingly agree. Until my knee is better, I'm stuck hobbling around and limited in what I can do. At least it's temporary.

"I was thinking, maybe you can run us through what you've learned so far?" Mirabel asks sweetly. She clasps her hands under her chin, blinking slowly. How could I say no to that face?

"That sounds like a distinct possibility." The thought of revisiting the crime board and adding a few notes gets my blood pumping. I'm nearly giddy at the thought of getting back to the case. "Should we wrap up here and get started?" Chairs screech as everyone around the table stands. I depress the levers and scoot my walker back from the table. Desmond takes over from here and helps wheel me from the room to our smaller community space with the crime board.

As expected, the room is musty. Doubtful that anyone has been in here in the last few weeks. Linda pulls the whiteboard to the center of the room for easy access. I stand from the walker and limp to grab a marker.

"Okay, here's what we know so far," I launch into the details of the theft. Within a few minutes, I outlined the basics of the case and move into the new details provided by Melody. Last night she had texted me with a handful of additional details. "Chandra and I met with Melody Deluca yesterday. She had some interesting images from their security cameras over the last month. It seems that the business had been under some sort of surveillance. The person on the camera feed matches the rough appearance of the thief chased from the store by Malcolm during the robbery. In the first event, he was seen on camera carrying a dark, oblong object that obscured his hand. With that, he, presuming it is a he based on the body type and stye of dress, had hidden all identifying factors. The only parts of him visible is a sliver of skin under each eye. They're observed staring directly into the camera but take no other action." Heads nod around the table as I speak and make notes. "In the second clip, the camera lens is covered, while a sticker is placed over it. One of the stickers from the lunch counter at Magpie's." A stomach growls at the mention of the local sandwich spot.

"How does your accident play in?" Alfie asks, he's dialed in on the crime board and seems eager to uncover more details.

"Ah! A great question and info to add to the board!" I scrawl out accident, placing my initials next to the word. "Witnesses that were on scene all mention a black two door car with a white sticker on the back. No one captured the license plate or details of the sticker, but it seems consistent with the vehicle from the robbery."

"Were you targeted, mija?" Elena's voice is tight with emotion. She's gripping Alfie's arm tightly, her nails press halfmoons into his forearm. To his credit, Alfie seems unbothered and gently pats her free hand.

"Chandra seems to think so." I clear my throat and readjust my posture. I've begun to lean too heavily on my left leg and it is growing sore. "Melody had stopped by Azúcar to meet me earlier in the day and a few of our regulars teased me about getting involved with another crime. So it was not a secret that I was an active part of the investigation. In our chat, she told me she had some new information. We agreed to meet after I got off work, but I don't remember saying where and when."

"Were they waiting for you?" Desmond questions, he too is staring intently at the board. "I can't figure out they would have known where you are."

"That's where it gets confusing for me too. How did they know I'd be there? It doesn't make sense. I'm leaning toward it being accidental."

"I don't know, it's too much of a coincidence for the same vehicle to have struck you and then driven off," Linda adds. "There are too many similarities in my book."

"Well, Chandra always says…" I start and am cut off by the group parroting, "At this stage, every detail matters!" We burst into laughter. How many times have we heard this? There's truth in the words. Nothing is too small for us to overlook. Thinking of the last case, we'd worked on together, the details mattered. A neighbor asking for help, a newspaper clipping. The details are how crimes are solved.

"What if we try to list who all may have been in the coffee shop?" Alfie asks. "Then we can see if any of them overlap with bakery customers?"

"Solid plan!" I say, the excitement catching like wildfire.

"Seb has cameras, right?" Linda asks, her wheels are turning. "If he gives us access, we can look for familiar people. The guy in the image is built like a small vehicle, I'm fairly certain he'll stand out in a crowd." Gathering closer together around the round table, Linda passes out paper for us to take notes. She's entered teacher mode. "On your paper, list anyone you recall from the shop in the days leading up to the break-in and CiCi's accident. Details will be key to putting the pieces into place." Silently, each of us get to work.

Straining my memory, I focus on the coffee orders from the last few weeks I'd worked. The details of the orders come easier than I'd imagined. Closing my eyes, I picture the beverages sliding onto the counter. For some, the smiling faces of customers fill in empty spaces of my memories. Their names come next. Elijah, Birdie, Colin, Jamie, Sofie, Inez, the list builds with dozens of names. These are only the to-go orders and I struggle to recall any of the restaurant patrons. Most are pick-ups from the counter by Wren or Gina. Using the back of my paper, I draw the cafe and mark the indoor and outdoor tables. Seeing the space helps and details flood in—the conversations, people, and smells. Mentally moving between the tables, it's overwhelming to picture them all. I keep returning to the patio. What is it about the patio?

"CiCi, do you remember when my book club came in?" Linda asks, she's intermittently scrunching up her mouth and appears to be chewing at the inside of her cheek.

"Hmm... the day of the theft?"

"No, the one before then."

"Was it the pirate book or the space station romance?"

"Space station," she confirms. I nod slowly.

"Matcha lattes with cold foam?"

"The very same. " Linda shudders slightly and makes a quiet *blech* noise. Not that there was anything wrong with the lattes. It was the first time the book club tried matcha and discovered the unique flavor. "What is it about that particular day?"

"The patio," we say in unison. Turning to look at one another, I grin. "He was in the corner, out by the street." Linda nods emphatically. "It's time to call Chandra."

15

Mugshots

After our revelations about the man on the patio, we were asked to come into the station this week. A sketch artist is scheduled to meet with us and then we're to go through mugshots with Detective Cassidy. In the meantime, Linda and I have been parked in a dusty beige room. The only sound is the hum of overhead fluorescent lights. The hum is occasionally interrupted by an ominous click and flicker. In no way is it welcoming or soothing. I sincerely hope this isn't where they have traumatized victims or families wait. Adding another item for my next dinner with Chandra. It leaves a lot to be desired and it's the county can most certainly do better.

Standing slowly, I exhale exasperatedly through pursed lips. The effect sounding like I'm blowing raspberries. Glancing at the clock,

I realize we've been in here for forty-three minutes, even though I could swear it's been closer to four hours. In hindsight, we should have clarified the time commitment. Linda has come prepared with her next book club read and a tumbler of coffee. I, on the other hand, brought my house keys, wallet, and a cell phone with ten percent left on the battery. In a lurching gait, I pace back and forth across the room to pass the slowly ticking minutes, sighing every few minutes.

"You may want to save some of that energy for later today," Linda suggests while turning the page of her book. "The sighing is delightful but I doubt I've got the strength to pick you up if you topple over." Despite how harsh her words may sound, there's a twinkle in her eye when she peeks at me over the edge of her glasses.

"Don't worry, I've practiced getting up," beaming at her, I'm proud that I no longer resemble a turtle on its back when I fall. And also, as someone who's spent her life falling down, getting back up is an acquired skill.

With a loud creak, the thick wooden door cracks open. Blair Cassidy pokes her head in the room, seeming out of sorts and more than a little rushed. Hot on her heels is Officer Malloy and a harried, young man in board shorts, sandals and a t-shift with a neon sea turtle. He carries an iPad and an oddly shaped black bag.

"Good Lord in heaven, it took me forever to find y'all. Nice of Tompkins to stash you in this dungeon." Blair shakes her head, staring around the room. "Malloy, can you secure us a spot to relocate? I cannot in good conscience leave anyone in here." He strides from the room, already grabbing his phone from the case at his waist. Clearly in no mood to waste more time, she continues, "While we wait, let me introduce you to our artist extraordinaire— Bento Jones."

"Hey ladies," he drawls out in the exact way you'd imagine. The stereotypical surfer voice. It's like a movie come to life. "Excellent to meet y'all. Don't let my vibes deceive, I'm killer at this." His confidence and smile are infectious.

"I'm CiCi Larkin and this is my friend, Linda Langston." I gesture to Linda. She closes her book and smiles sweetly.

"Have no fear, my dear, we aren't put off by your vibes," she reassures him. I love when she enters teacher mode, it's easy to picture her as the teacher everyone loved but knew not to push their luck with.

"Bet. Cool to meet you ladies." He smiles and bobs his head, his sunny curls flop with the motion and he pushes them back from his eyes. Granted, I have no idea what bet means, but I assume it is an agreement with Linda. In a different moment, I'd text my teenage niece to interpret for me.

"Detective Cassidy?" Malloy interrupts from the doorway. She raises an eyebrow and stares at him. "Conference room two just opened."

"Miraculous. Shall we?" she deadpans and waves us toward the door, pausing when she sees my crutches. "Uh...let's go at your pace. The walk isn't far, but I don't want you to push it." I nod appreciatively.

"Prepare to be impressed," I say as we make our way out of the room.

***

"Hmmm...maybe a little thicker?" Bento asks, he's staring intently at the sketch pad resting on a small easel. Linda and I have shared what we can remember of the man from the patio. Bento is refining the details.

"Perhaps, he did have an unusually thick neck. It was part of what drew my attention. He resembled a football player I'd seen on TV once." Linda leans in toward the drawing.

"I agree. His shoulders sloped a bit more." I roughly trace the shape in the air in front of me.

"Any additional facial features?" Blair asks, while Malloy takes copious notes of our descriptions.

"His sunglasses obscured most of his face," I lament. "Linda—do you think his beard looked odd?" She ponders this for a moment and then shakes her head. It must not be ringing a bell for her.

"Could it have been fake?" Malloy pipes up.

Interesting. This is exactly what was on my mind. The beard didn't seem to fit his face. I can't pin down if it was the shape or texture. It just didn't seem right. Bento tips back and watches my face. He studies me for an uncomfortable amount of time and resumes sketching. The room falls silent as we watch his pencil scratch over the paper. A rough outline of the man's face and body form.

"Hey boss lady, you got those screen grabs I can see?" he says without turning. All eyes go to Blair, but she points to me. Oh! He meant me? Pulling my nearly dead phone from my pocket, I quickly unlock and show the screen to Bento. He glances at the battery life in the corner and sends the images to his tablet. Smart man— that phone was not going to hold out for more than another couple of minutes.

Zooming in and out through the handful of photos, he studies each one for several minutes. I flash back to Chandra on the patio, inspecting every inch of the image. He sighs as he sets the tablet to the side of his easel. Assessing the drawing so far, he bends forward, then starts lightly sketchy the man's lower jaw and chin. In those few strokes, I see it. The face taking shape is the man in the security footage. Suppressing a gasp, I clamp Linda's hand tightly in mine. She squeezes back, she sees it too. This. Is. The. Man. Bento has filled in the gaps to give us a clearer picture of the man we'd seen in the cafe.

"Ladies?" Blair asks. Wide-eyed, I turn to her and nod excitedly. "Let's give Bento the chance to finalize his work and then we'll hit the mugshots."

A quick rap on the door and it swings open abruptly. Chandra steps into the room with her hand extended toward Blair. "Seb pulled the footage, you're going to want to see this." She presses a USB into Blair's hand. Together, they turn to leave. Naturally, I begin to follow. Chandra holds up her hand, halting me in my tracks.

"Nah, girlfriend, you gotta stay with Bento until he's wrapped up," Chandra advises. My disappointment must be written boldly on my face. "Don't sweat it. We'll show you after you've looked through photos. We can't let anything you see here taint your memories or give you a false impression." She pats me on the arm in sympathy and solidarity. Sighing, I remind myself she's absolutely right and I am still actively involved in helping. Having to wait is neither a rejection or exclusion.

"We'll be done soon, promise," Bento says. He's continued to refine the image with shading. It's now gone from an outline to a realistic drawing. The man on the page is square-bodied with a thick neck, shoulders that round down into bulging arms, and boulder-like jawline. His eyes remain hidden beneath oversized, reflective sunglasses, the kind popularized by sports fisherman, but he's now nearly recognizable. "Is there anything else with his hair or clothing? Maybe like the color or a style? Ya know, his fit..." He points to his clothing to emphasize the point.

"I only remember him as dressed similarly to the locals. Other than his size, he seemed to blend in rather than stand out," Linda recalls. "I don't think I can accurately describe what he was wearing or the color of his hair." I murmur my agreement. He wasn't memorable enough for me to have formed a distinct impression. Bento resumes his shading and refining the sketch. To my amazement, it begins to resemble a photograph.

"Nice work, dude," Malloy says, as we've chatted, he's walked over to stand directly behind Bento. In a congratulatory gesture, he claps him on the back. Bento throws him a toothy grin and a thumbs up.

"Gonna call it, ladies. We got a solid pic of the perp," he says, holding the drawing up for Linda and I to inspect. He's absolutely right. It's far better than the screenshots from the alley cameras. "Between this, the cafe cameras, and maybe shots from customers, you'll totally be able to find this dude."

"Thank you for your time," Linda says, her tone proper but pleasant. Bento bows at the waist and taps his right hand over his heart.

"Let's pack it up and I'll get them set up to look through the books." Malloy assists Bento in gathering his supplies and packing up. From their comfort level, and the ease of their efforts, this isn't the first time they've worked together. The two men are heading out the door within minutes. "Give me ten and we'll get started. I don't about y'all but I'm getting hungry, so I'll bring snacks too." Malloy is growing on me by the minute— might have to let Chandra know she has competition for police bestie.

***

Eighty-seven pages in, we're starting to lose hope.

"Anyone else alarmed by the number of criminals in our community?" it may come across as sarcasm, but I am genuinely shocked. Malloy and another office brought nine binders of images for Linda and I took through. We've not even finished the first book. Not a single picture has been remotely close to the sketch we created with Bento.

"The reality of this is, we are only reviewing the last five years. The storage room has dozens of binders with hundreds of pages," he confesses while prepping another binder for us to view. Linda's grumble mirrors my emotions. Today has stretched far longer than either of us planned and exhaustion is creeping in.

"The faces are starting to blur at this point. I'm having trouble remembering who we're looking for," I admit.

"Could we arrange a short break and then get back to it? My bones are starting to ache from these chairs." Linda shifts her position, attempting to find a more comfortable spot in the squeaking, ancient office chair.

"Absolutely! Let's take a stretch break and then plan to wrap it up within the hour," Malloy recommends. Linda and I heartily agree. I don't know how much longer I can take being here.

Laps in the hall loosen some of the stiffness in my leg, but don't alleviate the fatigue that's crept in over the last half hour. Our early success with Bento has given way to a growing sense that we'll never identify our guy. Discouraged but committed, Linda and I return to the stuffy conference room. My mind buzzes at the thought of

EIGHT additional books to flip through. Undercaffeinated and overstimulated, a headache looms behind my eyes.

"Why don't we divide and conquer?" Linda suggests. "I'll take these four," sliding the top binders to her seat and pushing the remainder to me, "you take these and if either of us find something promising, mark the page." Enthusiastically, I flip open the first binder I see.

A short while later, I've marked two potentials in one book, and am well into my second. Mid-way through, I freeze. He stares back at me from the middle row. Dark buzz cut hair, neck like a fire hydrant, square jaw, and broad shoulders. Unintentionally, I paw at Linda's arm. Her distracted, *hmmm* becomes a startled squeal of recognition.

"Did I just find him?" Breathless, I lean close to the photo. Malloy jumps from his chair and joins us at the table.

"Hey Cassidy," he says quietly, cell phone pressed tightly to his face, "you should come on down." Wrapping up his call, he snaps a picture of the mugshot and identifiers.

Name: Roland Emory

Alias: "Slug", "Big E", "rome"

Date of Birth: 07/17/1980

Arrest Date: 04/21/2019

Last Known Address: 487 Pelican Way, Unit 3, Parkland FL

Conviction(s): Breaking & Entering, Felony Assault

Blair and Chandra ease over to the table, their casual movements quietly contradict their obvious tension. This case just got to another level with the identification of a suspect.

"Ya sure?" Chandra asks me. I nod tightly— the longer I looked at the photo, the more convinced and creeped out I am.

"He's been to the cafe several times." I think back to the last few weeks. "He sat on the patio alone each time. I'm sure Wren would remember him."

"Send us the pics and check his last known," Blair instructs Malloy, "Can you also update the report with his details?"

"Already on it." Malloy has pulled out a tablet and is furiously tapping away while we've talked.

"Good work, ladies," Blair says, standing to shake our hands in turn. Chandra winks at me over head, beaming with pride. She offers to help us finish up and escort us back to the lobby. We say our goodbyes to Malloy and Blair. This has been the longest day and we're all eager to finish.

16

Back to the Grind

Finally, I get released from crutches and can go back to work. Seb has set a high stool up in the coffee bar for me to sit as needed. Gratefully, I drop onto the seat while steaming a pitcher of milk. The loud, long sigh escapes before I can stop it.

"Winding down, Slugger?" a chipper male voice asks from behind the espresso machine. Peering left then right, I see him. Desmond has arrived.

"Not gonna lie, this is way more tiring than I thought it would be. But, nothing I can't handle," filling my words with forced cheerfulness. It's too early in the day to give in.

"I'll keep it simple and only order a black coffee to go. Sound manageable?"

"You got it! Let me finish this pour and then I'll set you right up." Desmond always boosts my mood. He grins at me and tips his straw fedora.

While I work, he updates me on Karen's progress. The rehabilitation center specializes in stroke recovery. Ranked as one of the best in south Florida, if there's a place that can get Karen home, this is it. Desmond shares her physical and occupational therapy sessions today. Karen is now able to brush her teeth, comb her hair, and mostly feed herself with her right hand. The devastating news of complete loss of function on the left side was a bitter pill. Recently, she's lost function in her right leg due to prolonged immobility. When they received this news, Desmond knew Karen would not be returning home. He's struggling with the knowledge that their remaining years will be spent apart.

"How about you come for dinner tomorrow?" I ask, knowing that Desmond is familiar with my cooking skills. "I may have figured out meatballs and subs sound delish."

"I'm in. How about I bring the drinks?" Desmond is known for his cocktails in our neighborhood. "Hmmm...I need to figure out what pairs with meatball subs." Tapping his finger against his chin, he resembles an ancient philosopher pondering the meaning of life. Smiling, I slide his coffee toward him.

"We'll trust your judgement on that. See you at six?" Slurping his coffee, Desmond tips his hat and walks from the cafe.

The remainder of my shift passes smoothly with limited pain. Calling it a win, I clean up the coffee station before we close for the afternoon. Untying my apron to hang, a sharp poke in my ribs makes me jump. With a gasp, I turn to face Chandra. Smacking at her, I point down toward my knee. She blushes slightly and murmurs, "Whoopsie."

"Off today?" I ask, gesturing at her non-police issue shorts and tank.

"For now, I picked up the first half of a nightshift for Munoz, then will be back at it tomorrow morning" she replies as if I know who Munoz is. At least, I don't think I know who he is. "Came by to see Seb and give you some updates."

"Way to bury the lead!" I grumble. "Want to walk me to the car and fill me in?" My assumption is she will want a little privacy before sharing. She extends her hand for me to lead the way.

Exiting the cafe through the employee entrance, we slowly trek to my car. I may be free from my crutches and huge brace, but the healing is still slow. We chatter about each of our days and her upcoming shift until we're well away from the door or any prying ears.

"It's been a busy few days on our end," Chandra begins, making sure to match my pace. "We've issued a Be On the Look-Out, or BOLO, for the delightfully named, Slug. Unfortunately, he no longer resides at the address in his record. Which is a shocker to none of us." I snort at this. Things would have been far too simple if they'd found Slug chilling at home with his roommate. "His landlord hasn't seen him in nine months. Dude skipped out on his rent, leaving most of his stuff behind."

"Was he running from something?"

"Nothing we can find yet. He consistently seems to hang with the wrong crowd though. Drugs, thefts, assaults, he's dabbled in all of it. If there was something shady, Slug found his way into the mix."

"Has he been spotted since the accident?"

"Not since. But, the more we look, cher, the more we find." She's grinning like a cartoon cat. "Once we knew he'd been on camera behind the bakery and in the cafe, we started pushing harder on local businesses for footage. So far three more have agreed for us to review the footage— Delman's Market, Palmetto Pages, and Boba Baby—"

"If you don't hurry up..." I interrupt.

"Chill shug, I'm giving you context." We've arrived at my Jeep and both of us lean on the warm doors. "Guess who we spotted at Delman's? Specifically at Magpie's lunch counter?"

"Betting on our bestie, Slug." In lieu of agreement, she smacks me on the shoulder, continuing with her maniacal grin. Good lord, she's getting jocular, that means she's hyped with all they've found.

"Not just once but four times in the last two months." She pauses while I do a quick math check.

"Wait, that's before the robbery?" I sputter.

"Sure is. He was also seen on the ATM camera down the street. Cassidy has traffic checking all the red light cameras within a half mile in that time frame. That's gonna take a WHILE," emphasizing the timeframe. The fact that we have red-light cameras is news to me.

Momentarily, I am distracted wondering if I've run any red lights lately. "You back with me?" Snarling my lip at her, I nod. Hate that she knows me well enough to catch when my mind goes on a different path mid-conversation. "Great, cause there's more," she continues to list every business in the area with cameras that may have footage. Including those who've refused footage and those that haven't responded to requests.

"I feel like you're prepping me to ask for a favor?"

"First of all, I am offended," she flings a hand to her chest, as if I've wounded her, "As an officer of the law, I am simply sharing information with an interested party in an effort to keep the community safe and maintain relationships with local business."

"Righhhhtttt." I draw out the word to highlight my suspicion. Her PR style speech heightens the sensation that she's about to drop an ask in my lap.

"Fine. I was thinking that maybe when you're chatting with folks around h—," she starts.

I cut her off. This is not my first rodeo. "You want me to get them to turn over their footage?" I ask, getting to the point instead of dragging this out. My knee is starting to throb and the sun is getting hot.

"Oh my word! How sweet of you to offer!" Rolling my eyes, I stare at Chandra blankly. Now that she's gotten to the point, it's clear why she stopped by right before I left for the day. Which also leads me to suspect Seb is fully aware of what she's asking.

"You're a twit, you know that? All you had to do was ask. No need to add all the drama." I chastise, but she knows I love all the subterfuge.

"Well, now that you've offered to help, I can get the list to you tonight and you can start tomorrow?"

"Fine!" I sigh. "Come for dinner tomorrow around six?"

"Depends on what we're eating?" Sticking out my tongue, I open the car door and plop into the seat with a groan.

"Meatball subs and a surprise cocktail that Des is bringing."

"We're in. I'll bring a vegetable so we can pretend to be healthy." In a very cop move, she taps the roof of my Jeep and backs away to give me space to leave.

***

An obnoxious ping from my phone disturbs my reading blitz around 10 p.m. It's either my sister or Chandra.

Chandra: *Incoming list, check your email*

Me: *Can it wait til morning?*

Chandra: *if you must*

I send an angry devil emoji and attempt to get back to reading. Annoyingly, my interest is piqued and the temptation to review the list is too strong. As anticipated, nearly all the names on the list are familiar. Of the surrounding dozen small-businesses, only three have agreed to hand over what they have to Chandra. Copying to a note in my phone, I prioritize from those I'm most to least comfortable chatting with. Grateful to have good relationships in the community, I'm happy to see there's no one I'd dread talking with.

Me: *got it, will start mid-morning*

***

Brad is out the door before I'm awake. Despite most of a year passing since I was laid off, it seems I've not yet caught up on my sleep. All those years of getting up early for a commute must have made me permanently tired. Thankfully, I've got a self-sufficient husband. My job is to program the coffee to be ready when he wakes up.

Attempting to roll over, I can't seem to make the turn. Two small, furry bodies have me trapped in the tangled mess of bed linens. In unison, they sigh and stretch. Similar to me, they're not fans of getting out of bed. That is until I ask if they're hungry. In seconds, they've launched off the bed and are dancing in circles while running from the bedroom.

The dogs eat faster than is probably healthy for them and bolt onto the lanai. They fly out their doggie door and Zoom through the yard.

I hobble out the door with an overfilled cup of coffee. It's dark and strong, within moments, I swear I can feel it coursing through me. Based on how rough I feel this morning, I'm going to need plenty more before starting the day.

"CiCi! Are you out here?" Edna's nasal screech bounces off my neighbor's house. For a moment, I sit in absolute silence, pressing myself into the cushions of the lounge chair. "I can see your dogs and I know you can hear me?" Ugh...pretty sure they can hear her in the next town over.

"I'm here, Edna. Trying to wake up. Do you need something?" It may feel early to me, but Edna is typically out stomping through the neighborhood just after sunrise. I can't wait to hear the infractions she's imagined.

"Well," she gruffly begins. "As usual, your trash cans are improperly stored." Alarmingly, her voice is getting closer. Pressing harder into the cushions in a vain attempt to hide. "They've not only been out overnight, but they're covering a portion of the sidewalk." Flinging a throw pillow over my face, I scream into it. The pillow does little to muffle the sound.

"Thanks for the neighborly concern. Yet again, I'd like to remind you, we do not have an HOA. You cannot continue to make up rules for our street." This woman makes me weary. She's routinely on the hunt for fresh ways to terrorize the neighborhood, but trashcans remain one of her favorite topics.

"We may not have an HOA, but the county still has standards that you refuse to comply with. And I'd hate for you to be fined or worse for one of us to fall while dodging your filthy trashcans." Her voice is right beside the screen, but I refuse to look in her direction. Coco and Aggie fly onto the porch barking furiously. Using this as a distraction, I wordlessly go in the house and slam the door. The dogs can bark until she gives up and leaves. I hear her mutter. "little rats" as she walks down our driveway.

17

Lenses

"Hey CiCi! Welcome in, we just got in the cutest jeans and best of all they're in talls!" Mari Sandoval chirps out when I step into the Coral Belle Boutique. She makes it a point to know her customers and any locals that visit. We've had many chats about the challenges of finding jeans long enough to cover my ankles. Mari and her sister-in-law/business partner, Siobhan, make it a point to have a few things in stock that suit their regulars' tastes.

"Lead the way!" I follow Mari through the shop as she explains new arrivals and favorites. Before I can take in the inventory, she's pulled several items from racks we've passed, piling them into a changing stall at the rear of the store.

"Let me know if you need any other sizes!" she calls out while rushing to greet a woman and a teenager. "Welcome to the Coral Belle, y'all!"

Sadly, I loved every single thing I tried on. Reminding myself, I'm here to ask questions about the case, not spend my whole paycheck.

"Mari! How do you always pick the best? It's a gift," I tell her as I approach the register. "I've got to slim this down though," gesturing to the moderately-sized pile I've accumulated. Neither my closet nor my budget can handle this volume. Wracking my brain for an opener, I sort through the clothes.

"You're just supporting local businesses. Think of it as a community service." The most perfect opener has just appeared.

"Speaking of local businesses. What do you think of the robbery at the bakery?" Might not have been my most elegant segue but it'll work.

"OMG— I was terrified that we were next. You know, this store has a surprisingly high volume of sales. Between our inventory and sales, I do worry we're a target. It is not hard to swipe an outfit or piece of jewelry. Especially if one of us is with a customer."

"Definitely scary stuff! Have you had any incidents lately?"

"Nah," she pauses, "at least nothing more than our usual."

"Having incidents is part of your usual?" This suggestion shocks me. Conceptually, I understand that shoplifting and other petty thefts are on the rise. The reality of it boggles my mind.

"Unfortunately. During ebbs and flows of tourist season, our theft rates vary." Mari's chipper voice has dropped a few octaves to what I'm now certain is her actual voice. Softer, slower, with a thicker South Georgia accent. "We report the thefts to law enforcement and our insurance, but during peak we have thefts at minimum once a week. Last summer, we set a record. Thefts every day for two solid weeks. Totaled about $8000 in losses." My eyes nearly bug clean out of their sockets. Her casual tone belies how catastrophic the thefts would have been for the shop. "That's when Siobhan and I pulled the trigger on a better security system." Okay, well this might work in my favor.

"I am so sorry! That's hideous and I had no idea." Outrage on their behalf shimmers at the periphery of my emotions. "Has the new system helped reduce losses?"

She nods aggressively before answering, "Thankfully it has! In addition to discouraging thefts, it makes reporting far easier." Her eagerness to share the benefits, yet refusal to share footage with the police is confusing.

"Did you happen to catch any of the action during the day of the robbery?"

"I didn't." She stares down at the counter, picking at the edge of a flier. "That day, there was something weird going on with the camera. I noticed at the end of the day, our outdoor cameras were blacked out. Was the darnedest thing too."

"What do you mean?" I prompt, the back of my neck and scalp prickling.

"You know those stickers the sandwich counter at Magpie's puts on the paper?" she asks, gesturing to indicate a small circle with her thumb and index finger. Okay. Now I'm on the verge of jumping out of my skin, this is really happening. Instead of speaking, I nod and utter a squeaky, "Uh-huh."

Thankfully, Mari continues without seeming to notice. "Some prankster stuck them over the camera lenses. One out front and the other out back. Took forever to clean them off." She shakes her head, revisiting her attempts at removing the stickers.

"That is crazy. Seems like someone around here has been messing with those stickers." It's make or break time. "What did the police say when you told them?"

Blushing furiously, Mari sets to work organizing the counter. She straightens receipts and pens by the register. Clearing her throat several times as she fusses with anything she can get her hands on. "Well...I uh...I didn't tell them." She audibly gulps at her confession.

"Oh!" is all I can manage. How can I ask without sounding judgy or putting her on the spot? "Yeah, I can totally see that. Don't want to get drug into the situation if you can help it." Lame but it's the best I've got at this second. "Would you be open to telling them now?"

"Won't I be in trouble? I mean, I didn't come forward when they asked businesses on the street about cameras and footage we can share."

"Nah, they're still canvassing and recanvasing. I'm sure they'd be happy for any help you can give." I suggest, projecting an unfounded confidence. A large part of me knows that I cannot and should not speak for the police. Another part of me douses that thought, reassuring myself that I was asked to see if I can get any of the business owners to share.

"You really think?" I nod and force a smile, hoping that I'm right. "If you think it's the right thing to do, do you know who I should talk with?" Ahhh, progress.

"Do you know my friend, Chandra? She's also Seb's girlfriend." Pausing I let her try to remember, when the recognition dawns, I continue, "Let's start with her." Mari readily agrees, even the loose connection makes her more comfortable. Offering to connect them through a text, Mari shares her cell number with me. The cowbell above the door clangs as a new customer arrives. Mari excuses herself to greet them.

Me: *Progress. Mari at Coral Belle will share footage*

Me: *Same stickers over the cameras*

Chandra: *What?!? Hurry and send it*

Me: *Group text incoming. Know that you're a huge fan*

Chandra: *eye-rolling emoji*

She'd rather work back-to-back nights than be added to a group text. Sometimes it's the only way.

Me: *Hey ladies! Mari Sandoval meet Chandra Boudreaux.*

Me: *Mari has some odd camera activity. Can she show you?*

Chandra: *Hey! Thanks :)*

Chandra: *I'm out and about, could I stop by?*

From across the store, Mari looks at me and nods. She subtly points to the watch on her wrist.

Me: *Yep! Mari is with a customer right now*

Chandra: *Gimme 5*

Left to my own devices, I have no choice but to whittle down my clothing selections. Jeans for sure, I do one skinny and one wide-leg. Tops are harder. Narrowing it down to four, I'm stuck, when the bell clangs again.

"Don't get that yellow one, you'll never wear it. You love the color and want it to work more than it does," Chandra says, her head pokes around my shoulder. "Get the print tank and the black one with lace accents. Not sure about that green— you're better in emerald than mint." Sighing, she's right. I set the yellow tunic and mint button down off to the side. That was less painful than I imagined.

"You've got perfect timing. I was working on convincing myself I needed all four." Temporarily forgetting why she's here, I hold the yellow up next to her. Might not be my color, but Chandra glows next to it. Spotting the gun belt at her waist, I sigh and remove the shirt that has been draped over her shoulder. "I'll just set it down here, if you want to look later." Smiling and rolling her eyes, she knows I mean well. Even if I forget about priorities. "Mari is helping a customer back by the fitting rooms. She should be back here in a minute. She's not a hoverer and doesn't put pressure on her customers."

As if summoned, Mari appears between the racks of clothes. Her bronze-haired, spray-tanned pixie sized frame squeezes easily between the store displays. Chandra steps forward to greet her, Mari closes the gap and sticks her hand toward Chandra. Shaking vigorously, they introduce themselves. Chandra has her pleasant, neighborhood cop persona in place. Not that she's routinely unpleasant, but building rapport and putting people at ease is a specialty. Mari relaxes as they chat. The more comfortable she is, the easier it will be for her to share.

"I'm sure you're busy, so I should get to it," Mari begins, glancing at me for reassurance. I smile and shoot her a thumbs up. "It may be simpler to show you, can you come around the counter?" Chandra and I join Mari on the employee side. A bank of monitors is visible, the screens are small but there are internal and external feeds visible. Clicking a few times, Mari selects the day of the robbery. Her cameras are blacked out. The timestamps keep running. After about sixteen hours, there is a scratching of light as the covering is removed. A young woman's face, not Mari, fills the screen. She appears irritated and flicks whatever she's peeled off into a paper towel in one hand. Kudos to her for not littering, I guess.

"Siobhan, my business partner, discovered the lack of images and peeled the stickers off the day after the robbery. She was the opening shift. We'd missed the lack of images overnight unfortunately. I honestly focus more on the internal cameras. That's where our thefts usually occur." Throughout all of this, Chandra has silently watched and jotted down notes intermittently.

"Would you be willing to share this with us?" Chandra asks, pulling a business card free and passing it over.

Mari stops and stares the screen, biting her lower lip as she concentrates. She scrolls back to the initial loss of the feed. After saving the clips, she sends in an email to Chandra.

"I wish I would have come forward with this before. It just didn't seem to be a big deal. We honestly thought it was some sort of teenage prank or a social media thing." Her cheeks remain flushed, her voice low and slow, "Based on how we quickly you came to chat, I assume it is related to the bakery thefts?"

"Among other things," Chandra confirms. She's referencing my accident but Mari would have no idea. It wasn't in the news, by my request, it was scary enough without having to rehash it for weeks.. There was only a casual mention of an accident downtown and the suspected vehicle involved. She thanks Mari for the assistance and assures her, they'll be in touch soon.

Mission accomplished. I finish my purchases and make plans to meet for coffee the following week. Loaded with my new outfits, I check the list of businesses on my phone. There are eleven more to request or coordinate the footage with, which means more shopping. Sighing loudly, I head for the cafe. This requires caffeine.

18

Meatball Mayhem

"**I** got through eight on the list." Wishing I'd made better progress, I focus on stirring the simmering meatballs, silently thanking my mother for this slow cooker. For last year's anniversary, she got me a behemoth with more functions than I can understand. Literally a perfect gift for someone with below entry-level cooking skills.

"These smell amazing! How much longer?" Chandra whines. A stack of fresh hoagie rolls on the cutting board in front of her.

"Keep slicing and I'll get the cheese," spinning to get provolone from the fridge, I continue, "four don't keep the footage beyond forty-eight hours. Which feels kind of dumb, but not my decision."

Chandra grunts a laugh. "Two others said they need to speak with the board. That felt like a lie." I admit. "Two others said they had no suspicious activity in the last month. One told me this is none of my business and asked me to leave." Chandra is no longer laughing and seems put out. Time to get to the good news. "But...the last two were a different story." The slicing pauses and she perks up.

"Heifer, you better get to the point." Her tone is playfully menacing, the bread knife in her hand waves in my direction.

"Do you see? Isn't that irritating when someone buries the lead or takes forever to get to the point?" I ask. She rolls her eyes so hard that she may have seen the inside of her skull. "Like I was saying, the final two had interesting stories. My tenth stop of the day was at Sew It Was, you know the cute fabric store?" Chandra nods and I swear I see her eye twitch. "Brenda and Lori were just lovely. I probably could have spent an hour with them." Her eye does actually twitch this time. "They'd had an episode with a man loitering in the store. Brenda said he was a little too touchy-feely with the satins and she had to ask him to leave. Lori saw him two days later. He was standing by the spinning rack of patterns and staring out the window. Both felt uneasy with him. Would you like to know how they described him?"

"No neck and build like a small car?"

"Roughly," I say with a laugh. "Unfortunately, they don't have cameras. But, they gave me their phone numbers for you. Tomorrow is Brenda's day off and Lori's is Friday." Presenting the sticky note to her with a regal, "You are welcome." Chandra dips into a curtsy and snatches the paper so aggressively, that she nearly rips it in half.

"And the final one?"

" I talked to Mr. Ali's son, Joey, at Kebabbing Along. He said he doesn't know the password to the security system but to come by this week. He'll get it from his dad or uncle and help you with what you need. They've had random incidents over the last two months. Items moved in off hours, scratched paint on the back door. Motion alerts on otherwise blank footage. His dad was concerned it was racially motivated and was afraid to come forward. Where he was raised, the police cannot be trusted. So that fear has tainted his interactions here. Joey is happy to help and wants to reassure his father. He suggested any time on Thursday or Friday."

"You do good work! You know that, right?" Chandra says. The earlier irritation has gone and she seems proud of me. "Make sure to give me the details of the one who kicked you out."

"That'd be Lovella at Time After Thyme. She's friendly enough to customers but really hates Coco and Aggie. I was walking them downtown in the spring. She threatened to turn the hose on us if they "messed" in front of her store. I was not so friendly in return. So, today's interaction wasn't totally unexpected," I confess.

"Still, I'm paying her an on-duty visit." There are perks to having a friend on the police force. "She needs to respond to reasonable requests from law enforcement. I'll just stop in to chat and also mention concerns of citizens." Laughing, I ladle the meatballs and sauce onto an oversized platter decorated with dancing crabs.

"Ding Dong!" Desmond calls as he opens the front door. "In honor of the fun, picnic-style dinner, I'd like to introduce you to John Daly." He places the white ceramic pitcher and bag on lemon slices on the counter.

"Who or what is a John Daly?" I ask suspiciously, eyeing the pitcher.

"Both. It is an Arnold Palmer with a hefty dose of bourbon." He's clearly delighted by the addition to dinner. "The lemons are just for show." Before I can say anything else, Chandra is pulling glasses from the cupboard.

"Did I hear something about bourbon?" Brad hustles into the kitchen from his office.

***

With a satisfied sigh, Brad pushes his plate back and rubs his hands together. We're all feeling similarly stuffed. The meatball subs were a hit and not a single one was burnt or undercooked. The coleslaw was the right mix of tangy and sweet. Another dinner that came out as intended.

"Babe, you outdid yourself on that one!" Brad exclaims. "A perfect end of summer dinner." Desmond, Chandra, and Seb all agree. Every plate has been wiped clean and the mountain of meatballs has disappeared. Coco, Aggie, and Darla eye us from their spots on the lanai, all hoping there are meatballs in their future.

"Young lady, your cooking skills have improved!" Desmond says, he too is leaned back and patting his midsection. "Karen will be so proud of you." Tears prick my eyes, thinking of Karen's patience as I tackled simple recipes under her guidance. Most of which I ruined, but she was persistent in showing me basic meals that lower failure rates. The hours we spent in the kitchen are some of my treasured memories. I squeeze his hand as a thank you. Before I can answer, a horrendously loud siren erupts from Chandra's side of the table. She fumbles trying to quiet the alarm, nearly knocking over her drink and dropping the phone. All the dogs jump to high alert and silence falls over the table.

"Boudreaux," she snaps into the phone. Followed by several quick uh-huh, yes, and yes sir's. She stands quickly from the table and sprints to the front door. We all follow, not sure what is happening. Ending her call, she breathlessly tells, "Break in at Mr. Ali's kebab shop. There's apparently a fire as well. Stay here. I'll update you when I can." Instead of staying put, Seb races out the door behind her. Astonished, I step onto the porch and see his SUV is blocking her Jeep in the driveway. The engines rev and both reverse rapidly onto the street. To our continued surprise, he follows her.

"Huh, well I'll be," Desmond mutters, joining us on the porch. Linda pokes her head out of her front door and the Cohens stand from their porch swing.

"Looks like most of everyone is free. Should we have dessert while we wait?" I suggest. Brad waves our three neighbors over to the house. Each files from the steps and crosses the street.

"I'd call Mirabel but she's with Alfie and Elena in Montana until tomorrow," Desmond adds, appearing mildly disappointed.

"Don't worry— she'll be back in plenty of time to help us wrap this up." My words brighten his mood significantly. Movement across the street catches my eye. Edna stands on her porch with Hubert and the Avalons. Arms crossed, toe tapping. If I could see her face, there's no doubt its scrunched into a scowl. Raising my arm in a wave, I call "Helllloooooo neighbors," and blow a lip-smacking kiss. Spinning on my heels, I turn toward the house. Nothing gets under her skin more than denial of the last word or action.

19

On the Scene

Morning dawns with no word from Chandra. I tossed and turned throughout the night, checking my phone on the hour. The end result is me dragging from bed an hour later than usual, damp with sweat and the feeling I've been drugged. And still no messages from Chandra.

"How ya holding up?" Brad says, dropping a kiss on my clammy forehead.

"In desperate need of a scalding shower and a double espresso," I tell him in a whiney grumble. He leans in, gives me a sniff, then nods dramatically while handing me a espresso cup filled to the rim. Swatting him, I gulp the coffee in two quick drinks. It burns but does the job of perking me up enough to shower.

Before I can make it in the house, the doorbell rings.

***

"What do you mean?" My voice cracks with the you. It's an impossible situation for me to process.

"I know it's upsetting," Blair says soothingly. She clutches her coffee mug as if it's the only keeping her afloat. Her face is drawn and pale. Her under eyes are dark with streaked makeup and exhaustion. "We arrived on scene shortly after the alarm activated. Records show we were eight minutes from activation to arrival. Unfortunately, it wasn't fast enough." She exhales loudly through pursed lips, massaging her grip on the mug.

"Was he gone when you arrived?" Reconsidering my phrasing, I amend to add, "In the ambulance?"

Blair shakes her head solemnly, eyes shining. "No...when Munoz and Carolton got to him, there was a pulse. He was badly wounded. We weren't sure just how badly." Letting this soak in, she takes several slow sips of coffee. They're dainty to the point of inconsequential.

"There was too much blood lost before we arrived," Chandra adds, picking up while Blair pauses. "We estimate there were at least three bullet wounds. It was more than we could manage on scene." Seb grabs her hand in his and squeezes tightly. She tips her body to lean into him. I study her face carefully. She's tense and shows the same signs of exhaustion visible on Blair's face. The team must have been through a catastrophic night that's nearly pushed them to their breaking point. Nearly the entire department arrived to assist. Drive by shootings don't happen here.

"Were there any signs of a break-in?" Brad asks, glancing in his direction, I spot the open notes app on his phone. Thatta boy! Capturing all the details so none are lost.

Blair shakes her head again before answering. She stares into her nearly empty cup, swirling the remaining dregs of coffee. "As best we can tell, no. The entire glass front was shattered but the locks were intact. Nothing appears to have been missing at first glance. Joey's father, Bashir, and his uncle Samir, rushed to the hospital. It will have to wait until they're ready." We all nod in agreement. My heart breaks for this sweet family and the terror they'd endured last night. From chatting with Joey, I'd learned he is twenty-two and finishing an engineering degree. His father had insisted he attend college and avoid spending his life in the Kebab shop.

Brad has wordlessly returned with a full carafe of coffee, a plate of day-old Concha bread, and a small pot of honey butter I'd whipped up earlier this week. Chandra and Blair eagerly thrust their mugs toward Brad. He fills each as Seb scoots the cream and sugar in their direction. When she's stressed, Chandra needs her coffee extra sweet. Watching these men care of others in a time of need, my eyes sting with unshed tears. Brad smiles at me, winking as he refills our shared coffee, then plops beside me on the loveseat. Coco and Aggie are squeezed between us, maximizing the cuddle time they can get.

"How can we help?" I ask, my determination rearing its head. First my neighborhood was under attack, and now our precious downtown. I can't sit by idly.

"Hmmm..." Chandra murmurs, "How did I know?" She smiles at me over the rim of her mug, steam wafting in front of her face. "Seriously though, we knew you'd be willing." At this she raises her mug to me. "For the moment, we need to let the scene rest. Unfortunately, the mayor has decided to close off the majority of streets in the area. East and west 6-8th, Calendula, Iris, and Snap Dragon."

"What? But that includes the cafe? What will Seb do?" I shout, Brad places a hand on my thigh and squeezes while both dogs grumble at being jostled. Taking his cue, I pause my tirade and place a hand on my chest to steady my breathing.

"It can't be helped, CiCi. I do appreciate the enthusiasm nonetheless," Seb chimes in for the first time. "We'll be okay and can use the new coffee truck to make up for losses. Tev and Gilbert are setting up in the public parking by the pier. We've been overdue on getting it running. A terrible circumstance that has provided a perfect opportunity for the launch." Despite the positivity of his words, his face conveys his remorse. Now it is Chandra's turn to offer comfort.

"When the time is right, can you run an assist?" Blair asks, giving Chandra a pointed side-eye. "It will help tremendously if you can be our eyes and ears when we aren't around." Brad groans loudly with her request, but Blair pushes on, undeterred, "Our small force does the best we can, we're limited in how many officers we can allocate to surveillance round the clock."

Before answering, I stop and look right at Brad. Anxiety shows in the tightness of his face. A vein on his forehead pulses quickly. "You know I'd love to help, it's just that this one seems more dangerous than the last time. Missing wallets are one thing, but thefts and drive-by shootings have really upped the ante." My words ease a bit of the strain from his face. He nods subtly. "Let me talk it over with Brad first."

"I totally get that!" Chandra says, her voice low and soothing. "Just like last time, I promise to do everything I can to keep you safe." The last words are directed to Brad. They sit, locked in a staring contest of sorts. Finally, she nods and turns back to me. "You're right that this situation is more dangerous. The one bonus—this isn't happening on your street." A smile quirks one corner of her mouth and Brad huffs a small laugh beside me.

"It would be greatly appreciated by the department and the county. Your past behavior indicates not only can you be trusted, but that you offer valuable perspectives and insights into local cases. We also presume your neighbors will be involved. They seem to be as nosey as you are." She smiles conspiratorially. It's my turn to laugh. My little neighborhood group has proven to be helpful even when we aren't sure what we're doing.

"Let us know when you need help and what specifically it will be," Brad says, his words shocking me into silence. I stare, open-mouthed and bugged-eyed. He taps my chin, and flashes a toothy grin at me. "Don't forget, I helped with the last one."

***

"Does this mean I can get my own whiteboard?" I ask while locking the front door. Leaning against, I do my best version of a beguiling seductress.

"Jury is still out. Plus, where in the world would be put a six-foot whiteboard?" Gesturing around the inside of our home. He has a point. Our house is just over sixteen-hundred square feet which does not leave much room.

"You got any space in the garage?" I ask, flashing what I hope resembles puppy dog eyes.

"We'll figure it out. You need a shower and I need to log in for a meeting," he says, holding his nose and smirking at me.

"That sounded a lot like a yes," I cheer, skipping from the room. A hot shower and online shopping await, so now I'm in a rush to get the day started.

My shower is interrupted by persistent buzzing from my phone. Each message and call temporarily disrupts my shower playlist and has officially killed off the intended relaxation. As soon as I get the conditioner out of my hair, I'll deal with it.

"Hey!" Brad says, poking his head around the curtain. I screech and nearly waterboard myself. "Ha—sorry."

"What is the emergency?" I cry, rinsing the remnants from my face. "Between you and whoever is blowing up my phone, I'd give this shower a 0/10." Surliness is creeping into the edges of my voice.

"I'd give my view a 10/10 but that's beside the point." The flirty tone does nothing to reduce my irritation. Opening my eyes, I catch him staring.

"Creep!" I say and flick water in his direction. He easily dodges and presses the wet curtain to the backs of my thighs. He knows that grosses me out. Squealing I flip the water off and demand a towel.

Reluctantly handing me a fresh towel, he says "Chandra called me since you weren't answ—"

"Not answering? I've been in the shower for less than ten minutes and didn't even get to shave my right leg. What is so urgent?" I snap before he can finish.

"Well, she said there was a new development and thought you may be interested."

"Daggone her," I sputter and dig through the cast-off pile of clothes for my phone. "She knew it would get me." Opening my phone I have four missed calls and a series of texts escalating in urgency. Did she honestly think I was ignoring her? She'd been at the house for over an hour this morning and knew I looked like I'd rolled in a pig pen all night.

Me: *Do you know patience is a virtue?*

This is a common conversation between us. She was born with little to no patience, at least not in her personal life. I've seen the woman wait out a criminal case for months but blow her top over a ten-minute wait for lunch.

Chandra: *I've heard. Why didn't you answer?*

Me: *I was attempting to shower*

Chandra: *Good, you were musty this morning*

Me: *Didn't sleep because someone left me hanging all night*

Chandra: *Had other things to do than text you*

Chandra: *Can you come to the station today?*

Me: *Why? For how long? Last time I wasted a day*

Chandra: *2 p.m. One hour max*

Me: *Snacks?*

Chandra: *Bring your own*

Chandra: *And one for me*

I want to be irritated still but curiosity is getting the better of me. Brad leans against the doorframe and cocks an eyebrow.

"She gave zero details but asked me to come in for an hour this afternoon." Pouting I stomp from the bathroom. While I love getting to work with Chandra on cases, I do not love lingering in the mildewy conference rooms at the station. One too many hurricanes and few too many drywall changes over the last decade have left the place feeling slightly neglected.

"Take the girls for a walk and relax for a bit. I'd go with but the day is full of meetings until five." His suggestion seems like a primo solution. Today is supposed to be warm, clear, and sunny. The perfect combo.

"Walkies babies?" I chirp, rushing past Brad and into our room.

In five minutes, I'm out the door with Coco and Aggie in tow. We do our typical lap around the cul-de-sac, greeting our neighbors as we go. Edna's house is dark and closed up, I pray she's out of town again. There's only so much stress I can handle.

"Do you think Chip is out?" I ask as we exit our street and head to the nature trail across the street. Chip is our local alligator. He's on the smaller side at around four feet but he has a distinctly chipped tooth. The whole area has taken to the nickname and he's gained in popularity. We even tag Chip sightings in the neighborhood chat.

I quickly send a message to the group, *Chip out today?* and wait for responses while we walk.

As soon as we enter the path, I hear him. A guttural below and swishing sound clue me into his presence. For safety, I pick up the pups and pin them close to my body. We stand high above him on the boardwalk and watch. He's stretched to his whole four-and-a-half feet, belly rounded, and skin shining in the sun. Sliding my phone free, I snap pictures for our group. As I'm snapping away, he opens his mouth and that chipped tooth glints like a diamond. Watching him relax and bask in the warm, autumn morning is just the reset I needed. Raising my phone to record him stretching, it dings with a message.

Chandra: *Can you get here sooner?*

Immediately, I start sweating. Why does she need me to come in earlier?

20

Say it With Me

"Can I speak with Chandra Boudreaux?" I ask the desk officer. He dips his chin in the direction of a wooden door on the right. As I approach a buzzer sounds. Opening the door, I peek around the edge, spotting Chandra and Blair striding toward me. They're lock-stepped with rigid posture. Neither appears remotely approachable. Whatever this is about, it cannot be good.

"Come with us," Blair practically barks. Jumping forward through the doorway, I fall in with them. We stride through the halls silently. The quieter it stays, the more anxious I become. By the time we stop walking, my scalp is prickly sweat and heart feels like it may beat right out of chest. I attempt a smile, but my lips have gone dry and tight.

"We'll meet in here," Chandra says, snapping on a buzzing overhead light. Momentarily, I am caught in the realization that everything in this building makes noise. That's got to cause some sort of hearing impairment or psychosis. "Cees- now isn't the time." Busted. I drop into the seat Blair points to. What in the world is happening? Briefly, a shudder passes through me. I rub my arms to warm them.

"Apologies for all the drama," Blair begins. "There have been some significant updates throughout the morning." She sits behind the desk and it dawns that we're in what must be her office. The framed photo of her, a smiling tall man, and three small children confirms it. Off to the side, Chandra leans against a battered, avocado green filing cabinet. Tension radiates from her like mist off water in the morning. She's visibly upset by something, jaw is set in a hard line with hands clenched tightly on her gun belt.

"Wh—," My voice creaks, clearing my throat, I try again. "What has changed?" Chandra and Blair exchange a look, nodding in sync. Blair pins me with a hard stare.

"We're going to share information that cannot be discussed beyond the three of us." Her voice matches the unflinching stare. I don't speak, only nod my head repeatedly. "Not even Brad." At this I falter, and glance at Chandra. She softens and mouths, "Sorry girl." I weakly smile and look back at Blair. Knowing full well, I'm telling him.

"Great. Now that's covered." Blair opens the folder and slides the top page in my direction. "It seems there are more players than our bestie, Slug." Picking up the page, I review the series of mugshots. Three men glare back at me. Arthur 'Blitz' Maltz, Juan Diaz, Jin Ho Baek. Skimming the booking information, the only overlap I readily see is living in Florida.

"How are they connected?" I ask absentmindedly, studying the faces intently. Have I seen them before? Or do they look familiar because I'm forcing it?

"That's what we're working on currently. Initially, there was a single known accomplice— the driver of the black car. What the digital forensics team found changed our assumption," she slides two additional papers in my direction. A zoomed in shot of the driver's side of the car on a small street. A different view of the same car with another man driving.

"Two of the three?" I question, comparing the mugshots with traffic camera stills. "I see Baek and Maltz. Where is Diaz?"

"Good eye!" Blair passes another stack of photos across the cluttered desk. Diaz walking with Baek, Diaz eating with Slug. Maltz, Slug, and Baek sitting at a table outside of Gerardo's. Maltz and Diaz at Azúcar with Slug in the background. Maltz and Baek in the front seat of the black car two-door car. All the images connect the men. Too many to be coincidental.

"So no previous work together?" Work might be a stretch but I don't exactly know the lingo. The final photo taken on the same street where I'd been struck. My gut reaction screaming it is from that day. Palms sweaty and heart pounding, I wait anxiously while she shuffles more papers. The images crumbling slightly in my hands.

"From the information we received this morning, we cannot find a connection other than what is captured," Blair points to the printouts in my damp hands. "No overlapping sentences, parole officers, or addresses. By all accounts, there is no indication they know one another." Leaning back in her chair, she sighs loudly and runs her hands through her hair, tugging slightly at the ends.

"Why am I here?" None of this seems to have anything to do with me, other than the accident and my job at the cafe.

"We're hoping you can help us with finding out where they've been around town and how long they've been here," Blair again responds while Chandra watches silently. Normally, she's the one who talks to me about cases. Blair's openness and willingness to share makes me unusually tense. It seems there's more to this and waiting for that shoe to drop makes me twitchy.

"You're aware that I'm always..." I say slowly, waiting for either of them to interject, "willing to help. But you know Brad's rule." Blair shakes her head, noticeably confused. She shifts her gaze from me to Chandra.

"We have to keep her safe. Otherwise it's a no go," Chandra adds, "He means it too. Any time CiCi has helped, I've made a promise to Brad that I personally will ensure her safety. Her recent accident will make this more challenging. He thinks she was intentionally targeted."

"Well," Blair shifts in her chair, straightening papers, "he may not be wrong." I whip my head to face her so quickly that my neck cracks. Wincing, I hold the back of my neck and stare open-mouthed.

"What do you mean?" That earlier suspicion roars back. Does she have proof that my accident was intentional? Blair again stares at Chandra. "Alright, can we cut that out? It's like a low budget cop-drama. What is it that you aren't telling me?" Chandra leaves her post and sits in the chair beside me. She remains tense, perching on the edge of the seat. "Spill it sister."

"I knew you'd have questions." Her face relaxing for the first time. Realization hits, she's been uncomfortable at the thought of withholding details from me. She holds a hand out to Blair and is passed a second folder, thicker than the first. Sorting through, she extracts a printout with a wider angle of a photo we'd just looked at, Diaz and Baek walking on the street. With a gasp, I pull it from her hands. Diaz and Baek aren't simply walking down the street. They're following a woman. Specifically, me.

The series of images show them following me on different camera angles in town and ending at the cafe. The next photo I'm handed, another wider angle, shows Baek and Diaz waiting to be seated at Azucar. Slug is visible on the patio in the corner. Unlike before, he isn't alone. A man's back faces the camera. He's dressed in what appears to be a suit, a dark briefcase beside his chair. A shiver runs through me. Men in suits have made me nervous since my run in with Anton Dragovic. The paper trembles slightly. At this Chandra reaches over and squeeze my forearm, "It ain't him, cher." Nodding, I draw a shuddering breath, then focusing on relaxing the tightness forming in my chest.

"You sure?"

"It can't be. He's in prison for a long time."

"But, what if..."

Chandra interrupts, "There's no connection. I've checked and re-checked all morning."

Trusting her, I reach for the next image. Slug rushing to the passenger-side of that two-door, black car. The sight of it irritates me. He has a dark bag in his hand. Another shot, the car at a stoplight, miles from downtown. Baek driving and Slug in the passenger seat. At least now we know who the getaway driver is.

"This is the one we found most concerning. It was taken moments before your accident," Blair points to the photo in Chandra's hand. I look at it without understanding. "Check the timestamp." Chandra taps the bottom corner, 3:50 p.m.

"So...ten minutes before my accident?"

"Right. Taken ten minutes prior to you being struck. The car is parked in a metered zone, with cameras. It had been parked since 3:18 p.m."

"Okay. They parked and did what? Are they on any other cameras?" Blair and Chandra shake in unison, exchanging a quick side-eyed glance. Sighing loudly. "Don't start that again." I snap.

"They just sat. The camera takes a photo every seven minutes," she holds up her hand, "Yes, I know, seven is a weird choice. The city council picked it, not us." Blair smirks briefly, then her face becomes serious again. "The car was no longer parked after 3:58 p.m.. By your own timing, you were struck at 4:00 p.m." She pauses and leans forward on her desk, waiting for the words to sink in.

"Am I understanding this correctly?" I stammer. "They *waited* for me?"

"It appears so. Is there any way they would have known your arrival time?" Blair asks, a gentleness creeps into her voice that prompts tears to spring to my eyes. Standing abruptly, I nearly knock the chair over.

"No. The only people who knew were Brad, Chandra, and Melody." Biting my thumbnail, I think back to that day. "She came into work and asked if we could talk. But, it wasn't a great time and we made plans to chat when work wrapped up at two. I can't remember if we said anything in the cafe. I mean...maybe...did she mention a time?" Pacing back and forth, my head spins. "Where was I when I called you?"

"I don't remember, I was cleaning the car at the station. So I wasn't as focused as I normally would have been."

"Could you have called from a public place?" Blair asks. Her cautious tone is flat to avoid any hint of blame or accusation.

"Ummm...let me think. I left at the cafe a little after two. Walked to the car and sat for a minute," I drum my nails on the desk, trying desperately to remember the day. Since the accident, the events of that day have been a little fuzzy. "I was finishing a coffee I'd made and trying to figure out dinner." Making dinner remains my eternal struggle. What did I make that day anyway? Oh yeah, a turkey sandwich in the E.R. "WAIT!!!" I shout. The drumming ceases, Blair and Chandra flinch. "I called Melody on my way out the back door of the cafe. She suggested where we should meet." Snapping my fingers, I point at Chandra, "Remember how I've started to repeat instructions back?"

"Yeah, it's so you don't forget," Chandra says, smiling encouragingly. "Really has helped by the way."

"Thanks! I've hoped it was. Anyway— I repeated it back to her *out loud*. I said the time and location." That same prickling sweat returns, my scalp tingles and palms grow damp. "I need...I need to call Brad." Panic is beginning to seize me. Someone was listening, this was intentional.

"Slow and steady," Chandra says, guiding me back to the creaky wooden chair. "I already texted him to come get you. He's in the lobby."

"I thought you said—"

"Plans change girly. I want you to focus on calming down. This room is too small for the four of us, and I think we've accomplished enough today," Chandra says, glancing around me to Blair.

"Let's call it a day. Go home and try to relax. Chandra or I will check in later," Blair reassures, standing an extending a hand for me to shake. "We can't thank you enough for meeting with us. I know this hasn't been an easy discovery." The understatement of the century. My emotions are all over the place. I imagine a terrifyingly massive tornado filled with every thought and emotion running through my mind.

"But, you never told me what happened last night?"

"Later, there's plenty of time for that," Chandra says as we exit the office.

21

A Fine Line

I spend the next several hours waffling between anger and anxiety. How could I possibly have been the target? What would have prompted the group to single me out? I'm a nobody. There's nothing connecting me to the businesses involved. I make coffee for a living, not business decisions. It makes absolutely no sense, every angle leads to a dead-end.

"Hungry, my love?" Brad places a plate loaded with steak, crispy potatoes, and salad in front of me. The scent wafting upward resets my brain and the day is slightly less heavy. Grinning at my sweet husband as he refills my wine and leans down for a kiss. Thereby snapping in the final pieces into place. Relaxing into the chair, I inhale deeply. The steak-scented, evening air with a slight chill was perfect.

I'd given Brad the basics on the way from the station to the house. There's so much left to discuss, but it can wait until after we eat. This dinner smells too good to waste.

***

"They're sure?" Brad asks, leaning forward onto the table, clutching his wine glass with a concerning level of force. He's flushed with a vein visibly pulsing rapidly in his neck. He's taking the news about as well as I had.

"Not one-hundred percent," shrugging, "about as sure as they can be, though. Blair and Chandra presented some fairly solid evidence." The images of Maltz and Diaz following me into the cafe flashes before my eyes. I decide there's no benefit in attempting to be casual about the situation. It had already escalated to me being struck on a public street corner. How much further are they willing to go?

"Did you get copies of the photos?" Shaking my head, I admit that it didn't occur to me. With the strain of the afternoon, all I could think about was getting home to Brad. "I'm sure if we ask, Chandra may be willing to share. Was this the only reason they called you in?"

Grimacing, I mentally prepare my explanation. One I'd come up with while faking a nap earlier. "Well, the conversation began differently." Brad raises an eyebrow, gesturing with his free hand for me to keep going. So I do. "Blair was up front about Slug having previously unknown accomplices. That all four had been spotted around town in various combinations. Never all four together. The team can't find a connection other than Florida residency."

"Are you telling me, Blair asked you to look into them?"

"Sort of. Similar to my canvas of the businesses with cameras, she was hopeful I could ask around without drawing too much attention. Casual conversations can seem less suspicious and more people are willing to open up to me."

"Even though she knows you've been intentionally targeted?" His tension is leveling out, which does surprise me a bit. Mine was ratcheting up around this point in Blair's office. While taking a long sip of the crisp white wine, I wave my hand back and forth, indicating maybe. He doesn't seem pleased by this response. "And Chandra was willing to go along with endangering you?" There's the reaction I'd pictured. He stands from the table and paces around the lanai. Coco and Aggie following in his wake. It'd be comical if he wasn't on the verge of a coronary.

"She actually wasn't. The entire time, she stood by the stiff as a board with the most sour expression I've ever seen. When Blair said I couldn't tell you—" Brad lets out some sort of groan/grunt/growl combination that I've never heard before, ending "WHAT?!?" I put up a hand to halt him, "Chandra looked like she'd swallowed a cup of curdled milk and apologized. Let's be clear, I was telling you whether I had Blair's blessing or not." He nods his head and blows me a kiss. "To death, babes."

"Dear God, let's not use that word right now," he says with a frown. Point taken.

"Anyway, once I brought up your rule for my involvement, Chandra took the lead," I can't help but sound proud of her, "She finally relaxed and opened up. The reminder of keeping me safe was the ammo she needed to move the conversation in the direction she wanted." Brad finally stops pacing, drops into his seat and refills his wine. Both dogs jump on the chaise and eye him warily, unsure if he's staying put or they'll need to spring into action. "From that moment, the weird tension finally ended. For the first time since I walked in, it felt like they were both being honest."

"Tell me where you're at..."

"Torn. You know staying out of it will now be physically impossible. At the same time, I'm scared of what the next escalation might be."

"Solid and I am right there with you." He clicks his glass to mine and murmurs, "To death." All while grinning widely.

"So we're in?"

"We're in. With rules. Your safety comes first, no matter how badly they want your help." I readily agree. Dying won't be worth solving the case. Poor Joey Ali nearly lost his life already. No one else should.

"Tomorrow?" we say in unison and then burst into laughter. My mind is already racing a mile a minute and I'll need the night to not only organize my thoughts—I also need to rally the troops. Kicking things off, I send a group text. Talking through today with Brad has moved me from anxious, to readiness. We need to get this case solved and get our town back.

Me: *Community center at noon?*

A flood of thumbs up and heart emojis pour into my phone immediately.

***

The doorbell camera chimes at 5:36 a.m. Jolting awake, I picture Slug lurking on the porch with a rocket launcher.

"Relax, it's just a delivery," Brad reassures, holding his lit phone screen in my direction. A driver jogs back to their van in the pre-dawn darkness.

Sighing loudly, I flop back on the bed and pull the covers over my head. Questioning the improbability of returning to sleep, I scrunch on my side and wake up two hours later to the smell of coffee. It's inches from my face and I can't resist flinging the covers back to take a sip.

Muffled barking hints at Brad and the dogs on the lanai.. I grab an oversized cardigan and stumble through the house toward the back door. On the way, a huge box leaning against the living room wall catches my eye. My undercaffeinated brain can't even begin to guess at what it could be. From what I can remember, I hadn't been the one to order anything in several days. Deciding it's a mystery for later, I squeeze into the chair with Brad. He wraps me in a hug and steals my mug of coffee. Laughing, I take it back and drink as much as I can before scalding myself.

Today is off to a much better start than yesterday. Settling in to snuggle and enjoy my coffee, I contentedly heave a sigh. Brad presses his cheek to mine and asks, "Better than yesterday?" I nod slowly, replaying the events of yesterday— a day full of too many emotions for me to have processed yet. For now, I'm enjoying this moment and will deal with the day as it comes.

"Did you see your present?" Brad murmurs into the top of my head. I attempt to crane my neck to see him but end up only giving him a bizarre whale-eyed gaze. Covering my eyes with his hand, he mutters, "Creepy."

"What present?" I ask, fighting to free myself from his hand and look around the lanai.

"You didn't notice the nearly six-foot box in the living room?" he asks incredulously.

"Oh...that...yes, but I had no idea what it was," I confess. In hindsight, it does seem slightly ridiculous to have stumbled past it with no questions.

"Interesting approach," he teases. "Would you like to see it?"

Scrambling from the chair, the dogs and I race into the living room. Sliding to a stop in my sock feet, I inspect the box in an effort to guess the contents. Finally spotting the logo, it's a well-known office supply store. Which doesn't really help me guess. Did he get a new desk or something? The sound of scissor blades click together behind me, Brad strides past me, brandishing them with a flourish. He quickly slices the tape and stands back, "M'lady? The honor is yours."

Peeling the layers of the box away, I screech with excitement. A gleaming, unblemished whiteboard. The blankness is a thing of true beauty and my imagination runs wild filling it with case details and notes.

"It's on wheels," Brad says triumphantly. This is a dream come true. Standing with my hands clapped on either side of my face, tears fall easily. For a moment, I am embarrassed to cry over office supplies, then that emotion is replaced with pure joy. This represents so much more. He's fully supporting my silly dreams and giving me a space to organize my thoughts.

Flinging my arms around him, I topple us onto the sofa. Crying, laughing, squealing, and covering his face with kisses.

22

Fill in the Blanks

The door of the community center clicks open with a blast of heat. So much for the allegedly cooler weather. Today is forecasted in the low nineties. We'd had a reprieve for less than a week.

Mirabel arrives first, escorted in by Desmond. Her outfit of the day is built around brightly pattered floral pedal pushers, topped with a lemon yellow-eyelet blouse. Her glasses were her favorite lime green frames. She looked like a walking citrus grove in those colors and brings immediate sunshine to the space.

"We've got to put a refresh on the agenda for next year's budget. This place is getting dingy," she says while cracking open a container of fresh fruit and a second of madeleines.

"I already have it in the notes for next month's meeting. Between the carpet and the scuffed walls, we're starting to be a bit sad," Desmond confirms. He opens homemade fruit dip and caramel sauce. We position the items on the table with the coffee I've brewed and a carafe of cinnamon iced coffee. Which for full transparency is mostly for Linda and I. She's taken to the iced coffees and cold brews I make at Azúcar, to the point that I keep some on hand for when she drops by the house.

"Is the gang all here?" Linda calls out from the doorway. She swoops in, placing a platter of warm scones with whipped butter next to the other treats.

"Nearly. Waiting on Moshe and Francie. Chandra and Brad can't make it," I tell her, sniffing the scones like a bloodhound. "Orange and vanilla?" She nods approvingly. "A last-minute meeting has pulled Brad out of the fun and Chandra is caught up with the case."

"Don't worry, the guests of honor have arrived," Moshe booms, leading Francie in by the hand. She's holding a tray of peach caprese salad. The uncertainty on her face breaks my heart. Over the last several months, her dementia has rapidly advanced after a brief hospitalization. Which is apparently not uncommon. Either way, it hurts to see her intermittently confused by her surroundings.

"Shall we load up and get down to brass tacks?" Desmond asks, while loading a plate with treats from the table. Murmuring in agreement, we line up buffet style. Within ten minutes, we're seated around the table in the conference room. While the fishy smell has dissipated, there's still a vague musty smell.

"Adding to the list," Desmond says before Mirabel can ask.

"There have been quite a few developments since our dinner a few days ago," I begin. "This can't leave the room." I make eye contact with each of my friends around the table. They nod solemnly in turn. "As you know, Chandra was called in emergently with most of the police force. It sadly ended with a shooting," gasps erupt. Walking to the partially filled in crime board, I add the details of Joey's injuries and notes on the new accomplices. When I get to my accident, Mirabel and Linda sniffle softly, clutching hands. Mirabel whispers "Nieta!" softly. She was crushed by my accident and spent an entire day cooking for me. She and Linda refused to leave me alone for most of the first week. "Unfortunately, Detective Cassidy and Chandra believe it was not accidental and I was intentionally targeted."

More muffled gasps. Moshe stands red-faced and tense, striding back and forth across the side of the room. If I didn't know better, I'd be concerned he would punch a hole through the wall. Desmond grips the arms of his chair until I'm convinced he'll rip them off. Francie watches Moshe with confusion. Linda leans over and pats her gently, easing her anxiety.

"What can we do?" Linda asks, the tight set of jaw the opposite of her red-rimmed eyes.

"Figure out what they're doing here and why me—" To emphasize, I tap the board with the marker, the clicking brings Moshe and Desmond back to the task at hand.

"How are we going to do that?" Desmond asks.

"Exactly how we did it last time. We talk to our friends and neighbors. We keep an eye out around here and in town. Keeping Blair and Chandra up to date on *everything* we find." Momentary silence falls over the room as each considers what the best approach is.

"I can get with my book club ladies, we're often downtown together. Someone will have seen something, whether they realize it or not." Linda kicks off the planning.

"I've got the Jenkins and Browns. They've been in business the longest in the area and will be tuned into the happenings." Desmond begins scratching notes on a yellow legal pad that has appeared from nowhere.

"My in is with the bank. A former colleague is the manager. They'll be willing to chat with me. This is personal and time to call in all the favors," Moshe says. "Francie and I can arrange a dinner for any that are willing to help. The patio is ready for a party." They've spent the last several months redoing their outdoor space in preparation of a granddaughter's graduation in the spring.

"Alfie has friends at the insurance office and Elena's niece runs the bookstore. They'll help us get what we need," Mirabel adds and points to Desmond's pad. "Write that down for me."

"I'm on it in the cafe. So many of the locals are regulars, I can probe to see if anyone remembers them. It's super important that we all keep an eye out. These men are not above potentially fatal violence." My voice cracks on the last word. I push away the image of a smiling Joey, promising to help however he can. While none of the men involved were caught on camera, I'm convinced they were involved. "When do we get this party started?"

"I'll call Bernice and Emmet Brown once I get home. Time for an older-timer's reunion," Desmond says while grinning. This man loves to be in the thick of it.

"Seems like a fine afternoon for a visit to the bank to me," Moshe chimes in. Now that we've got a plan, the raging giant has calmed and is sitting peacefully, holding Francie's hand.

"The book club is due for a check-in anyway, I'll put in a call and assemble my troops," Linda says, snapping a photo of Desmond's notes and another of our crime board.

"Alfie and Elena are coming over for dinner. Every good plan starts with a good meal." Mirabel smiles conspiratorially. Her cooking works miracles and I'm convinced the right meal from her kitchen can get any problem solved.

***

Chandra: *your club needs a name*

    Chandra: *I can't keep listing them all by name, it takes too long*

    Me: *open to suggestions. We can add it to the next meeting*

    Chandra: *about time*

    Chandra: *solve the case, yet?*

    Me: *solid start to it*

    Chandra: *pizza night?*

    Me: *when have I ever turned that down?*

Dinner arrived sooner than I'd planned. Brad had a free spot in the afternoon to help me put the whiteboard together and find it a home. We opted to relocate some patio furniture and place it against the wall on the lanai. Tucked away, the whiteboard is protected from rain and prying eyes. We rig up an old bed sheet to cover it when not in use. Running through the meeting at the community center, I fill in notes on a corner of the board.

"Put me down to chat with Paul and Marco." Brad points to the list of who we're planning to interview. I must look confused about adding his friends' names to the board. "They've invested in a few of the buildings downtown and are in the process of outright purchasing another. It's taking a while though. There's some developer intent on out bidding anyone local. They'll have some scoop on what's happening." My confusion disappears into delight. Who knew they were so involved? Love seeing our community work to preserve local businesses.

Darla sprints onto the porch at the speed of a hippo launched from a cannon. She shoots through the doggie door with Coco and Aggie on her tail. Well, not literally, but close enough.

"Guess dinner is here?" Brad asks wryly.

"What? You can't match her pace?" I shout into the house.

"Y'all need to lock that door," Chandra says while dropping a salad and garlic bread into the center of the table.

"As if she doesn't have a key," Seb chimes in, peeking over at us over three boxes of pizza. Sheepishly saying, "I was hungry when I ordered."

"No complaints, my man." Brad claps him on the back while going into the house for drinks. He returns with sodas and iced tea.

Chandra points to my human-sized whiteboard, "This is new..."

"Gift for my sweet. I can't have her at the community center all hours of the day. Way easier to let her crack the case from here." Brad smiles at me proudly, ignoring Chandra's miffed snort.

"Pizza then spill it," Chandra says, whipping the pizza boxes open.

***

"Put me down for whatever businesses are left over. We have a town hall scheduled for Sunday. There is growing fear over our safety and we are meeting to discuss what we can do," Seb offers. Chandra glances at him, clearly this is news to her. "We decided this afternoon. I'd planned to tell you at some point tonight."

"You betta," she says with mock menace.

"Do you know if Paul and Marco will be there?" Brad adds, chomping on a pizza crust. He casually dips the pieces in hot sauce before throwing them into his mouth.

"No. We didn't open it to the investors and building owners. Only the business owners. There will be a separate meeting once we have all had the chance to talk."

"Makes sense. No need to have all those voices around the table. I'll keep it quiet until after weekend. Don't want to start a mutiny." Brad waves a crust in Seb's direction. We all agree that is likely the best course. The town can't take more drama at the moment.

"Remember—this cannot turn into a community event with vigilantes taking matters into their own hands," Chandra admonishes.

"Noted! I swore everyone to secrecy. Plus, we're all pretty darn scared and don't want to attract too much attention."

"My point exactly. For whatever reason, you've earned a target. I can't keep you safe if there are too many people in the way." Brad shifts uncomfortably in his chair at Chandra's words.

"Speaking of that," he says slowly.

"I've installed extra cameras overnight. Inside and outside the cafe. We've also put three more in the employee lot. There isn't an angle uncovered," Seb reassures him.

"Didn't they cover the lenses at the other places?" Brad's stress over my safety, returning in a fierce wave.

"I thought about that. We've taken the precaution of making sure most are not visible. Unless you know where to look." He proudly opens the app on his phone to share the feeds with Brad. "Tev was with CiCi while she waited for the ambulance. He was pretty shaken up and is concerned for our staff. So, he and a few of my cousins have volunteered as security." Chandra cocks an eyebrow, again displeased with this announcement. "It was on my list to tell you."

"Do they know what they're doing?" Brad questions, no doubt picturing his cousins, Todd and Barry. Neither would be able to hold their own in a verbal confrontation, let alone a fight.

"Without saying too much," Seb tips his head toward Chandra, "I'm fairly sure they can hold their own." Message received. Brad relaxes knowing I'll be safe at work.

"Park only in the back lot," Brad tells me, his tone not allowing for any argument.

"What about around here?" Chandra points to the security light and camera above the garage.

"I ordered more today." Brad points to the fence line and other side of the house. "Enough for all corners, back door, and motion sensor lights. We'll put CiCi's Jeep inside the garage. No way we're replacing the top again." I make a face and mouth, "eww," the last time it took an eternity to fix. I have no desire to repeat that event.

Satisfied, we switch topics and chat about Chandra's family coming to town next month. We've all had enough of this case for the day.

23

Pulling Shots

Wren twirls up to the counter and hands an order slip to me. Two coladas, a black cold brew, and a hot latte with cinnamon and nutmeg.

"If you happen to have an extra shot free, let me know. I could use it!" Wren admits, sliding her skates back and forth. The skaters equivalent of tapping your foot. "Today is dragging." She gestures to the nearly empty cafe. The only customers we've had are a few out of town visitors and a handful of police officers patrolling downtown. Blowing a mouthful of air through pursed lips, I made a loud sputtering sound. "Same girl," Wren says before skating away.

Pulling the shots, mixing the sweetened brew, and prepping the hot milk doesn't take long. I pull an extra shot for Wren and set it aside. My final step in the order is the simple cold brew. When I first started at the cafe, I wished for orders like this. Simple, quick to assemble, with a limited opportunity to mess up. Today, I could really have used something to pass the time or at least a few customers to chat with.

"Thanks!" Wren squeaks, reaching for her espresso. She downs it in one gulp, wiping her mouth and smiling widely. "Absolutely perfect. Hope it does the trick." She whirls away, her tray loaded with our only order.

Discouraged, I occupy myself cleaning the coffee bar. Stopping short of disassembling the espresso machine, everything is cleaned to within an inch of its life. Staff pops by asking for anything extra that might be laying around. On the fourth drop-in, I make a decision. This is the perfect day to practice. Pulling out the recipe list kept under the counter in a notebook, I call any of the free staff over. Together we peruse and select three coffees to sample— two hot and one iced. Whatever we don't drink we can share with friends who stop by.

Hitting the storage room for supplies, a buzz erupts from my back pocket. Sliding the phone out, I see a message from Brad.

Brad: *holding your own?*

Me: *yeah, trying to keep busy*

Brad: *slow day?*

Me: *practically dead*

Me: *come in for lunch?*

Brad: *no can do, meetings all afternoon*

Me: *everyone is avoiding downtown*

Brad: *you blame them?*

He's not wrong. If I didn't work downtown, I probably would avoid it too. Break-ins, creeps caught on camera, drive-by shootings. Our small town is known for relaxing beach trips, great food, and a unique historic downtown. Now, that reputation is at stake. It's daunting to think how long the damage will take to recover from.

"Hey, Cees?" Wren's voice calls into the storeroom. "You got some customers." Abandoning my task, I hustle back to the coffee bar, only to freeze in my tracks. Standing at the counter are Arthur Maltz and Jin Ho Baek. Stammering, I struggle through my usual greeting. Turning to start their orders, I slip my phone from the apron pocket and text *911* to Chandra. The buzzing indicates a video call. I answer as smoothly as possible with violently trembling hands. Chandra smartly stays quiet.

"Can I get a name for the latte? And one for the breve?"

"Uh, yeah sure. Artie for the latte and Jin for the breve."

Thanking them, I end the call and begin making their beverages. In the process, I scatter espresso grounds across the counter twice while prepping.

"You need a hand?" Seb asks, crossing behind the counter. I nod, indicating the grounds everywhere.

"One of those days, ya know?" I joke. "You do the espresso and I'll prep the milk." Seb jovially agrees, passing by me, he squeezes my arm. Good, that means he's spoken with Chandra. He makes polite small talk with the two men, even making light of the slow day we're having. When he asks what they think is going on, I nearly drop the milk pitcher. It clatters a little but remains upright. My word— I can't decide if I want them to rush out or stick around until the police arrive.

"Sheesh, I've got it bad today. Might be time to eat." Attempting to cover my jitters with humor, a garbled laugh bubbles up. Moving as slowly as possible, I finish both beverages and demo a new latte art I'd seen online. In the background, I see Seb's cousins move into tables on either side of the restaurant. Having never questioned who they are or what they're capable of, I am relieved by their presence in the room. Safety in numbers, right? Isn't that what saves gazelles on nature shows?

Try as we might, the men decline to sit in the cafe and take their drinks to go. Even faking that my card reader is down, we call over Hannah to use the mobile. Maltz and Baek suddenly grow antsy and offer to pay with cash. Dropping a twenty-dollar bill on the counter, Baek gruffly says, "Keep the change," aggressively snatching his cup from the counter.

Before we can stop them, they're out the door and down the street. Seb is on the phone with Chandra immediately. He nods at his cousins and they silently exit the cafe, following the men onto the street. I collapse onto the edge of the counter. The moment they left, my chest began burning with the pent-up fear. I grip the edge of the countertop, white-knuckled and dripping sweat. A cool cloth is placed on the back of my neck by Wren.

"Honey, I have no clue what just happened. But, geez am I sorry that I called you back up here," she laments while continuing to soothe me. One hand presses the cloth to my neck, the other rubs my back.

In a few moments, I've collected myself enough to speak. Turning to face Wren, I smile and squeeze her hand reassuringly. "Don't sweat it." Despite her smile, she seems unnerved by my lack of explanation. Tightening the strings of my apron, I remove the cloth from my neck and stand straighter. Coffee will help settle us all. Getting to work, I begin setting up three cortados. The small, sweetened coffees are just what we'll need. The door chimes and I resist the urge to turn. Giving into the anxiety won't do me any favors.

"They're gone," Seb murmurs from across the counter. "By the time I got outside, there was no sign of them. It was like they vanished. Chandra and Blair are on it, both assume they'd parked nearby and left quickly. The biggest issue, there weren't any cars on the street..." His words freeze me in place.

"No cars?" Surely, he's mistaken. He must have missed a parked car, or a vehicle rounding the corner before he made it onto the street. Seb's face makes me reconsider questioning him He seems as confused as I am. "Will the cameras help?" Snapping his fingers, he points at me and rushes away from the coffee bar. I'm left standing with a half steamed pitcher of milk and flat espresso. Sighing heavily, I dump the dead shots and begin again.

***

Collapsing onto the sofa, I'm slathered with kisses from Coco and Aggie. The unexpected afternoon thunderstorm has left them frantic and they dance all over, begging to be held. After the weird day I've had, there's nothing I want more than to snuggle them and close my eyes for a bit. Draping a blanket over us, I curl onto my side, pulling both dogs to me. In seconds they've calmed. My eyelids become impossibly heavy, the pull of nap irresistible. Just a few minutes, I tell myself.

"Babe, you awake?" Brad's voice rumbles distantly. Faintly, I feel the sofa shift as he sits on the edge. Reaching for him, I attempt to pull him to lie down. Instead, he places an arm beneath me and lifts my body into a semi-sitting position. Grumbling lightly, I crack my eyes open. The house is dark other than the light above the stove. Rubbing my eyes, I stare at my watch. It's 6:48 p.m. More than three hours have passed since I'd laid down. The intention was a quick nap but the emotional exhaustion of the day clearly had other plans.

"You're home so late," I croak out, the hours-long nap leaving my throat dry.

"I tried to call," we say in unison then laugh. Standing, Brad pulls me from the couch and we stumble into the kitchen together. "I had a late meeting and wanted you to know it would be close to seven before I could get home. You didn't answer, so I assumed you'd gotten busy after work."

"I was so tired, I laid down with the dogs, and crashed. Guess why I called?" He shrugs and indicates for me to continue. "Artie Diaz and Jin Ho Baek visited the coffee bar this afternoon..." Brad's jaw drops so quickly that it cracks. Rubbing his jaw, he stares at me. "It was right after we talked last. Wren called me back to the coffee bar and I nearly passed out when I saw who it was." From here I explain that they disappeared from sight after exiting the shop. Immediately after leaving to check the cameras, Seb had the hostess tell us that we were closing for the day. I never heard if the men were caught on the security feed.

"Have you checked your phone?" he asks, as stunned as I'd been earlier in the day. Having woken in a stupor, it hadn't occurred to me that Chandra may have called. I half-jog to the couch and search through the discarded blanket and throw pillows. Cheering for myself, I pull my phone from between the cushions. Seven missed calls, twenty-three text messages. Sheesh— I really must've been dead to the world. Brad leans in, reading over my shoulder. Two calls are him, one my mother, three Chandra, and one Blair. Groaning, I open my texts. It's a barrage of messages asking where I am, if I'm okay, and why no one has heard from me. There's no way I'm going to respond to those, instead I tap Chandra's number.

"My God! We thought you were dead." She shrieks into the phone. "You had like ten minutes until I sent a unit over."

"You need a deep breath or two," I suggest. "A nap was in order after the day we had. Plus, my phone disappeared into the couch."

"Cool. So, two violent criminals appear at your work today. Then you go off the radar, do you see why I may have been concerned?" She's no calmer than when she answered the phone. Actually, she may be more irritated now. Her harshly whispered words sting slightly. It hadn't been intentional.

"When you put it like that. Admittedly, it sounds worse," I confess, "I was exhausted and passed out. Also, you could have just come over."

"I'm mid-shift and can't just pop by to see what you're up to," she gripes, but at least her voice has softened a bit. "I won't be able to get away until after nine. This afternoon got weird."

"You're telling me!" Turning the day over in my mind, it was confusing and unsettling, leaving me exhausted. "Drinks tonight or coffee tomorrow?" I'm torn between wanting all the details and wanting a quick dinner before bed.

"Coffee is the better option," she starts, her tone turning cautious. "Gotta jet but I'll text you the details." The call disconnects before I can say anything else. I wish this was unusual behavior— it isn't. Chandra is prone to dramatic endings to calls. Turning to Brad, I would tell him about the call but his face was millimeters from mine and he's no doubt heard every word.

"That was weird," he says and turns to the kitchen. "Let's find something to eat," his tone brightens at the idea of food. Following him into the kitchen, my phone buzzes.

Chandra: *Not downtown. Your house or Community Center?*

Chandra: *Too many details.*

Me: *My house. I've got my fancy new whiteboard* with a star-eyed emoji.

Chandra: *God help us. See you around nine. I'll bring bagels.*

"Tomorrow, you work from home, right?" I confirm with Brad. He nods emphatically as he scoops out leftover spaghetti. I'd been pretty proud of that dinner, the meat was only slightly overcooked and the sauce was delicious. "Good. Chandra has news and plans to come over in the morning to go over it. Always easier when you're here. Saves me from calling you to debrief after."

14

Taking a Stand

"That makes no sense, Chan," Brad sputters around a mouthful of bagel.

"You're tellin' me!" she retorts then bites aggressively into her own.

"They just disappeared?" Incredulity making my tone nearly mocking. How could two grown men disappear on a street lined with cameras? It would take a team to pull that off in a movie. There's literally no way that happens in real life.

"Well, they didn't vanish. The poorly timed outage shut everything down," she mumbles while chewing. "No one could have predicted the Wi-Fi would go out in that moment." Unbelievably, the moment Diaz and Baek stepped through the doors, the entire block lost Wi-Fi. Worse yet, the outage was a mere ten minutes. Long enough for them to get away, short enough to barely raise suspicion. It was only discovered when the officers were canvasing businesses and requesting footage. A request has been submitted for records from the internet provider.

"Have there been any other sightings of them or reports of crimes in the area?"

"Interestingly, no reports of sightings. But..." She pauses and I scowl. Smirking at me, Chandra continues, "Mr. Alban reported a door ajar alert in the back of the store." My eyes bug. Mr. and Mrs. Alban have run their art store, HeArtWorks, since 1981. They not only sell supplies, they host classes and support the arts community with exhibits and shows throughout the year. In June, the Albans sponsored an art festival to support a local family who'd lost their home in a fire. The community raised over $5,000 to help the family resettle in the area.

"Was there anything missing or moved?" Brad asks, since I am still rendered speechless.

"From their quick assessment, no. But it unnerved them enough to let us know. Malloy and Munoz responded, took photographs, dusted for prints, all the normal things. There was about a dozen different fingerprints they pulled. No obvious damage to the door or frame." Having polished off her bagel, she readjusts and sits cross-legged to sip her coffee. From her posture change, I assume she's done sharing. Standing, I head to the whiteboard. "You may want to sit back down," she suggests with a knowing smile. Without another word, I plop back into my chair and lean forward, prompting her to go on.

"We've asked for any in the area to share pictures or videos they may have from around that time." I try to figure out how the police department would have spread the word so quickly. "Remember we hired the Chief's nephew to build us a few social media pages?" We nod in sync. "Using those, we put out a public request. Pretty smart right?" She seems pretty proud of the way the community has been included. "We've had dozens of photos and videos sent in the last eighteen hours."

"That's pretty genius!" I cheer. The community will have angles and shots that the installed cameras may have missed. "How did you ask?"

"We're testing a new approach to safety and piloting a short window to see how it goes. As cover, we asked for anything in a four-hour window. It gave us two hours before and after." I clap, startling the dogs and rocketing them from their beds. Rounds of shushing quiet them enough to carry on. "The AV tech team has the files and are reviewing with facial recognition."

I am genuinely impressed by the changes in the department. Maybe the new Chief has been exactly what the department needs? Rafe Mercer arrived in town after the dramatic events earlier in the summer. The former Chief decided the turmoil was too much and the time to retire had come. With the change in leadership, there came a change in policy and roles. Chandra moved from a patrol officer to a blended patrol and community outreach position. She sincerely loves having the opportunity to keep the community safe all while building relationships with residents and business owners.

"How long before they've got results?" Brad has shifted over to the whiteboard while Chandra has talked. He's begun taking notes on the photos.

Chandra holds up her cell and waves it back and forth. "We've already had a couple snaps with Diaz and Baek visible." I gasp, delighted that progress is being made. "It's only the backs of their heads. But the techs have determined it is them leaving Azúcar with coffee." Even better, they've got them as they exit. "The system scans the photos as each arrives. This morning, the tech team will review what's come in and make adjustments as needed. We're hopeful at this stage." As if she's summoned the team, her phone screen lights up with an incoming video call. "Eek...let me take this." She swipes and barks, "Boudreaux" into the phone, springing from her chair.

The call doesn't last long. Before another pot of coffee has brewed, Chandra swings back through the doorway onto the lanai. She sniffs the air like a bloodhound and reaches for her now empty mug. Without telling us about the call, she refills her cup from the still brewing pot. The pot clinks into place, and she once again pops onto the porch. Brad points to the whiteboard with the uncapped marker in his hand.

"Any guesses what they found?" she murmurs over the edge of her mug, eyes twinkling.

"The getaway car?" I suggest.

"Close but not quite," loud, dramatic slurp, "the duo were spotted by the front door, in the image you saw on my phone. The next series of images show the backs of their heads. Then they dip into Gerardo's." Brad and I gasp.

"Why would they have gone into the bakery?" Brad asks, chewing on the cap of the marker.

"That is still unclear. We do know they did not reappear on the street at any point for the next two hours." She swipes through several photos before finally turning her phone toward us. "The proximity to the buildings prevented owner mounted cameras from picking up their movements." Something about that strikes me as very intentional, almost premeditated. Looking back up to Chandra, she's nodding and I can tell I'm on the right track.

"How did they know the angles of the cameras?" I ask and Chandra grins broadly.

"Still working on that, but it is obvious they were aware of dead spots."

"Obvious to who?" Brad asks, staring down at the phone and shaking his head.

"See how they move along the front of the building. Passersby might think they're squeezing to the side to avoid bumping into others. I see them weaving in and out to avoid cameras," I tell him, zooming in and out of the photo as I talk. He finally nods, having recognized the pattern of movements.

"How long would it take to plan that?" he asks, holding the phone closer to his face.

"Wait!" I shout, grabbing Brad by the forearm and squeezing. He whips to face me, eyes-wide. "It's a trial run! They're practicing." His eyes bulge even further and Chandra pumps her fist in the air.

"Knew you'd get there!" she cheers. "The assumption as of this morning is exactly that. We believe this was all to determine a safe path of travel down the main street. One that will keep them off camera and free to move between businesses."

"Who are they targeting?" Brad asks from the whiteboard. He's quickly making notes from our conversation.

"That is the big question, cher." Leaning back in her chair, Chandra stares off, watching the dogs play. Her tells are all there— death grip on the mug, chewing her cheek. She's playing out all the scenarios she can imagine. I picture a silent film flying through her mind.

"What if we shifted the cameras?" Brad asks. Chandra pulls herself back and angles to stare at him. She gestures for him to go on. "Obviously, they'd notice if the cameras were physically altered. But, you can make small adjustments in the app for some." He grabs his phone from the table and opens our security application. Pulling up the camera from the yard, he pans left, right, and zooms out, creating different views of the same scene. Chandra fist bumps him and reaches for her phone.

"Seb! Baby, I need a favor," she begins.

***

The local business owners file into the community center, one by one. Each handing over their cell phones to Chandra and Malloy. Detective Cassidy stands in the front of the room with Chief Mercer. It's like watching a weird parade. One laced with tension, it builds from the anxiety and irritation being given little information or little choice.

"We know it feels somewhat over the top, but please bear with us," she calls out pleasantly as our visitors take their seats. When this plan was hatched earlier, we were sworn to secrecy with our co-conspirators, Desmond and Linda. We prepped the main room and gathered what we could for refreshments. Our paltry collection is accented by cookies from Linda's freezer stash. Thank goodness she keeps extras put aside for emergencies. Despite the grumbles, the cookies and drinks are quickly being snapped up. Linda is the reigning queen of the chocolate chip cookie in our neighborhood. She credits stress-baking after long days in the classroom.

"Any hints?" Mari whispers, sliding into a seat near me. I shake my head, hoping to project disappointment and solidarity. "Shoot! Was banking on you having the inside story." To soothe herself, she dips her cookie into the steaming coffee and takes an enormous bite. A happy dance while chewing, distracts her from further questions. Using it to my advantage, I pop out of my seat to rearrange the platter of dwindling cookies.

With a nod from Chandra, Blair steps up to the front table and claps her hands. The echo draws all eyes to her. She briefly introduces herself and Chief Mercer. He thanks her for the introduction and then addresses the audience.

"I'm sure the invitations you received may have been confusing. It isn't every day that an officer invites you to a local community center for snacks and a chat with the cops." Chuckles erupt through the thirty or so seated around the room. "There was unfortunately a reason for the secrecy." His tone changes from light-hearted to serious. "Our downtown has been under attack for several weeks. Events escalated and have led to significant injuries for a member of our community." A few sniffles from the group, at the mention of poor Joey Ali. "Based on information received from credible sources, it is our belief that portions of downtown are under observation from the perpetrators." Gasps replace the sniffles. Several in the audience have shifted to the edges of their seats.

"Through a community project, we've captured the movements of two males suspected of involvement. Neither of them have been directly connected to the crimes but are known associates," Blair adds. She and Mercer place a poster onto an empty frame beside their table. Diaz, Maltz, Baek, and Emory's mugshots stare blankly into the crowd. "On camera, these men have been observed in combination at local businesses and on the street."

"It is our belief, that they are continuing to observe downtown. Think of it as them casing the joint." Sporadic, nervous laughter from the audience breaks the tension. "In line with these assumptions, we need your assistance."

Mercer and Cassidy step through the plan in detail, answering questions as they go. Each business owner is asked to adjust cameras digitally if able to provide better coverage of the streets. Still images are shared of Diaz and Baek skirting along the edge of the sidewalk with hats and strategically placed coffee cups hiding their faces. There was a technical explanation provided on height, body measurements, and gait patterns given by the Chief. It was a little too technical for me but seemed to land well with the majority of the audience. Whispers and nods indicate the growing agreement with the plan.

"With your cooperation, we'd ask the cameras be adjusted overnight. The tech team has compiled a list of the known security camera brands in use around town. There are additional instructions for resetting the angles and customer service contacts. I'll take this opportunity to thank y'all from the bottom of my heart. The department appreciates the community support." A smattering of loud claps, cascade into thunderous applause from the small group. "In the event you spot any of these men," he gestures to the poster, " DO NOT attempt to engage or follow them." He pointedly glances in my direction and I feel the warmth of my face flushing. I pick at the hem of shorts, refusing to look up. "Our department has issued a county-wide alert for officers to be on the lookout, commonly known as a BOLO, for Diaz, Maltz, Baek, and Emory. If you see them, call 911. We will have an increased law enforcement presence downtown. A mixed group of uniformed and plain closed officers. While the officers are on duty, even if you recognize them, do not acknowledge their role. This is for their safety, as well as, your own." This does not seem to be his first rodeo. I'm picking up that man hunts might have been slightly more common in eastern North Carolina than our little pocket of Florida. "We appreciate your discretion and willingness to assist."

As he leaves the front of the room, the group begins to disburse. Officers pass out the promised information sheets as attendees collect their cell phones. While it may have seemed unnecessarily cloak and dagger, Mercer had been adamant that we collect phones. The idea was to reduce distractions and to limit the amount of photos or videos that may be shared. Rather than grumble, most were compliant. The recent crimes have everyone rattled, and people are eager to cooperate. Before long, the crowd has thinned and Desmond ushers us out the door, into the warm night air.

25

Downtown Depression

A dreary week of rain has put me in a righteously foul mood. And I am not the only one. Our entire town seems to have fallen victim as well. The dozen or so customers we do have are quick-tempered and don't spend much time in the cafe. It seems the whole spirit in the area has changed. I've finished the last of my mid-afternoon rush, two jumpy receptionists from the insurance company up the road. I'd hoped to ask about the events downtown but they were not up for it. Beyond giving their orders, neither was in a chatty or even pleasant mood. They snatched their coffees a split second after I called their names and they were out the door.

Leaning against the counter, I sigh loudly and stare out at the falling rain. The noise catches Wren's attention and she nods solemnly. She's seated at our biggest table, with salt and pepper shakers lined up to be filled. Earlier in the afternoon, she and the hostess counted the sugar packets at every table and wrote inspirational messages on each. Peak boredom activities right there. We've had a grand total of eight customers choose to dine-in today, everything else has been takeout. I don't really blame them, sitting in restaurants and visiting shops has become downright dangerous.

In the midst of working up the courage, I prep to ask if I can call it a day. With only an hour to go, there shouldn't be any harm in going home early. And then the bell above the door chimes.

Linda has arrived with her book club. A flock of brightly attired women in their mid-late seventies pours into the cafe. All chattering loudly, happily discussing their latest read, shaking rain from coats and umbrellas. From Linda, I know it's a romance in a space station, something about a sentient lifeform and a scientist. I'd tuned out at the mention of slime trails.

"Are we too late?" one of the ladies trills. Her name escapes me, despite having met several times.

"More like right on time!" I say, her infectious smile has me grinning in return. "Table or to-go?" Fully expecting the group to take their orders and leave.

"Table of course," Linda says, "we didn't get to finish our book autopsy." A mischievous smirk makes her eyes twinkle.

"That's my department then." Wren glides over with a handful of menus, having abandoned craft time with condiments. She beckons over her shoulder and skates away, delighting the group by skating backward and transitioning into a swanlike move. The mood inside the cafe has shifted, rain aside, the afternoon seems a little brighter. Listening to the women laugh and tease one another, I smile. Sometimes all you need is a happy group to turn your day around.

While I'm steaming milk, the bells above the door chime again. I don't look up to avoid disrupting the process. Seconds later, I dread not preparing myself. The counter squeaks slightly as a body leans against it.

"Huh," the nasal voice drones, causing a shiver up my spine. "You do still work here." Edna. She sniffs her nose and gazes at me over the edge of her glasses. The effect is a schoolteacher about to lay down a punishment. "I'm surprised it's lasted this long." Thankful for the task in progress, I finish and force my best customer service smile.

"Welcome in, Edna. I don't think you've been in for quite a while." Considering myself fortunate, she's not terrorized me at work before. "Are you here for a coffee or would you like a table?" Silently, I pray she wants a table and will vacate the coffee bar.

"There's no way I'd stick around long enough to eat here. This area has gone down the tubes." Sneering, she takes in the mostly empty cafe and deserted street in front. "I'm surprised you've got any customers."

Continuing to grin manically, I reassure her that she doesn't have a reason to be fearful. I'm mid-explanation of the efforts of the police force when she raises her hand to stop me.

"First of all, I know full well what's going on around here. Second, stop grinning at me like that. You look unwell." The sneer has been replaced by an all-out glare. Why does this woman insist on making every interaction so unpleasant.

"Well, look what the cat dragged in." Linda's voice drips with an artificial pleasantness. "I didn't realize you ventured out much." The friction between these two fairly crackles. Edna snarls in her direction. Linda smiles with saccharine sweetness.

"Black coffee to go," Edna barks, smacking the menu onto the counter. "I assume you can handle that?" Turning my back to the pot, I stick my tongue out and imagine telling her off. Instead, Linda intervenes.

"Come on, now. Why don't you sit and visit with us?" Linda's group waves at us, oblivious to the tension.

"Not on your life. I've survived the bank and if I make it out of here uninjured, I'll consider it a win." Edna draws her purse tightly to her chest and gestures for me to hurry up. Linda cocks an eyebrow at me and tips her head toward the coffee pot. Taking her hint, I skip the next order for her table and pour Edna's coffee. She snatches it and throws a five-dollar bill onto the counter. With a brusque grunt, she leaves. I am begrudgingly appreciative for the fifty percent tip she's unwittingly given me.

"Have a lovely afternoon," I call after her. Even though she grates on my nerves, this is still a business and we need all the customers we can get. "You don't think anyone overheard her, do you?"

"Not likely, my book club is all keyed up and it's not exactly a full house." We both take in the three occupied tables. She's not wrong, there is no one within ten feet of the coffee bar. "Don't worry, my dear," Linda pats my hand, "business will pick back up. The snowbirds are arriving soon, then we'll have families visiting for the holidays. That will make up for this." Her hand flutters around the cafe. I reluctantly agree, in another few weeks the downtown will be unrecognizable. In a good way.

"How have your chats gone?" I quietly ask.

"Better than planned," Linda admits with pride. "Should we schedule a session at the community center?" And just like that, my good mood returns.

***

Walking to my Jeep, I tap out a text to Chandra.

Me: *Linda has updates. Meeting this evening at six.*

Chandra: *On nights for the next three. Fill me in later?*

Well that shoots my plan out of the sky— guess we won't have an excuse to order takeout. Groaning and opening my phone to the list of recipes I've been accumulating. Since Chandra and Seb won't be coming over, there isn't need for ordering out three nights in a row. Scrolling through, nothing is sparking joy. I've been dreaming of Crab Rangoon and Mongolian Beef all afternoon. This is why I like ordering food, way less of an investment and it never arrives burnt. Cold occasionally, but not burnt.

Throwing my phone into the passenger seat, I tip my seat back and enjoy the warmth of the car before hitting the road for the grocery store. Eyes closed and practicing a few yoga breaths, the pull of quick nap begins to overtake me. Right before I drift off, a text dings and the car reads it aloud.

Elena: *Heard we're meeting at the community center. Ok if I bring something for the group to eat?*

Salvation! I yank my seat lever and sit bolt upright. Elena's cooking is restaurant quality and will be way better than Tom Mee's China Palace.

Me: *Of course! Whatever sounds good to you.*

Elena: *Perfect :) I've been roasting pork and potatoes all day.*

Me: *Oh yum! Should I grab some bread?*

Elena: *Covered, mija. Mama and I have been baking.*

My mouth waters at the thought of slow roasted pork and fresh bread. Throwing a heart on her message, I call Brad to let him know. We're saved from another terrible dinner. His response fills the screen with confetti. Bless his patience with my abysmal cooking, it has improved over the last year but not by much. Soaring with my strengths, I'll prepare the tableware and the conference room.

***

Once the clattering of silverware has calmed and after dinner coffees have been poured, I take my spot by the whiteboard, uncapped marker in hand. Quietly drumming my nails on the edge of the board, I survey the notes so far and who was supposed to chat with whom.

"I spoke with Bernice and Serena. They didn't have many additional insights but did share progress on the reopening. If all goes according to plan, they'll be back in business within the next two weeks," he pauses, collects his thoughts and continues, "mid-way through, the grandson and his wife came in. Seems to be a little undercurrent of tension with the granddaughter-in-law, at least from what I pieced together. She's got some hesitations about reopening and mentioned finances several times when we talked. The best I can tell, that conversation didn't seem to be new and the family was irritated when she brought it up." Interesting the things you learn when families all come together, whether they realize it or not.

"Any word from the folks at Delman's or Magpie's?" I ask, squeaking notes on the board.

"Not really. They loosely inventory the stickers, not well enough to tell if any rolls are missing. There was an explanation about the boxes and how each is shipped. Was neither interesting or relevant." He grimaces. None of us blame him for tuning that out. Inventory is rarely exciting to discuss. "When I asked about any new visitors or regulars, there wasn't anyone who matched the descriptions of our perps." Lately he's been working lingo from cop dramas into our conversations, it's received mixed reviews but he persists. "Only a few fellas in suits. They mentioned being in town for business and meetings at the bank. Then the conversation devolved to what specials Mr. Brown is planning for the upcoming holiday season. Can you imagine a roast beef with candy cane horseradish? Absolutely horrifying if you ask me." Groans and gags erupt around the table.

"Quite the segue, Des," Moshe speaks up, his face still creased in a frown over the roast beef comment. "I met with Townsend, yes that's his real name, at the Savings and Loan. He was more than happy to have lunch and catch me up on the local financial situation. Telling actually. There is a significant amount of debt within the business community and a handful of commercial developers are circling," his tone ominous. "Spells a little danger for our current downtown. Changes may be on the horizon. One in particular stands out as the most aggressive, a man by the name of Alain Forde," he withdraws a small notebook from the chest pocket of his crisp Oxford shirt. In a startling realization, I've never seen Moshe in anything other than pressed slacks and a highly starched dress shirt. Even when he is doing yardwork now that I think of it. "His company is the Faltmann Group. Based in St. Augustine. They've acquired more than a dozen properties this year," he summarizes his notes. "If need be, I have the dates and locations available on my computer." Francine beams at him throughout. I catch a glimpse of the doting wife she's been for many decades, by his side at dinners and fundraisers. She may be losing her memory, but not her love for this man. To prevent tears from springing loose, I face the board and note Moshe's findings.

"Can it be my turn?" Linda pipes up, hands pressed together in a pleading pose. She's clearly been dying to share. We all nod and give her our full attention. To my surprise, she jumps from her seat and joins me at the whiteboard. Extending her hand to me, she gestures at the marker. Happy to relinquish it, I drop into a chair beside Brad. He stops making notes on his tablet and pulls me in close . After a long day apart, I am delighted to snuggle with him while we investigate.

"This is more about connections than new information." She flips the board to the clean side and begins listing the names of the fourteen women in her book club, affectionately called the Bad Biddies. I can't help but giggle, she's never mentioned the name before. Laughter catches in my throat when I see the trend on the board. The majority of the women are business owners, connected by family, or employed locally. I'm not sure why that's a surprise, yet it is. List complete, she sketches a Ven diagram. The common connection is Azúcar. I gasp and mutter, "Wait.."

Linda holds a finger up in my direction, she's got more. "I'm not insinuating that Seb or his business are at the center of the crimes. What I am highlighting is the frequency the of interactions, the commonalities of who is in the cafe, and proximity to the most significant of crimes." While speaking, she fills in more details with the source. "How I see this, the perps, as Desmond refers to them," he tips an imaginary hat in her direction, "appear to be using the cafe as a centralized meeting place or perhaps even as a dead drop." Oh geez, now she's doing it. As punctuation, she snaps the cap into place, and rests in on the tray with a bang. No one speaks, we all stare at the board taking in what she's shared.

"It makes sense," Elena speaks up first. "My niece at the bookstore hasn't seen any of the men. But they sit all the way at the end of the block, separated by the public parking lot. If the men are mostly by the cafe, I can understand why she hasn't seen them." We murmur in agreement.

"Similar to Moshe— the owners of the insurance company, Javi and Samantha Martez, mentioned a few corporations sniffing around," Alfie takes his turn, "Two have asks for rates on occupied buildings and businesses. One took it well and one did not. The name Forde does sound familiar. He took the refusal badly and caused a scene, shouting at the new receptionist. Mrs. Martez threatened to call the police if he did not leave the premises. That seemed to do the trick and he left. Neither of them have seen him since. None of the other men were spotted."

Listening to all their contributions, mine seem paltry. I've had scattered conversations and made no real progress. I may be imagining it but people seem to be avoiding conversations with me, other than Edna that is. Every day used to be filled with getting to know my customers but now they order and leave. Earlier in the week, I scared a bank teller while talking to her. She backed away from the counter and offered to wait on the patio for her coffee. Wren took it to her because I felt so bad about the whole interaction.

Chandra texts for an update and a request for leftovers. I take a few photos of the board, impressed by how many details we've filled in. It's almost like we're real investigators. I do a little shimmy of pride as I send off the pics of the board and an overly full plastic container. No one wanted her to feel left over, so her dinner was packed up before we started eating to make sure there was plenty.

The conversation winds down and we slowly go to the door, overstuffed but ready to head to our respective homes. Most have brought their golf carts but Brad and I opt to walk. We haven't reached the golf cart age bracket yet. We agreed at forty, we'll give in.

Strolling down the street, hand-in-hand, Brad fills me in on a new client. He's in the middle of describing a cringey moment when tires screech beside us. Started, we freeze in our tracks. Everyone has already passed us and are probably home by now. It can only be one person. In unison, we groan, "Edna". Then laugh. As anticipated, she does not appreciate any of this.

"Hmph," she grumbles, leering at us from the driver's seat. It's not nearly as intimidating as usual, she has to lean around Hubert. Irritated, she smacks a palm into his chest and presses him into the seat. He makes an oof sound with the impact. "If it isn't our local sleuths. What prey tell has our illustrious porch patrol gotten up to this evening?" Okay, I may despise this lady but porch patrol is kind of a fun nickname.

"Oh, the usual. Good food with our friends. Jealous?" I say, the snarkiness dripping like acid. Instead of responding, she presses the gas to the floor and lurches away from us. The cart fishtails and she fights to correct their trajectory. Poor Hubert grabs the roof as he nearly topples out the side. Brad stares at me, displeased with my rudeness. My relationship with Edna has soured further after her visit to the cafe. I shrug and keep walking, "Don't tell me you feel bad for her? She's the absolute worst and had that coming." In an attempt to defend myself, I gesture at her rapidly disappearing cart. He sighs and jogs to catch up to me. "Although, I didn't hate the name she gave us." Brad continues to look at me wordlessly. "I've got to give her credit, the Porch Patrol is pretty funny. Reminds me of that kids show."

Breaking into a smile, he nods, "It is pretty good. Weren't you and Chandra talking about this a couple of weeks ago?" He throws an arm around my shoulder, we walk on with our peace restored. In a few steps, we're back to laughing about the lunch meeting with his client.

26

Enough Out of You

It was an easy decision for us to agree on the Porch Patrol. Partly because we loved it and partly to annoy Edna. Pettiness has no age limit. Mirabel, at ninety-three, was the first to agree and offered to make us T-shirts with her granddaughters. Linda requested yard signs to put on display. Chandra was delighted because she has become tired of listing us individually and had started referring to our group as the Chain Gang.

Having coffee on the porch before work, I come to an overdue decision. There are plenty of ways I can connect with customers, it doesn't need to be direct questions. Bouncing the ideas off my sister was a perfect way to practice, she'd called as I was leaving, giving me a captive audience anyway. We came up with a few more casual options. Interrogation only works for the police, chit chat is the key to my community's heart.

The chance to try it out came earlier than planned. I was putting my bag under the counter when Mari and Siobhan from the boutique silently appear. They are paler than usual with dark circles under their eyes. Mari's chin quivers when I tell them good morning. It can't be anything I've said. Siobhan reaches over, clasping Mari's hand tightly. Neither says a single word. It's unnerving.

"Hey gals, everything ok?" Trying to be casual but growing increasingly concerned. Sniffles instead of an answer. I slide a small stack of cocktail napkins in their direction. From beyond them, I catch Seb's eye. He gestures at them and I shake my head slightly. I've got no clue and clearly this is going to take a moment. Cafe Cubano is in order. I set up the moka pot and prepare for the first precious drips of coffee. While I work, they whisper and work their way through the napkins. By the time I've blended the hot, sweet coffee, they're ready to talk. Each sips the super strength coffee and lets out a shuddering sigh. Despite not being related by blood, the sisters-in-law are bizarrely in sync.

"We found it this morning," Siobhan starts. Mari softly sobs, so she continues. "The back door was dented but closed. When we checked out ba—" gulping sob, "the mural was," the two cling to one another, "destroyed!" A gut-wrenching sob and they collapse into one another. I remember the detailed mermaid mural covering the wall on the back of their building. A local artist had been commissioned last year. It was unveiled in a community ceremony. The work was stunning and one of a kind.

"When you're ready, it's okay to take your time," I reassure them, sipping my own coffee. Seb and Wren have inched closer. I tap my cup and both nod. I turn my back to prepare more coffee. The whispering resumes and no matter how quietly I move, it's beyond what I can hear. At last, when I pour, Seb and Wren join us. Wren has positioned herself between Siobhan and Mari, an arm around each. They cry quietly into her shoulders for several minutes. The duo had saved for more than a year to afford the custom mural. Plus, the destruction is more than simple vandalism. It's the equivalent of painting a target.

"Not only did they spray disgusting words, whoever it was blacked our Coral's eyes and teeth. Then also sprayed over the camera lenses. None of it was caught by the security system," Mari says, her voice much stronger. She sounds not only hurt, but also angry. "It feels so malicious." It does indeed.

"Does it look like they made it inside?" I ask. Mari shakes her head.

"We'd installed a reinforced lock on the door. There's a bar that drops down and prevents it from being forced open." Confusion spreads across my face. "We enter and exit through the front. The rolling gate protects the front door." I can now picture the metal gate that drops down and secures at the curb. "I swear that's what saved the store."

"Even if they took it out on Coral," Siobhan adds, still sniffling, "we called the police but told them we'd wait here. It was too much to stand on the street and wait. Feels safer to be here." On cue, the doorway fills with Malloy and Munoz, imposing in their dark uniforms. They approach the coffee bar to speak with Siobhan and Mari. Having had an opportunity to release their emotions a bit, the women straighten and stand to greet the officers. "Thank you for coming," Siobhan's voice has resumed it's quiet, deeper tone.

"Can you take us over to your shop?" Munoz asks, then gestures to the doorway. Before I ask if they want either of us to come, they're walking out with the officers. Wren tosses her hands and shrugs. Our work is done here.

Now, to occupy myself until I can learn more. I shoot a text to the Porch Patrol with an update. A flood of thumbs-up emojis barrages my inbox. Not exactly the responses I'd expected but this is very much on brand. Since my phone is out, it's time for a coffee bar brainstorming session. Which should I tackle next? Seb and Wren weigh in. With the approach of cooler weather at some point in the next few months, we settle on a warming latte. A base of medium roast with cinnamon and nutmeg mixed in with the grounds, topped with a caramel drizzle and optional chocolate shavings. Seb requests I brew a few to test the coffee-spice ratio. More than happy to oblige, the prep begins before the lunch rush arrives. Or at least what passes for a rush these days.

Before long a flight of coffees with varying ratios are set up on the bar. The kitchen and waitstaff cast their votes on the brews. We informally tally the favorites on my chalkboard and decide on the version heavier on cinnamon. Mini pots of three caramels are placed for tasting as well and the salted caramel wins by a mile. As anticipated, our dessert chef makes it in house and the blend of salty and sweet will be just what the coffee needs. Caffeinated and satisfied, the group splits up to finish our preparations for the day.

While brewing a pot of drip coffee, I see the lunch specials posting and my mouth waters. A steaming bowl of Ajiaco is just what I need. The savory broth filled with meat and vegetables will fill the hole skipping breakfast left. The sooner I get to work, the sooner I get to take lunch. Kicking it up a notch, I speed through prep and am ready when the doors open at eleven o'clock.

To the entire cafe's surprise, customers are waiting outside the doors. In minutes, we have eight tables filled and to go orders piling in.

"I have no clue what's happened, but I couldn't be happier," Seb announces when dropping a ticket off to me. "Our community is back!" Clapping his hands, he nearly sprints to greet more customers at the hostess stand. Smiling, I glance around at the mix of familiar faces and complete strangers. The snowbirds are trickling in at the perfect time.

***

In a flash, it is after 2 p.m. and the crowd has thinned to a few of our loyal customers. The older men sit in groups of four at tables on the patio, laughing and sipping coffee. Seems like the balance of the neighborhood might be on the cusp of returning.

Wren wheels over with two steaming bowls of soup and fresh, crusty bread. I nearly collapse at the first bite. The flavors are what I've dreamt of all morning. "Yeah, I know!" Wren says as she blows on a spoon filled with broth and yuca. Glancing past her, I see men seated on the bench in front of the cafe. One faces toward the street, the other stares into the cafe. From this distance, I can't make out their faces. But, immediately, the back of my neck prickles. Today has been too normal for these goons to ruin things.

"One sec, huh?" I ask, ducking around the counter. Wren is too engrossed in her lunch to do more than nod. She's been moving non-stop since the doors opened and nothing is going to interrupt her break. Moving as quickly as possible without startling anyone, I walk onto the patio. Only to see...Moshe and Desmond.

"Pssst—" I hiss. Both pivot to look at me, like owls perched on a brand. "What are you doing?"

"Enjoying the sunshine," Moshe says evenly. "You've had a busy day. Finish your lunch and we'll catch up later." In a synchronized move, they collectively ignore me and return to whatever it is they're up to. Sighing, I go back to the counter. No sense in wasting time guessing, for all I know they really are people watching and soaking up the sun.

***

The remainder of the week passes without incident. Other than seeing Moshe and Desmond sitting in the sun most days, there's nothing abnormal happening downtown. Each day we have more visitors arrive, to the point that our streets are bustling with newcomers. For the first few weeks of snowbird season, shops around town do a brisk business while everyone settles in for the season.

Other good news keeps coming in, the gals at Coral Belle Boutique are working with their insurance company to have the mural repaired. In a stroke of impeccable timing, the artist has a free block on her calendar late next week and is willing to get started while Mari and Siobhan work out the reimbursement. She's made some sketches to improve what was already a beautiful piece of art. The town council is planning a reopening ceremony for Gerardo's and an unveiling of the mural. Should be quite the party and we're overdue for some celebration.

Humming to myself, I pour coffees with the hostess and a busboy. As I work, I'm picturing the party planned for next month. Swaying to the unknown tune, I daydream of dancing with Brad. Swirling around in a vintage Hollywood inspired gown, pressed close to him in the cooling night air.

"What do you think you're doing?" a voice shrieks, drawing the attention of everyone in the cafe and a dozen or so on the sidewalk. "I've seen you for days and that's it. I don't know what kind of perverts you are!" The elderly female voice shakes with rage. Nearly dropping the coffee, I sprint through the patio to see a tiny woman attempting to hit Desmond and Moshe. On their bench, arms swatting to ward off her blows and making a valiant effort to explain. She doesn't tire at all, raining blow after blow. Her pocketbook makes a thwacking sound each time it connects with an arm or an unprotected spot on their bodies. In true form, neither tries to harm her, only flailing their arms when she strikes.

Before we can reach them, Officer Malloy sprints over. His presence stopping her assault mid-swing. "Ma'am," he huffs. "What seems to be the problem?" Leaning slightly forward to catch his breath, he mumbles a nonsensical combination of letters and numbers into his radio. It squawks in response.

"I keep seeing these two men here. All the time. All day. They're up to no good! I'm sure of it," she shouts, thrusting an arthritic finger at Desmond and Moshe. Both flinch when her hand flies out, but the bag is now at her side.

Malloy does an excellent job of hiding his smile. "These gentlemen?" He now points in their direction. "You're concerned about them?" She scowls and nods her head slowly, not taking her eyes off the duo. "I can assure you, they may be up to something, but nothing dangerous or illicit." She falters slightly, still staring them down. "Mr. Canistel and" pointing at Desmond, then at Moshe, "Mr. Cohen are respected members of the community. You are not in danger." The woman finally breaks her gaze, aiming it at Malloy. He puts his hands up in front of his chest, almost in surrender. "Whatever they're doing sitting here, it likely has nothing to do with any of you." He gestures at the assembled ground. Moshe and Desmond blush and smile sheepishly. "If you'd be so kind as to carry on, I would like to speak with them." Begrudgingly, she crushes her pocketbook to her chest and stomps away, head held high. She appears confident in having done her civic duty, what precisely that is remains to be seen.

Seb speaks up, "We've got a table free and fresh coffee if you'd like to step inside." All three men follow him to a table in the corner. Desmond beckons for me to join and Seb nods his approval. We haven't officially opened yet, so there's no harm in me stepping away.

"Well that was fun," Malloy begins, his face slightly reddened from his jog and the interaction. Before speaking, he fans himself with one of the menus on the table.

"Yes, we could not have seen that coming," Desmond answers, laying on the charm with his best southern gentleman voice. Malloy makes a face at the attempt. "To answer the unspoken, we have indeed been sitting on the bench for a few days. But—as you said, no malicious intent. Only..." He tapers off, throwing a side-eyed glance at Moshe.

"May we be frank?" he booms. When frustrated or stressed, Moshe has a tendency to ratchet up to the volume. It ends up sounding like a foghorn. Unfazed, Malloy asks him to continue. Moshe clears his throat and makes an effort to lower the volume. "With all the events downtown, we've become concerned for CiCi's safety." I nearly drop the mug of coffee I'd brought with me. They're here to watch me? "The rash of crimes have made us nervous. While there has been a break, we don't feel it's entirely safe yet." My mouth gapes wide open.

"Did you know about this?" Malloy spears me with a hard look.

"Do I seem to have known?" I retort. "I'm as shocked as you are!" Shaking my head, I stare at each in turn. "Is that why you've been out there for days?" Heads nod and cheeks blush. "It started the day of the mural incident," I recall. Again, more nodding.

"I have to insist that you not. Find another way to check in with her. Creeping out the snowbirds is not a great solution. We've got enough to deal with at the moment," Malloy's smile is barely concealed, "Have her share her location or check in during the day. We cannot have another purse beating on the sidewalk. Understood?" To his relief, Moshe and Desmond agree to find another method. "There's nothing more to do now. How about a coffee and you can fill me in on anything you've seen?" I scurry off to grab coffees and place an order for a plate of pastries with Wren. I'll have more than enough opportunity to discuss this with them later.

Over dinner, Seb and I regale Chandra and Brad with the events of the morning. We'd promised to save it until we were all together. They're as delighted and shocked by it as we were. Thankfully, the remainder of the day passed with no other friendly stalkers or attempted citizen's arrests.

"Did they think no one would notice?" Chandra asks incredulously.

"With the influx of visitors, they assumed the crowds would hide them," I lamely defend their actions.

"Babe, there are not that many people downtown. Two men, one of them is nearly my height, are going to stick out," Brad half teases-half scolds.

"No one could have predicted that Lovella's sister would be in town and keeping an eye on the mean streets of Palmetto Breeze," considering the lady, I add, "should have known they were sisters. They could be twins."

"They actually are," Seb quietly adds. It only increases the ridiculousness of the situation.

"Listen. Just cause y'all came up with a squad name, do not assume you're an actual crime fighting team," Chandra raises an eyebrow, daring me to defend them again. "We love the help, but don't make it harder on us," she then smiles, "Wish you'd grabbed a pic," poking Seb in the ribs.

Despite the teasing, I know she's mostly serious and I don't blame her. What if something had happened and Desmond or Moshe were injured? The thought makes a shudder pass through me. Goosebumps form along my upper arms. Using it as an excuse to release some tension, I get up to go into the house for a moment. When Brad looks my way, I rub my arms to indicate a chill. He smiles and returns to his dinner.

Continuing the charade, I grab the lightest sweater I can find. Struggling into it, I nearly knock into Chandra in the hallway. Awkwardly, I yelp and topple into the wall. She grabs my arm to steady me and steers me into the kitchen.

"What?" I ask, slightly alarmed. Fight or flight mode activated.

"Have you put anything thought into the license?" My mind goes blank. License? What license? I bobble my head in confusion. "I know it's been months."

A text message flashes in my mind— *call me, I have an idea.* Months ago, after the theft cases resolved, Chandra had texted me.

"The...PI license?" I ask, unsure if there's another one that I'm missing. Her smile tells me I'm on the right track. "I searched online after we talked and printed the forms."

"And?"

"And... nothing. I lost my nerve. Brad and I talked, he thought it would be right up my alley. But, then, I got in my head and convinced myself to drop it."

"You need to get out of that head," she points at my forehead. "Do you think we'd lie to you?" Scrunching up my face, I feign being deep in thought. She flicks me on the arm. "We wouldn't you dweeb." I know they wouldn't, but that's not the same as believing I can do something. Support is great, failure is not. Losing my job did a number on my confidence and I don't think I'm ready to leap into another career. "Think about it, okay? Talk to Brad?" she urges.

Without agreeing to apply, I agree to consider the process. This does the trick and she's willing to let it drop. Whatever level of tension from earlier has dissipated. Linking our arms, we stroll back onto the patio. Chandra whispering to me about an upcoming surprise for Seb. I'm only half listening, the idea of the PI license has taken over my brain. Could it really happen?

27

Briefcases and Bad Suits

F unky and out of sorts, Coco, Aggie, and I hit the neighborhood for a walk, in an effort to clear the fog that's settled over my brain. So far this morning, I've spilled two cups of coffee, dropped my phone in the sink while brushing my teeth, and burnt toast until it resembled charcoal briquettes. Brad was legitimately concerned for my safety and rightly so, I woke up in walking disaster mode. Only after I promised not to cook or bake would he leave for work. Which made me feel even worse, by the time he'd left, traffic will be an absolute nightmare. He swears it's fine, but it only added to my mood.

Putting in my earphones, I start a new mystery that has been on hold in the library app. A bright spot this morning was the notification of its arrival. Maximum noise cancellation and high volume is the right combo for a reset. In a rare twist, not a single one of our neighbors is out and about yet. Not even Edna.

Rounding the corner, the community center comes into view and in a flash my decision is made. Two weeks ago, Desmond had gifted me a key. This morning seems like an excellent first use. The security code is easy to remember...it's the address. Wouldn't rate it as foolproof but it is simple.

As usual, the air is cool and slightly musty. Inhaling deeply, the tangles in my mind loosen. Unclipping their leashes, I release Coco and Aggie to sniff until their hearts are content. Racing away from me, noses to the ground, in seconds they've disappeared from sight. Brad set me an article that sniffing is more enriching than an hour-long walk. True or not, I agree that it's good for their little brains. We call them sniff-ventures and they soak up every second.

Half a mug of coffee later, I'm parked in front of the whiteboard. Staring at the notes, I read through all the information we've collected. The words blend together, swirling into patterns as I relax my eyes. Taking a few of those yoga breaths that my mother and sister swear by. Meh. I'd rather inhale the scent of coffee instead. Sighing, I stand to get a different perspective. The diagram on the back of the board catches my eye. And then I see it. How many times have we stared at this and missed it?

***

"I don't think I've seen you here before?" he croons, a slick voice, greasy and smooth. Sending a shiver up my spine, I whip my head up at the man talking with Wren. He's several inches taller than me, but skeletally thin. Dressed in an olive, double-breasted suit, he is out of place on an eighty-degree October day. At his side is a shabby briefcase that makes me pause. Too many briefcases and suits have been mentioned lately.

Wren deftly dismisses the man. She's a mix of polite and firmly not interested. He persists in attempting to draw her into conversation at his table. Several of us have taken note and are ready for a sign to intervene. Wren discreetly shakes her head at Tev and Seb. They're hovering in the kitchen doorway, seconds from springing into the dining room. She holds her hand up, once again respectful but definite in her rejection. This time she adds that her boyfriend wouldn't appreciate her going to dinner tonight without him. Faltering at the mention of a boyfriend, the man tells her he's just being "friendly." A phrase that has made millions of women nervous. Wren smiles graciously and mentions another server will be taking over for her shortly. Wheeling away, she nods at Seb then points to him. Seb is on it and approaches the table. After a brief chat, the order is changed to takeout and he exits the restaurant within the next several moments.

When she glides to the counter, I check in to see if she's okay. "Nothing I can't handle. I've been a server long than I haven't. Plus, the staff here is on it." She gestures at our coworkers sprinkled around the cafe, proud to work in a safe environment.

Itching to ask for details but careful not to pry, I simply ask, "Boyfriend?" with eyebrow raised and a smirk.

"Still new, but good!" Her blush and smile give more information than her words. "Very good," she adds, with a tinkling laugh. "We're still new, but I really like him," she gushes, clutching her hands to her chest. Her giddiness is precious and I'm over the moon for her. She's been single since her divorce two years ago. Her ex was a complete dud and the last we'd heard he is running sport fishing tours in the Gulf from a cousin's boat. It's been almost a year between text messages asking for money. No one is sad that he's leaving her alone.

A sudden spike in customers cuts our conversation short but she promises to tell me more over lunch.

Despite the customers, there's a lull in coffee orders. To pass the time, I scroll back through photos of the crime board I snapped this morning. Examining each corner, the pattern I noticed earlier this morning stands out like an emergency beacon at night. Making notes on cast off order slips, it occurs that I should be using the journal Brad gifted me last week. The pastel turquoise leather peaks at me from inside my tote under the counter. Feeling the soft cover, my heart swells. In the card, he said for my deepest thoughts or newest cases. It can be both right?

Tucking the order slips in the back, I draw out the board on an entire page. Filling in notes from the pictures, another idea strikes. It's time to ask the Porch Patrol.

Me: *thoughts on the businessmen with briefcases?*

Alfie: *nothing positive*

Desmond: *making folks nervous*

Linda: *Brenda and Lori think they're creeps. I am inclined to agree.*

Me: *do we have an exact count?*

Moshe: *Bank manager estimated eight in town*

Me: *seems like we need a headcount*

Everyone agrees. An estimate isn't enough. We can't figure out who they are and what they want without knowing how many are lurking in town. I cast my eyes around the cafe, none in here since Seb gave the last one the boot. Scratching out details I can recall, a description fills in. Could it be my memory is improving? Granted, I can't remember if I ate breakfast, but his face comes into view clearly when I focus. Unfortunately, he reads more like a cartoon villain than a real-life person. Oh well, it's more than we had this morning.

Drumming my nails on the counter, I try to come up with a plan to figure out how many of these men have been in town and are currently still here. Other than following anyone we find, how will we keep track. A hand locks in place over mine, forcing my fingers into stillness.

"I swear, I could hear that from the backdoor," Chandra teases. She's arrived right on time. I've run out of ideas and need someone to chime.

"It's like you can read my mind." Grinning widely, I spin my notebook to face her. Filling her in on the morning's encounter and thoughts running through my mind at a million miles an hour. "If we can get a better idea of how many players there are, we can plan a little better."

"Cees— plan for what?" Her tone and furrowed brow broadcast her feelings.

"Wellllll.....I'm not there yet. First, I need to understand what's going on. Why are there so many men with briefcases suddenly? What is their agenda? A fleet of badly dressed men in suits doesn't appear for no good reason." We banter back and forth about the alleged motivation for their arrival but my suspicions are there's a different explanation, one that none of us will like. Without my whiteboard, we use a fresh page to list out possibilities from plausible to ridiculous. Giggling, we add anything we can think of, most of which are not likely.

Our conversation is interrupted by Seb's arrival. He wraps his arms around Chandra from behind and drops a kiss onto the side of her neck. She laughs and curls herself deeper into his embrace. I'd tease about their PDA in a place of business, but in the moment, the place has emptied out. Checking my watch, I realize it's nearly closing time. Re-energized, I shoo them away to begin cleaning up and shutting down the coffee bar for the day.

"Dinner still on for tonight?" Chandra asks before walking away with Seb.

"Yep! Moshe has it under control. He's antsy to debut their new patio." Smiling, I picture the hand printed invitation he'd delivered a few weeks ago. Our little group was asked to attend an actual dinner party. We usually keep things more casual, dropping in and out of one another's homes after a text message or phone call. Having a formal invitation is a nice change and makes it special.

***

The Cohens yard has been transformed over the last several months. A generic concrete patio has been replaced by sand-colored flagstones extending out farther than the original footprint. In the middle, a tall wooden pergola draped with twinkling lights with a table for twelve at the center. A seating area with an L-shaped sectional and chairs surrounds a firepit. Scattered around the yard are matured banana trees, palms, and birds of paradise. It's absolutely stunning! We'd stayed at a resort last year that had similar outdoor landscaping. I took dozens of photos for inspiration. Not that I did anything with them but it was briefly motivating and we talked about our dream yard.

We ooh and ahh over the changes, genuinely impressed by the transformation. Francine beams at the praise. Today is a good day for her and we see glimpses of who she is—the sparkling hostess, engaging with her company and making sure we feel comfortable in her home. She laughs, shares stories, refills cups before they're fully empty. In an effort to save her from strain. dinner was provided by a local Italian restaurant. We feast on lasagna, salad, and crusty bread.

Before we've finished our meal, talk shifts to the ongoing situation in town. I've been holding back from bringing it up and am delighted when Linda kicks off the discussion. She and some of her girlfriends met downtown for shopping earlier today.

"Brenda swears she saw Diaz and Maltz with two men in suits." She crosses her arms and leans back. "Not saying she didn't, just that none of the rest of us did."

"Did she say where?" Brad asks, sliding his phone from his jeans pocket and opening his notes. We've officially slipped into investigation mode and I couldn't be happier. My brain has been buzzing all afternoon, it's time to straighten it out.

"In the public parking area. There were four men and one of those big, black SUVs. You know the limousine for hire type?" We nod, easily picturing the vehicle. "Sadly, she didn't have great descriptions of the unknown men with briefcases. One was described as balding, middle-aged, in a gray pinstripe suit. The other was more sharply dressed, navy suit, silver hair brushed away from his face. According to Brenda, it looked like a boss and an underling. But, she is a tad on the dramatic side," Linda concludes. Chandra types rapidly into her phone, when she catches my eye, she mouths "Cassidy" and carries on.

"That sounds a lot like the fellows we saw," Desmond says, "before our unfortunate incident that is."

"Can Cassidy get security footage from the lot?" I'm hopeful we can get images of the group. Chandra nods and resumes texting. "If we can get the pictures, we can start to identify them." An idea strikes like lightning. "Can Bento help?" Again, a nod and smile from Chandra.

"Bento would be perfect!," Linda exclaims. "He was such a nice young man and so talented." Have to agree with her there, Bento was fantastic and helped us get where we are.

"Totally do-able," Chandra chimes in. "I've updated Cassidy as we've been talking. She's talking with the AV tech lead and assembling the group to review footage. By tomorrow evening we should have some more information."

We celebrate the progress by diving into heaping portions of tiramisu that materialized while we talked. Through an unspoken consensus, we move on from the case. The rest of the evening passes with rounds of stories from past and present. As usual, we hear replays of old stories blended with new versions. Laughter echoes around the table. Moshe and Francine smile at one another, holding hands, and savoring their company.

28

Things Get Personal

This week has been heavy. A little too heavy if I'm being honest.

Brad and I decide on an escape to the Keys for a long weekend to find a sliver of peace. Leaving by Thursday afternoon, we'll arrive in time to have dinner before settling into our rental cottage.

Between the thefts last year and the break-ins downtown, crime has worn thin. I'm left feeling disheartened and overly exhausted by all of it. This case feels like it's dragging on without any progress. As a group, we've spent most of the week trying to track down any of the men in town, without any success. They seem to have completely vanished. The last sighting was in the public parking lot. No one has seen or heard from any of them. Alfie and Moshe have been in touch with their contacts, and it seems that the men have ghosted there as well. Currently, I've decided my role has come to a close for this case, and I am more than happy to leave the rest to the professionals. This hasn't done much to quell my concerns of what the life of a PI would entail for me. Is this really how I want to spend my time?

Waking up to the sound of waves crashing outside, I croak out, "Coffee?" Brad mumbles a yes and turns to face the patio doors. Weak morning sun filters in through the curtains. Groaning loudly and stretching, I flip the covers back and prepare myself to exit the luxurious bed. Coco and Aggie have puddled themselves in the center and make no attempts to move. They're as exhausted as we are. The ability of dogs to absorb our emotions never ceases to amaze. Padding to the kitchen, I glance toward my phone but make a conscious decision to avoid picking it up from the charger. This weekend is for us to unwind, part of that is staying off my phone. Reaffirming my resolve, I pop a coffee pod in the machine and press the lid closed. The satisfying snap feels like an exclamation point to my thoughts.

Recommitted, I step onto the patio to take in the warm, salty breeze. Inhaling deeply with my eyes closed, my muscles relax and the tension I've been holding onto dissipates. What is it about the beach that makes stress disappear? Well, maybe not disappear, that feels slightly overdramatic. At least, it lessens my stress to a manage-able level.

The coffee maker sputters, signaling it's time for me to go inside. A splash of cream, before crossing to place the mug on Brad's side table, then I drop a kiss onto his lips. He stretches toward me and pulls me to sit on the edge of the bed next to him. Instead of reaching for the cup, he curls onto his side and wraps his body around me. With his busy schedule, we don't have many mornings to linger before life begins. I'm more than happy to sip coffee while soaking in the comfort of having him near me. Resting my arm over his back, I pull him even closer. In moments, he's snoring softly.

By the time I've drained the cup, Brad is solidly back to sleep. Watching his steady breathing is the equivalent of a tranquilizer and a singular coffee isn't enough to keep me awake. Back under the covers I go. That's the beauty of vacation, no schedule and no pressure to be up early. Sleep crashes over me like the waves on the shore.

Hours later, we wake to a room warmed with mid-morning sunshine and two wiggly dogs ready for some fun. They snort and grumble, making tunnels in the sheets, giving me time to shake the cobwebs of sleep free from my mind.

"My turn," Brad says, swinging his legs free from the covers. I nod appreciatively, pushing myself into a seated position.

"Coffee and a beach walk?" I suggest, pointing to the rambunctious duo, wrestling on the duvet. Aggie has Coco pinned, eight legs flailing in the air. They've been cooped up for too many hours and are going wild.

By the time Brad returns with coffee, they're hopscotching all over the bed. My coffee sloshes, nearly spilling on the crisp white linens. Brad and I make an "ACK" sound in unison, freezing the dogs in mid-run. As we rushed to protect the coffee, our phones drop from the bedside table onto the tiled floor with a smack that echoes through the small space. I screech at the sound.

Brad holds up my shattered phone. The screen smashed beyond usability. My hands fly over my mouth, too shocked to speak. Granted, I hadn't planned to use my phone this weekend, but I'll need it at some point. Brad grimaces and picks at the shattered glass.

"It's okay. Really. I wanted a break," I say, attempting to be casual. I'd gotten the phone earlier in the year after breaking the previous version. Looks like it'll be three for me this year, which is a record unto itself. Two phones has been my max. "I'll get a junker at a gas station before we head home and pop the sim into it." A strained smile plays across my lips, holding the mug toward Brad, I clink them in a lackluster cheers.

Despite the last few moments, I am committed to a relaxing weekend of beach walks, swimming, and more seafood than is reasonable. Extending his phone in my direction, he powers it down, and says, "Solidarity." Instead of a second cheers, he stands and pulls me up from the bed. Dancing in me in a circle, we head to the patio. Two furry missiles launch themselves in the direction of the doors. Laughing, we spin our way outside to the small yard.

***

Before I know it, we're more than halfway through the trip. I've read two of the three mysteries from my outrageously large pile of unread books. Disappointingly, the villains were easily identified early on. Doesn't matter though, they were still fun reads. A few times, I've caught myself reaching for my no longer functional phone. It's just so tempting to scroll or shop when there's downtime. Maybe I'm more attached than I want to admit?

Closing my book and resting back, I settle in for a nap in the sun. Brad and the dogs have gone for a jog on the beach to burn off energy, so no distractions. The challenge will be turning off my brain. It's like a blender running full tilt with the top off most days. Flinging an arm over my eyes, I picture the crime boards at the community center and in our garage. We really need to consolidate. Shaking my head, I force an image of clearing an old Etch-A-Sketch. No luck though, I shake until I'm dizzy, but the board filled with notes and printed images. Walking myself through the case from day one, I outline the crimes, suspects, and possible motives. That's where I get stuck. What is motivating this? Chandra and Detective Cassidy think it's something to do with me. Which doesn't make sense. I'm a previous marketing minion at an accounting firm turned barista with a reading and coffee addiction. How does that mark me as a target? Or is the cafe? Could Seb's business be the real target and I'm collateral? Jumping up from my chair, I grab my journal and make notes.

The sound of running feet accompanied by panting pulls me from the building storm of thoughts. A red and sweaty Brad stands in front of me, a sandy little dog tucked under each arm. His glistening chest and biceps distract me from his words. The little bits of sand caught in his chest hair really makes me stare.

"Babe? Are you having a stroke? What are you staring at?" he pants out. The heavy breathing isn't helping me listen either. "Graciella Louise!"

I snap to attention, he hasn't used my full name since our vows. "What? You're sparkling and I like it," I say coyly, a blush creeping into my sunburnt cheeks. "Shouldn't you be flattered?" He grins and shakes his head.

"Yes, but did you hear what I said?" Dropping onto my chair, he releases the dogs from his grip and wipes sandy hands on my pristine towel. I murmur an "eww" but he keeps talking. "I know I wasn't going to turn my phone, but I did. Figured a podcast or some music would be nice on the walk." He doesn't need to justify, I do appreciate the effort, though. "I had more than a dozen missed calls and close to thirty texts. Most from Chandra." This gets me and I reach for his phone. He hands it over, open to the messages. Scrolling through, the first is wishing us a happy vacation and an ask to bring a bottom of rum back as a gift for Seb. From there, the messages progress in urgency.

C: *Hey! Tried to call. Guessing you're at the beach. Can you have CiCi call me?*

C: *Not trying to be a pest, need to talk to y'all*

C: *Call me*

C: *Okay. Not sure what's going on. You guys ok?*

C: *I've got updates. Call me or Seb.*

C: *Break-in at Azúcar. Smash and grab. Fire in the kitchen. No injuries.*

C: *Starting to get worried. Can one of y'all call?*

C: *Been a full day and nothing. Call or I'm sending a unit by.*

Without another word, I tap on her number. She answers by the second ring with a string of swear words that I didn't know could be combined. When she takes a breath, I say, "My phone broke." A poor excuse, but it's the truth. "Brad turned his off in solidarity. Also, why are you so much nicer when you text him?"

"Do you know, I actually considered you may be dead or injured?" Her tone is still fiery, with a hint of fear. I may have imagined it cracking, she's clearly deeply upset. I spend the next several minutes sincerely apologizing, explaining what happened the first morning. At one point, she does chuckle softly. The tide is turning, thankfully. This gal has a hurricane force temper that can be hard to turn.

"Tell me about the cafe?" I ask, wincing slightly and grasping Brad's forearm in a death grip. He furrows his brow and wraps his fingers tightly over mine.

"Wren and Tev were scheduled to open yesterday at 5:30. Seb's policy is openers arrive and enter the building together. No one goes in alone." Despite being well aware of the policy, I don't interrupt. "The smoke was what they noticed first. Tev said when the door opened, it rolled out. He initially thought the whole place was on fire." The way she says it sounds like *fy-uh* with her slow drawl, in these moments, I take comfort in her intentional downshift. "He foolishly rushed in. Wren called 911 when she saw the smoke. He tracked the source to the kitchen. One of the oversized metal trashcans was smoldering. It had been stuffed with paper products and table linens, then set fire. Tev's quick thinking prevented the spread, he used an extinguisher to douse the small flames and topped it all off with a big 'ole bucket of ice." She sounds proud of him, but also irritated by his lack of personal safety. I can absolutely guarantee she would have rushed into a burning building to investigate, she just doesn't want others doing it. "Arson is investigating what accelerant was used. Currently, it suspected to be cooking oil. The bottles next to the griddle were found empty and scattered behind the trashcan."

"No injuries?" Brad asks.

"None that we know of. Tons, and I mean, TONS of damage. This went beyond a robbery. The level of destruction is outrageous and appears to have a revenge or rage element." I hold off on questions, sensing she's building up to more. "The POS devices are missing, phones ripped from the walls, dishes and glassware were shattered. There's more—" she pauses, sucking in a deep breath, "the coffee bar—it's wrecked."

Groaning aloud, I hate having to ask, "Can you define wrecked?" Anxiously waiting the seconds it takes her to reply, I chew my lower lip, still gripping Brad's arm fiercely. He reaches forward and touches my lip, the action is enough to reset. I release my lip and the claw-like grip on his arm. He mimes taking deep breaths. I swear everyone in my life is always telling me to take a breath.

"Picture your worst, then double it. And maybe double it again, shug," she says with a sigh. "Equipment smashed beyond repair, coffee thrown everywhere. If it could be broken, they broke it."

"Suspects?" Brad asks.

"The usual, we actively are searching for our four crime-loving besties. Maltz and Diaz were spotted with a rented moving truck late the evening before a few blocks away. Cameras picked up no discernable images, but it is assumed they were involved. Would be super nice to catch at least one of them," Chandra laments. The entire department must be feeling the same frustration. These guys seem to disappear every time we get close.

"Should we come home?" I'm torn between finishing our trip and the need to support our friends. All we'll do anyway is talk about what's happening at home until we get back.

"Do I think you need to be here? No. Would I rather you be home where I know you're safe? Yes."

"Hey now, you're starting to sound like me," Brad teases. Chandra lets out a gruff chuckle. Not only has this impacted the town she serves, but it has directly hit the man she loves.

"Give us an hour to get packed up, we'll text when we're on the road," Brad assures her. I nod appreciatively, relieved that it wasn't my call to make. "We'll get CiCi a phone on the way home."

29

Out of Service

Words fail as we survey the inside of Azúcar. Horrifyingly, this is the view *after* the police have processed the scene and removed some of the damaged equipment as evidence. It's so much worse than Chandra described. I realize she'd taken it easy on the phone, only sharing a portion of how bad this all is. Bad is an underwhelming description. Malicious is the only word I can conjure to describe the destruction surrounding us. There is little chance this much aggression is only for money.

Not only are the dishes and glassware decimated, but every corner of the cafe has something damaged. Heartbreakingly, the oversized hand-painted mirrors on the walls are smashed. They're from the previous owners of the cafe, which was once a pharmacy. Seb once told me the mirrors had been painted in the late 1930s and salvaged from a hotel set to be demolished. The most grotesque is the ominous message scrawled on the coffee bar. In ugly red spray paint, "LEARN YOUR LESSON," mars the antique wooden surface.

Tears slide down my cheeks, dripping off the edge of my jaw. Yet again, the crushing weight of losing history hits me. All those feelings of letting go and turning this case over the professionals fly out the gaping hole in the front window.

At this point, I no longer have a job to get to. Might as well dig in and help however I can. This situation strikes me as all too familiar. With a weighty sigh, the kind I feel pulling up from the soles of my feet, I slide the flip phone from my back pocket.

***

During our drive, Brad offered to get the garage in order so I'll have a space to work from. He told me that I can't be effective if I'm splitting time between both boards. A valid point if I've ever heard. We've got work to do after all and I can't do it alone. My excitement to get started feels a tad inappropriate, but rather than let guilt creep in, I'll use the emotions to fuel getting back on track.

On the way home, we stop at the Community Center. The time has long past for officially consolidating the crime boards. Brad photographs while I collect printouts and the file folder we've accumulated. While it may only take a few minutes, texts ping my phone non-stop. My technology hiatus has caused quick a disruption and a mild panic. Linda is already at our house and Mirabel has dinner nearly ready. The Porch Patrol is prepping for a long evening.

Desmond and Moshe sit in the rocking chairs on our small front porch, they've been waiting for us. Not sure how long they've been there, but both are visibly relieved as we pull into the driveway. Desmond launches from his chair and waves excitedly. Moshe is slightly more tempered in his reaction, waving like a politician on a balcony. They make their way cautiously down the stairs to the truck. Coco and Aggie bolt in their direction when the door opens.

"Nice of you to join us," Desmond says, eyes sparkling as he reaches to help me down. Moshe has the back door open and is pulling bags out. He and Brad load their arms, while Desmond escorts me to the porch. They must have been seriously worried about us. "Wait til we fill you in. Linda and Francie got some photos when they went to run errands the other day." Intrigued, I pick up my pace heading for the house.

"Darling, CiCi!" Mirabel walks toward me with her arms extended, wrapping me tightly in a hug. "When none of us heard from you..." She trails off, leaning back and patting my cheek. Her own cheeks are damp with tears. I squeeze her into another hug, and kiss her on top of her head, her fluffy cotton candy hair tickling my nose. Suddenly, guilt lands on me heavily. I went completely off the radar with no warning. All the strain Chandra felt was shared by my friends. I murmur, "sorry," as I continue to cling to Mirabel. Seemingly satisfied, she releases me with a pat and reaches for Brad.

Linda stands behind us with her arms crossed over her chest, her face a blend of relief and irritation. I go through similar steps and apologize. She quickly smiles and swats me. I wish I had a better justification than it feeling like the right decision at the time.

"Alright then, we've all had a chance to chat with these youngin's. Are we waiting for anyone else or can we dig in?" Desmond asks, clasping his hands eagerly while eyeing the food spread on the counter. As if on cue, the front door opens.

"Did y'all start yet?" Chandra's slightly muffled voice calls out from the hallway. She appears behind a stack of grocery bags with Seb trailing in her wake. We all stare at the volume of food. "What? It's gonna be a long night."

"She overexaggerates," Seb clarifies, "I had to clean out some of the food from the cafe. This is your share, CiCi." In true Seb fashion, he's split up the food amongst the team. Nothing goes to waste and everyone is taken care of.

"Shall we?" Brad asks, he's more than ready to eat after a long day of driving and stress.

Plates and silverware clink as each of us scoop portions of rice, beans, grilled flank steak, and salad. I can barely contain myself from sampling while walking onto the lanai. At some point, Brad has turned on the lights, porch heaters, and candles. It may be in the sixties at night, but that's way too cold for me. I park in a chair near one of the heaters and prepare to dig in as others join me around the table. In moments, banter is replaced by spoons and forks clanking against the vintage bone-china dinnerware I inherited from my grandmother. My mother is still horrified that I use it routinely, refusing to save it for special occasions. Using the floral-patterned dishes with gold rims may seem extravagant but really— shouldn't every meal with people we love be considered a special moment? Grandma would have celebrated instead of criticized, she was joy and sunshine wrapped in a patterned Mumu.

Once the ooh's and mmm's have settled down, we begin chatting again, getting to the real reason we've all gathered.

"You should have seen Azúcar when we got there," Seb says, patting the edges of his mouth with a napkin. Chandra reaches over and squeezes his knee, leaving her hand on his leg, she pats him reassuringly. No doubt, they've had many emotional conversations over the last two days. Seb has developed a new crease between his brows. Despite the newness, it's deep and matches the dark circles beneath his eyes. The strain is written in his face, even if his tone is casual. His livelihood is at stake, and there's no obvious reason why his business is in the crosshairs. Azúcar was hit harder than any of the other places in town. "It was so shocking, I couldn't process what I was seeing. Every corner of the cafe was damaged, they left nothing untouched." He grimaces and passes a hand over his eyes. Chandra leans in, resting her head on his shoulder.

Moments pass before Chandra speaks, "For the foreseeable future, the cafe will be closed," I groan loudly. I'd anticipated it, obviously, but hearing it hurts more than I'd imagined. "Not only do we have the local investigation, but we have the Arson unit involved now. The process will be far slower. And..." she pauses and pointedly stares at me, knowing I hate when she does this, "there was mention that this may require federal involvement as well." Dropping my into my hands, I picture FBI agents swarming downtown and taking over, refusing to allow any assistance.

"Define 'federal'?" Moshe gruffly asks.

"I wish I knew which agency, I've heard FB I but also whisperings of ATF notification."

"What in the world would ATF have to do with the crimes?"

"The misleading Alcohol, Tobacco, and Firearms doesn't fully encompass what their teams cover," Chandra notes, her tone has turned sarcastic, and I can tell she's not pleased about the outside agencies weighing in. "Above my paygrade anyway."

"Sounds like we need to get crackin' before this gets more complicated," Linda chimes in. Heads nod around the table.

Brad stands and rubs his palms together. "Gents, can I get a hand?" he asks, eyes flashing, cheeks pink. He's clearly delighted to have a project. Glasses raise and chairs scrape back from the table. "We need to make a bit of space in the garage. Having a single space to work from will simplify things for us all." Seb, Desmond, Moshe, and Brad make their way to the driveway from the lanai.

"Dibs on dish duty," Francie says, standing and gathering plates, "I'm not sure how much help I'll be with details, but I can clean like a pro." She smiles widely and picks up the tower of plates. Chandra and I spring into action, assisting with clearing the table.

"Mir and I will hold down the fort until your return," Linda chuckles and clinks her water glass to Mirabel's. They did cook most of the food, so no one is going to object.

Walking through the doorway, I fill Chandra in on my work at the community center earlier. She agrees that now is the time for us to get to work. "The clock is ticking, and I've got no idea when it will chime, cher." From the driveway, the men's voices and laughter echo amongst the scrapes and bangs of their progress. Offering a silent prayer of thanks for my husband's tidiness, this should not take long.

***

"This has gone a bit chaotic, y'all. We need to reorganize before we get started," Chandra shakes her head, taking in the notes, scribbles, and arrows between columns. "Cees, photos and wipe it down." Saluting, I step forward and snap pictures of the board section by section. Linda comes behind me with cleanser and paper towels. Ever the efficient teacher, I can easily imagine her cleaning blackboards at the end of her day.

As if she can read my mind, she adds, "Years of practice will make quick work of it." She spritzes dramatically and swipes her paper towel. Off to the side, Chandra recruits help in sorting the papers from our multiple folders. Surveying the growing mound of papers, Brad snaps his fingers and beckons for Seb to follow home. They drag an oversized pegboard from behind his toolchest.

"Better than a corkboard?' he asks, shaking a box of small pin sized nails. "Worth all the extra holes." I beam at him and he winks. Chandra mutters, "eww," then laughs. She's like the bratty sister he never had.

"Alright, gang, let's get started." Chandra passes out folders, then says, "Got any tape?" Brad opens a drawer, revealing not only multiple colors, but widths and types. Chandra pursues and selects a roll of off-white masking tape and a black marker. "Ya know, you may have the perfect set up for this." It's like all of my husband's dreams of an organized garage have been fulfilled. He's always on me that one day I'll appreciate his system. Today seems to be that day. Cracking the wrapper on the tape, Chandra rapidly tears off strips to define regions on the peg and white boards, barking out directions to Brad and Seb, she outlines the categories. Within ten minutes, a new format has taken shape. Desmond is taking up photos in the order they're handed to him. I tackle drawing out a timeline on the backside of the whiteboard, beginning with the first sighting of Slug on the bakery cameras, moving forward to the break in and fire at Azúcar. As I write, the board wobbles lightly, Chandra and Linda fill in notes on the other side. Returning to the patterns from days ago, I see a trend. Slug and his comrades on camera, seemingly innocently spending time downtown, followed by an incident of some sort.

Slick dude with the briefcase is always spotted in the interim. There are a few things that I have trouble connecting still— why they're here and my accident. Tracing their arrival has been unsuccessful, the police cannot find how the four men intersect with each other and our town. Without thinking, I whisper, "Why here?"

"That's the million-dollar question, ain't it?" Chandra mutters back, a crunch tells me she's biting down on a marker cap.

"Umm...those are new, get it out of your mouth," I say in a blend of mock and true disgust. A marker cap launches over the board and sticks to my hair. It's covered in bite marks and spit. "Classy!"

"Mijas— focus," Mirabel corrects and we snap back to the whiteboard, both feeling the sting of her kind correction.

"I do believe this is officially a crime board," Desmond pipes up excitedly, standing back to study our work over the last half an hour

"Should we make a space for questions we've got circling around?" I ask. "My brain is getting full and I need to clean some of these out." Chandra taps a blank space and hands me the capless pink marker. I curtsy and take it from her hand, thankful that she only chews caps, not the whole marker.

1. Why are they here?

2. When did they get here?

3. Briefcases?

4. Connection to downtown?

Before I can list point five, a throat clears behind us. We all spin startled, including my useless watch dogs. They bark but it's definitely too late to warn us of the new arrival.

"Looks like I missed my invitation," Detective Blair Cassidy stands, scowling with her arms folded tightly across her chest. I sputter, attempting an explanation. She stops me, holding her hand up in my direction.

"I can help with a few of these." She reaches out and Brad places an unchewed maker in her outstretched hand. "We now know that Baek and Diaz have been in town for two months, Emory for three, and Maltz, the most recent at about six weeks." Explains why he hadn't shown up in the earlier images from cameras around town. "As for the why and the connections, we're still working on that." Not extremely helpful and I can't help but frown. "We have determined there is one connection—" She repositions herself to write under the list of suspects. Crossing out Mr. Slick, she fills in Alain Forde, a name we're familiar with even though we've never met him. Moshe grins like a cartoon cat, he was the first in our group to uncover the name. "This is where we are at a bit of a dead end, but don't stress, the Chief has called in a favor and a team is working on identifying a connection." Satisfied, she steps back and passes the marker back to me. "My next question is— any food left?"

30

This is Why You Shouldn't Hang Out in Alleys

Finding myself once again jobless and caught in the middle of a series of crimes, I do what I did before— make coffee and walk my dogs. Part of me wishes I was kidding or being dramatic, but I'm not. These are two things that settle my mind and bring me peace. So here I am, walking the dogs at 8 a.m. on a Tuesday, polishing off a thirty-ounce iced coffee. Notably, my barista skills have drastically improved over the last six months. I've moved past celebrating learning how to set the timer on the coffee maker and onto crafting custom coffees complete with latte art. Seb tried to balance the schedule and keep as many as possible working, I volunteered to take the time off. To be clear, I work because it's fun and gives me extra takeout money. I'd rather know those who need the work have access to it.

Linda managed to convince me that the next book club selection is right up my alley. As promised, the novel is free from sci-fi and slime trails. Thankfully, it's a historical romance with a bit of mystery. I'm four chapters into *Moonlight in the Cavendale Library* and am hooked. Marching through the neighborhood with the audiobook blasting at 1.5X speed, I'm in the zone.

Rounding the corner onto the next block, Coco and Aggie pull on their leashes, yanking nearly free. Caught off guard by their burst of energy, I shriek.

"Always so dramatic." Edna's harsh, nasal voice audible over my noise canceling ear buds. Matching her scowling stare, I stop in the center of the walk. She and her little posse are dressed for pickleball, bags, rackets, the whole nine yards. If I wasn't so irritated, I'd compliment Mrs. Avalon on her matching set. It's absolutely adorable! Magenta and lime florals cover the top with a coordinating striped skirt. Maybe later I can ask where she got it, just not right now. Edna would latch onto it in a second and turn on poor Dina.

"If you weren't always prowling around, hunting for issues, perhaps we wouldn't all be on edge," I retort. Not my best work, but she did scare the crap out of me thirty seconds ago and my heart feels like it's about to climb out of my chest. She sniffs loudly and steps OVER my dogs. How an eighty-year has that level of balance and dexterity is beyond me. It's a tribute to the new medicine I'd heard she's started. While it hasn't improved her mood, it has helped her hip. Momentarily, I'm happy for her. Then in a split second, I am back to her stepping over my dogs as if they were trash on the walk. "EDNA!" I shout. She continues to ignore me, beckoning to the Avalons and Hubert with her racket. Because they aren't psychopaths, they offer tight smiles and step around us. Mr. Avalon even stoops to allow Aggie to lick his hand. He whispers "sorry," looking chagrined. The trio carry on down the walk, trailing behind Edna the Evil like ducklings.

The real question— do I let her ruin my morning or keep going in the hopes of spotting Chip by the pond? I opt for the latter. Why let her take away the nice time we were having. Coco and Aggie sit at attention, mouths open, and eyes sparkling. Decision made. It's time to see what Chip is up to.

Despite Edna's best efforts, the day improves the longer we walk. By the time, we spot Chip's pond, all of us are bebopping along. I'm imagining walking the halls of Cavendale Castle while the dogs march in front of me, ears flopping, bandanas flying in the wind. Today is peak Florida fall. Sunny, low-eighties, with hints that there might be rain later in the day. The air has that pre-rain smell mixed into the breeze. I inhale deeply and savor the beauty of the morning.

Plopping onto a bench, leashes around my ankle, we settle in to await our neighborhood gator. It may not seem sensible to every one, but it makes sense to me. Moments later, the center of the pond ripples as the tip of a nose breaks the surface. I get so excited that I fumble with my phone and nearly drop it onto the bench. Having just got a new smartphone, the last thing I want to do is break another one. Brad will restrict me to flip phones from the gas station if I shatter or lose this one. Not that I'd blame him at all, I'm even over it. Recovering my grip after a few weird oomph and oopsies, I firmly hold onto the phone and open the screen to the camera. His face breaks through the surface as I hit record. And...my phone rings, canceling the recording.

Chandra's face fills the screen. Part of me wants to decline the call and go back to watching Chip. But, the nosey part of me can't handle the idea of missing what she has to say. I tap to accept the video call, leaving it zoomed in the slowly surfacing gator.

"Good God, why are you so close to that thing?" she screeches, as her voice echoes, Carl tucks his head back under the water with a loud splash. Zooming out, I show her how far we are from the water's edge. Flipping the camera to face me, I ask what's up. Not that it is unusual for Chandra to call, but there's typically a reason, she doesn't love chatting on the phone and prefers to text.

"Can't I call to see what you're up to?" she responds, batting her lashes in a faux demur posture.

"We both know that's a lie," I tease with a smirk. "I'm out for a walk and enjoying the sunshine, nothing else on the radar. Ya know, jobless and all." She gives a mini-grimace and a twinge of guilt hits me. "So...what are you up to?" Hoping my lighthearted tone will reduce the awkwardness.

"I'm glad you asked," she begins, her face lights up in a genuine smile. "We've had Bento in to recreate sketches of some the notorious briefcase men that have been spotted around town." My interest is now piqued. Straightening on the bench, I lean into the screen. "Thought you may be interested. We haven't made ID's but did get four solid images to add to the investigation." Nodding my head, I drum my free hand on the bench. We've already identified Mr. Forde, perhaps some of his associates, or competitors, can be added to the list with the new drawings. "Would you be up for taking a look?"

As if there's any way I'd say no! Reaching forward, I untangle the dogs from my ankle and stand quickly. "Should I come to you or will we meet later?"

"Do you have time to come into the station this afternoon?" I tip my head and stare into the phone. "Right, right, you're off work. Can you be here in an hour?" I nod enthusiastically. "Any chance you can also grab me lunch? I'm starving." I promise to bring her a meal from Magpie's and a coffee from home.

With a fresh pep in my step, the dogs and I nearly jog home. This feels like good progress! After all the recent stalls, solving the case seemed far off. The sketches from today could be just what we need to wrap this mess up. On the way back to the house, I call Brad to fill him in. The call rolls over to his voicemail and I leave a quick message, "Chandra has some leads, heading down to check things out. I'll be before dinner."

Good enough for now, I think as I end the call. He'll call when he's free. Tucking my phone in my pocket, I take a quick look around as we enter our neighborhood. Running into Edna isn't on my priority list, one interaction in a day is more than enough.

***

Magpie's is shockingly busy, with a line nearly to the store's check-out counter. Ten minutes into the wait and I regret not calling ahead. The quiet tension of the last few months has lulled us into a sense of complacency. We've adapted to shorter lines and quicker interactions. Snowbird season is officially upon us, meaning things have changed quickly. Over the last week, foot traffic in town has blown up. Which is shocking considering the damaged and closed businesses. For an outsider, it may not seem out of the ordinary. A lot of smaller towns have revitalization projects that appear more of destruction than construction. Our repeat visitors have a lot of questions about what's happened, especially if they keep an eye on local news when they aren't here. To that group, Palmetto Breeze is their second home and the crimes hit them hard.

Texting Chandra about the line, I warn her that I've hit a snag and won't be there on time. Dramatically, I add that this is killing me and I've got to do something. She doesn't respond in the seconds my phone is out of my bag. I opt to people watch for a bit, distractedly stuffing it into a side pocket. Maybe I'll be able to recognize some of the visitors in here? Plus, it's good to train my observation skills. On the side, I've been reading up on this PI license idea and decided that I will apply. The worst they can say is no, right? There are so many things I need to work on, primarily not constantly losing my phone and paying more attention when out in public. You never know what you'll stumble on, the town's recent foray into citizen photos is a prime example.

Before I know it, I'm next to order. The devil on my shoulder tells me to order that horseradish monstrosity Desmond mentioned. Instead, I get her a classic club sandwich, jalapeno chips, and a sweet tea. Would have been funnier to order the other one though.

***

Hurrying out the door, I check the time. It's 1:15 p.m. I'd told Chandra my ETA was 1 p.m. As usual, my hands are overly full. The bag from Magpie's is bulkier than I thought it would be. Fighting around the top of it, I grab my phone. Before sending off a text, I decide to pop down the alley. It will shave the tiniest bit of time off my walk to the car. In the moment, every second seems to count.

Me: *Goods acquired, took longer than planned. Too many people around.*

Chandra sends back an emoji with a face palm.

Continuing to stare at my phone, I run back up to my last message to Brad. Super odd that I've heard nothing from him. Normally, he texts me all throughout his day. Keeping me up to date on the random happenings or anything he finds funny. Shuffling along, my foot strikes something with a dull thud.

Please do not be a dirty diaper.

I gag at the thought and am tempted to step over whatever it is without looking. In the end, I can't help myself. Peeking over the bulky carry out bag, I see something *far* worse.

Stifling a scream, I clamp a hand firmly over my mouth. Shrieking won't be helpful to anyone, I've seen enough made for TV crime movies to know that.

Filling most of the alley, sprawled on his back, the infamous Slug. His face is a dusky blue with his mouth gaping open. One eye bulges, staring directly at me. He is very clearly dead, yelling for help won't make a difference. Without thinking, I drop to the ground next to him, careful to avoid touching. A thick, black cord circles his neck at least twice. He's dressed in a dark suit with a brightly patterned tie. Not the usual look he sports, I've only seen pictures of him in jeans and t-shirts or hoodies. One arm is tucked behind his body. The other clutches a familiar, battered leather briefcase. It's almost like these are part of the uniform if you're up to no good around here. Could what we're looking for be right here?

Desperate for answers, I frantically search through the bag. Pulling out his photo ID and two other wallets, I set them on the edge of his splayed-out jacket. Deeper within the bag, several file folders are held together with a rubber band. Just as I slide them from the briefcase, I hear a scuffling sound behind me and I spin to look.

"Keep your hands where I can see them and don't move!" a harsh male voice barks at me.

31

Jailbird

An imposingly broad police officer stands behind me in the alley. I sputter, trying to explain who I am while scrambling to my feet. He rushes at me, gun drawn. I scream and drop back down, heart hammering. He's shouting, but my brain can't process a word. A crowd forms, filling the opening of the alley between buildings. Embarrassment compounds my terror. I freeze in place, ice cold with dread but flushed with shame. He mutters into the radio clipped on his shirt, none of it making sense to me.

"Please. I...I...found him...tripped...on..." I sob, "himmmmm...." Horrifyingly, I dissolve into a wail, the last word drawn out. Admitting aloud that I'd not only found a dead body (again), but that I'd kicked him makes my stomach flip. I turn to the side, doing my best to avoid Slug's body, and lose the remainder of my breakfast behind a pile of cast-off trash bags. The officer continues to shout, ordering me to stay still. A voice overrides his from the crowd.

"Can you not see what's happening? Give her a second." Instead of escalating, it tempers the young officer's response. He lowers his gun and addresses me in a lower tone of voice.

"Walk toward me with your hands in the air, palms facing me." Nodding, I wipe my mouth and walk slowly toward him. He remains tense but holsters his weapon, keeping his hand in place over the grip. Murmuring an unintelligible phrase into his crackling radio, he beckons for me to step closer. "Place your hands behind your back." Shock ripples through me. He's arresting me. Surely, he can't imagine I'd killed Slug. "Anything sharp in your pockets?" he demands, working his hands from my shoulders down to my waist. I can't speak, shaking my head I stare at the ground. What were whispers from the observers has now grown to outright talking. The shame is too great for me to even glance at the group.

"What is going on here?" The voice is sharp and nasal. Groaning, I couldn't have imagined this getting worse, yet it has. "Young man, did you hear me?" Edna's sharpness, snaps everyone in the crowd to attention. The officer stiffens, his grip tightening on my upper arm. She has elbowed her way through from the middle, and now stands in front of us. Arms crossed, scowling, toe tapping. Classic Edna stance.

"Ma'am," he addresses Edna, "the situation is under control. There's no need for you to be concerned. Please refrain from coming any closer." On that last bit, his voice trembles ever so slightly.

"I highly doubt this is as under control as you profess." She's moved from scowling to sneering, the tips of his ears redden. "Do you know who the young woman you've apprehended is?"

"We haven't gotten that far," he protests, standing straighter and puffing out his chest slightly. Obviously in an attempt to regain authority.

"Why don't I fill you in? You must be new here." I've been the recipient of that tone many times and promise, it stings like a jellyfish wrapping around your leg. It's a burn that builds the longer you're exposed. "Whatever you believe to have occurred, I can assure you—" pausing for effect, and running her eyes over him with disdain, "you are incorrect. You've apprehended CiCi Larkin. She is many things, nosey, intrusive, sloppy," okay, ouch, "but she is not, and never will be a murderer. I suggest you find out more details before continuing to manhandle a respected member of the community." Wait—is Edna defending me?

Several others step forward in my defense as sirens scream. With a screech, multiple cars skid to a stop. I may not be able to physically see them, I mentally picture armed officers running in our direction, full assault gear, guns raised.

"Clear a path, NOW!!!!" the words echo, bouncing between the buildings and fence of the alley. Detective Blair Cassidy has arrived on scene and she does not look pleased. "Officer, undo those cuffs," she spits. Slightly relieved, I attempt a smile. My salvation is here, or at least it felt that way until she makes eye contact. "Wipe that look off your face." Uh-oh. She about as happy to see me as Edna usually is. Speaking of Edna, she's stepped back a few feet and is talking into her cell phone, a satisfied smirk on her face. Pretty sure, she's telling everyone she knows that I messed up and she had to save me. Blanching, I force myself to relax and appear neither stressed, relieved, or sad. The effect is certainly delightful for those watching, probably like one of those B-rated shape-shifting alien movie scenes. "Stand to the side and touch NOTHING. I mean absolutely nothing other than the ground under your feet." Backing a foot or so away, I stand rooted in place, hands clasped so tightly that my knuckles crack. Other officers file in around us, placing ribbons of yellow crime scene tape at the perimeter.

Facing the unnamed officer, she barks, "Walk me through it." His retelling does make it sound worse, especially the part where I frantically removed items from the dead man's briefcase. Grimacing, I am tempted to explain myself but recognize this is not the time for it. Drumming my folded hands on the waistband of my jeans, I collect my thoughts. The drumming must be louder than I imagine, as both Cassidy and No Name are staring at me suddenly. Opening my mouth to speak, I am halted by Cassidy's glare. Cool, so not yet. Back to gripping my hands until I break a knuckle.

"Pssst..." a hiss from beyond the tape. Without moving, I turn my eyes to spot Edna. Phone held in my direction. "I called your husband. He's on his way. I told him this serves you right, about time you learned to stop interfering." Gasping, I turn my head fully in her direction. She stomps off through the crowd, offending as many people as possible, shouting sweet things at them, "Move!" "Get out of the way!" "What is wrong with you people?" A delight to all around her.

"Your turn," Cassidy says, now standing about six inches from me. She's so close that I see a tiny ruptured blood vessel in the white part of her left eye. My efforts to organize my thoughts prove useless the moment she speaks.

"Ummmm," off to an illustrious start, "I waited forever in the deli line to get lunch for Chandra, Office Boudreaux," I clarify for No Name, who now seems even more uncomfortable, his ears are flaming red and he's refusing to make eye contact. "Since I was so behind, the alley seemed faster. Between texting Chan and Brad, my husband," again for No Name, "I wasn't looking where I was going," I pantomime staring at a non-existent cell phone. "My right foot struck something, which I assumed to be a dirty diaper." Why did I need to include that tidbit? More flustered now, I lose my train of thought. "I mean," gesturing at the dead man, a grotesquely altered chuckle bubbles up, "clearly not a diaper." Oh dear God, get it together, I prod myself. "Once I realized it was Slug, his real name is Ren Emory," smiling at No Name, who is looking increasingly confused, "anyway, when I saw who it was AND the briefcase, it was like I was possessed. My brain told me not to touch anything, but my hands were yanking the bag open and emptying it before I could stop myself. That's when Officer...I'm sorry I didn't catch your name."

"Galvin," he mutters.

Got it. "That's when Officer Galvin appeared and began shouting at me, waving his gun around." The last part might not have been necessary, but the withering look Cassidy gives him feels worth it.

"I wouldn't describe it as waving," he weakly defends himself. I notice for the first time that he is young, very young and gives off fresh from the academy vibes. He probably thought he'd stumbled on a career making scene. Instead, he's in the crosshairs of a no-non-sense detective.

"Where were you headed with the lunch?" Cassidy continues her interrogation. Can it be an interrogation if I haven't had my rights read to me?

"Chandra asked if I could come down to check over the sketches Bento had done earlier today." Before I can explain who Bento is, Cassidy holds up her hand. Okay, so no explanations warranted from here on out. Message received. "We were supposed to meet at 1 p.m." She checks her watch and I catch the time. It's now nearly 2 p.m.

"Galvin, escort Mrs. Larkin to the station," she orders. He steps forward, reaching for his handcuffs. "Did I say take her into custody?" He releases his grip on the cuffs, instead taking me by the elbow. "I'll let Chandra know you're on your way in and have her radio where to meet." Galvin does his best to keep a relaxed face, despite the turn this has taken. "CiCi, you don't have any of his possessions with you?" She tips her head toward Slug's body. I aggressively shake my head no.

"No ma'am, whatever I took out is on the ground next to him," I confess, pointing to the papers and multiple wallets. With a nod, she turns and walks away. Galvin quietly directs me to his squad car. "What are the odds I can use my phone once we're in the car?" His face gives me an answer even if he says nothing.

***

Chandra, it seems, is even angrier than Cassidy. When she opens the conference room door, she nearly rips it off its hinges. I'd joke about her hitting the gym, but this does not appear to be the right time for humor.

"How many times have we discussed crime scene etiquette?" she whisper shouts, which is way scarier than if she'd simply yelled. I'd have preferred if she came in screaming instead of quietly seething,

"I fully recognize that I acted like an idiot and violated everything you've taught me about preserving a scene. Something took over in my brain and the next thing I knew I was rifling through his bag and

Danny Do-gooder was pointing a gun at me." Was that a hint of a smile?

"We will have a lot to discuss about this later. For now, take me through EVERYTHING that happened."

I retell the story, leaving nothing out and making sure it is consistent. Telling a story precisely goes against my personality, I don't think I've ever told a story the same way twice in my entire life. Not that there's anything to hide, just that even slight variations could be suspicious. By the end, Chandra is leaned back in her chair, mouth agape.

"Edna? Edna defended you?"

"Yeah, but she was mean about it."

"Doesn't matter, I'd assumed she hated you enough to convince him to arrest you on the spot." She shakes her head, she's not wrong. Edna has never once had anything kind to say about me and often berates me over nothing. I was more shocked than she is. "Also, thank goodness Cassidy was there, if Galvin had seen your texts to me, you'd have been in hot water."

"What's that mean?" All I'd done was text about how long it took to get her lunch.

"Do you mean other than them sounding like you'd pulled off a crime?" She reads the messages back to me and I redden.

"Yikes! Those make me out to be a low-level criminal," I groan.

"Guessing you didn't get my food?" I shake my head, picturing the bag sitting beside Slug's dead body. Not saying she wouldn't have eaten it but the thought makes me gag a little. "Let's hit the vending machine and then I'll show you the sketches."

***

"After all that, you recognize any of them?" Brad asks, tipping his beer bottle against his lips. We decided that today was bizarre enough, it required pizza and beer by the firepit, pulling out all the stops to relax.

"Ya know, that would have made today a little less brutal," I lament, poking at the fire with a stick. The sketches and proposed mugshots were a bust. None of them were familiar to me. "Can you believe Slug is dead?" He shakes his head, eyes locked onto the flames.

"Anything noteworthy on the papers?"

"No, but I did catch the names on the other IDs." This catches his attention. "Alain Forde and Albert Emory."

"The mysterious, Mr. Forde, Wonder who Albert Emory is," he ponders, now peeling the label from his bottle. "With the same last name—"

"Was weird..." Pulling up the images of the licenses, I only see the faces and names. No addresses, no other details. "Alain and Albert were strikingly similar." Not enough to be the same person, but could realistically be related. "Do you think they could be connected?" Brad shrugs and rests his head against the Adirondack chair, what starts as a sigh ends as a groan.

"Do you know how weird it was for Edna to call me? I almost didn't answer, figuring she was calling about trash cans or dog poop." I giggle at his choice of offenses. Edna is always after me for one or the other, real or imagined. "Glad I did." He stretches a hand over and I take it squeezing three times, our unspoken code. Three squeezes, three words. I. Love. You.

"You've had a lot of strange phone calls over the last couple of months." Thinking back to the day of my accident, he now squeezes three times and smiles sadly. "I don't do it on purpose you know." This gets a genuine smile. We both know, trouble finds me. For as long as I can remember, if there's something that can go wrong, I'll find myself in the thick of things. We sit in relaxed silence, soaking in the evening.

"Want to update the board?" Brad asks, mischief twinkling in his eyes. In sync, we jump from our chairs and head into the garage.

32

Clearing the Air

A week of my being called in and out of the police department follows. I've recited what happened so frequently, that
I could do it in my sleep. It's almost a default answer. By Chandra's
recommendation, the dirty diaper comment no longer makes an
appearance. She deemed it non-essential information.

Chief Mercer was justifiably angry over my actions. Having never
been screamed at by the Chief of Police, it was life altering. The man
really is skilled at dressing you down to the bone without making it
personal. A wild experience to endure. He threatened to charge me
with tampering with a crime scene if I ever behaved this way again.

Thankfully, my involvement did not seem to have impacted any of the evidence. The wallets were covered in fingerprints, only two of which were mine. The briefcase contained Slug's and mine, otherwise it appeared to have been wiped clean. Which is bizarrely suspicious.

Having felt the wrath of Mercer and Cassidy, I lay as low as possible. The brief, but memorable, terror of wearing handcuffs also did a number on me. There are plenty of things to fill my time and give me an excuse to avoid investigating. We're all hands on deck at Azúcar, helping to reset before we reopen early next month. With my height, I've been given the honor of painting. Specifically edging around the crown molding. Seb has turned the tragedy into a hidden blessing. He claims to have never liked the pale salmon color on the walls, that it felt right a few years ago, but no longer "fits the vibes" of the place according to the younger staff members. It also does not photograph well. The color distorts depending on the lighting, varying from a garish orange to mauve, rarely ever the actual color. He's now chosen a mint green, the color is somehow both cool and warm, giving a tropical touch and improving the lighting. While the vintage mirrors were a total loss, Seb and Chandra are on the hunt for similar pieces. They've gone to auctions and estate sales around Florida and Georgia each free weekend. Brad and I have been invited, but there's one thing my husband hates— driving for hours to go shopping. Instead, we watch Darla while they shop. A fair trade if you ask me. We get puppy snuggles without hearing Brad mutter under his breath for hours.

Tomorrow night, the local business owners are hosting a town hall with Chief Mercer. It's a big event, catered by several local places, among them are Azúcar, Kebabbing Along, and Gerardo's. Our kitchens have remained functional, allowing for our coffee truck to offer a limited selection of food. With us approaching re-opening, we're able to make deliveries and increase the foods offered on the truck. Because of this, Seb is able to provide a significant portion of the food. And the entire cafe is aflutter. Not only are we in a push to open, we're pushing to get food and drinks ready for the town meeting. Based on the effort being put in, there's no way I would miss it.

***

Plates empty and bellies full, the attendees fill into the rows of chairs. Standing in the back of the room, I've got a good view and note who is present. In a surprise turn of events, Joey Ali is here. He'd been discharged from the hospital and quietly recovering at home. He's wheelchair bound for the foreseeable future, the full prognosis remains to be seen, but he's here. There were many days when it wasn't clear if he'd make it. Due to the circumstances, the family requested privacy and declined any company while he was at his most vulnerable. When his father wheeled him in, they were swamped by well-wishers offering hugs and kisses. A stark reminder that we've had so much more than property damage. Glass can be replaced, walls repaired, but the life of human is irreplaceable.

Chief Mercer and the Mayor, Milton Fugate, call the meeting to order by striking a wooden gavel on the podium. A zip of excitement runs through me, there hasn't been a reason for us to attend one of these in the past and frankly, they seemed boring. Passing motions for begonias versus petunias, bulb wattage, and street cleaning schedules has always felt like none of my business. Tonight though, it feels strangely adult to be at a town hall session, like a scene from a small-town movie set in New England.

The meeting kicks off with a review of the agenda, followed by a reading of last month's minutes. Whipping out my notebook, I jot down a few notes. Business changes, parking adjustments, potential new investments. This is pure gold! Why have I never come to these? All the information shared is perfect for us nosey folks. And they're giving it out for free. I seriously undersold these meetings.

"Now, it's time for why we've all assembled. The safety of our downtown and your business. Would anyone like to open?" Mayor Fugate extends a hand to the audience. A microphone on a stand is placed in the center aisle. Awkwardly, no one moves to speak. There are plenty of side eyes, glances back and forth, and whispers. I don't have anything to do with the proceedings, yet I find my face flushing and a sweat breaking out on my lower back. Someone will speak up, right?

At the moment when I'm about to twitch out of my skin, Mari and Siobhan stand. Walking to the microphone, arm-in-arm. Their husbands quietly cheer them on. They're faces are plastered with tight smiles, neither seems to be comfortable speaking in front of the crowd.

"He—" The microphone screeches before Mari can get out a greeting. With a frown, the Mayor turns to the duo in the AV booth. Apologies are made and there's a "Try it now," shouted.

"Hello?" A little meeker this time to test the sound. Mari relaxes when there is no feedback or crackling. She holds onto a small bundle of index cards with handwritten notes. "For the record, Mari and Siobhan Sandoval, co-owners of the Coral Belle Boutique." Siobhan weakly smiles, she is less outgoing than Mari, and public speaking is way outside of her comfort zone. "After a series of tourist related thefts, this past summer, we increased cameras in and around our shop. We thought that would be sufficient, but then our beautiful mural was destroyed." She pauses and looks at Siobhan and the brothers in the row behind. All three smile encouragingly at her, she briefly checks her cards then continues, "The measures we'd taken to reinforce the door did prevent a break-in, but unfortunately, it would appear the vandals knew the location of our cameras and were able to avoid being on film. Since then, we have received permission to install cameras with audio facing the back door of our shop. Thankfully, the only recordings are of raccoons and a couple of iguanas." Her final words prompt chuckles throughout the room.

"We're committed to making any and all recordings available to law enforcement should the need arise. I would like to suggest a vote on a new standard requiring businesses to cooperate in sharing footage on request." Applause crackles when she pauses. "Sadly, over the last few months, there have been several business owners in the community that have refused requests for camera feeds and it is my," Siobhan steps forward slightly, "*our* opinion that this may have hampered the investigation into thefts, vandalism, and injury to members of the community." Again, the audience applauds, and several shout, "Here, here!"

As she steps back, heads in the audience turn to face Lovella from Time After Thyme. Word gets around and it has become widely known that she repeatedly refused to cooperate. There's even talk that she has contributed to the crime streak or may even be in on whatever is going on. Her face reddens and she fans herself with a napkin. Good, a bit of shame can go a long way.

Seb strides confidently to the microphone next, he shares about the instances he observed on the street, at the cafe, and my injury. Next, he outlines the cameras and added security put into place. Notably, he leaves out any mention of his armed cousins guarding the entrance out back. The week of the break-in, he'd told them there hadn't been much activity and they were okay to come in later. He's kicked himself for that every day since, lamenting that if they'd been at the cafe, maybe they would have spotted the offenders. We've all reassured him that he couldn't have prevented it. The arson investigator shared the fire was a slow burn and had been smoldering for several hours by the time it was discovered, meaning it had likely been started overnight.

"I would like the record to reflect my support of the standard proposed by Mari and Siobhan." The audience again shares their support.

One by one, the business owners line up to share their increased security measures and support of the requirement to cooperate with police. Lovella snuck out without a word, but her Irish goodbye did not go unnoticed. Time will tell if she falls in line or not.

Nearly an hour later, Chief Mercer steps back to the podium. "It's my turn to share." His easy manner, prompts chuckles and smiles throughout the room. "We hear your request for the new town standard, there will be some legalities that need investigation before we can proceed." A handful of groans from the group prompts him to give wave his hands in a gesture of peace, "Not saying it's a no, but we have to do it proper. Before we wrap up, I want to ask Detective Blair Cassidy to join me. She will provide updates on the status of the investigation."

"Thank you, Chief," Cassidy graciously accepts the offered spot in front of the microphone. "Many of you have not only been victims of these shameful, cowardly crimes, but have also actively assisted in the investigation," Brad taps his shoulder into mine and wraps his arm around my waist. "As you know, recently, our primary suspect, Ren Emory, also known as Slug, was found deceased. It has been ruled a homicide." Gasps from the crowd, clearly some knew and some just learned of it. "At the time his body was discovered, a briefcase with incriminating documents. The details of which, I cannot release but do directly pertain to this business community." I barely contain my celebratory whoop, I knew those papers meant something. If only I'd had more time to check them over. "Since this is an active investigation, we would ask for your help again. If there are any, and I mean any, information relating to the crimes or to Mr. Emory's death, please do not hesitate to reach out to our department. I am happy to share my cell phone number with the group." Whispers abound, folks glance around wide-eyed. "Chief, if I may?" He nods and she continues, "I'd like to introduce, Agent Darius Patton." A broad-shouldered man in cowboy hat and jeans steps forward from the back of the room. "He is leading an investigatory team through a division of the Bureau of Alcohol, Tobacco, Firearms, and Explosives. Agent Patton and his team have stepped in to assist our department." Polite applause ripples as he approaches and removes his hat.

I gawk at Chandra, she stands stiffly, facing the front of the room. How in the world has she kept this from me? She also does not seem delighted at the ATF's involvement. Brad's grip tightens slightly, a cue to fix my face. Clearing my throat, I relax my face, and return my attention to the podium.

"Thank y'all for the warm welcome." His Texas drawls puts Chandra's accent to shame. Why does this man look so familiar? I swear I've seen him but not in person. We've never met, as far as I can recall. "I appreciate the collaboration of Chief Mercer and Detective Cassidy. Our help isn't always wanted, so this has been a pleasant surprise. Our department has been aware of Mr. Emory's dealings in the past. He has connections to a small-time arms dealer, has traded in stolen weapons, and considered a suspect in a money laundering scheme. Our Miami (pronounced My-am-uh) Field Division was following his activities for over a year, then he went off the radar. Other known associates of his have been spotted in and around the area. We will continue to search for connections and to assist in understanding his dealings in your town."

OMG!!!! Recognition hits. I suck my breath in so harshly, that my nose pinches and squeaks loudly. Brad turns to face me, startled. Agent Patton. He's Wren's boyfriend. The very new, very good guy. She'd mentioned once that he was new in town, and this explains it. He looks familiar, because Wren has shown me a picture of him. Craning my neck, I attempt to find her in the crowd. Shockingly, she's nowhere to be seen. Which kind of makes sense, launching a relationship in this forum isn't exactly romantic or appropriate.

There's no way I can communicate this to Brad right now. I gesture to be chill. He shakes his head and rolls his eyes. Let's be real, my public awkwardness is neither new, nor unexpected. For all he knows, I've suddenly remembered where I left my keys that went missing last week. I almost wish that's what it was, I loved that keychain. Linda got it for me on her trip to the Great Lakes last year.

Forcing my mind to focus, Agent Patton is now hosting a Q&A session for us. Try as I might, I cannot pay attention and will need Brad to fill me in later.

***

"I didn't tell you because I wasn't aware. Cassidy introduced Patton to me about an hour before the meeting. And spoiler, I already know all about Darius Patton. No introduction needed." Her tone is acidic, the embodiment of spitting nails. I most definitely need this back story. Rather than ask, I refill her margarita and wait. "We've been acquainted for years." That doesn't feel accurate. Tapping my toes in my sandals, I do my best to stay still. "He and my cousin went to college together. And before you ask, we did go on a date or two. I can see it causing you physical pain to be quiet."

"What do you mean a date or two?" My brain is spinning, there has been too much information shared tonight, "Does Seb know your ex is here?"

"Oh knock it off. I was a senior in high school, he was a college freshman. It never amounted to anything," she admits, some of the viciousness leaving her voice. "After winter break, schedules got busy and I never heard from him again. I was focused on getting into Louisiana State, he was at Tulane." I nod, having no clue what that means, but relieved that she's sharing without prompting. "My irritation is less with him ghosting me, which wasn't a thing then, and more with having ATF involvement sprung on me right before the meeting." That makes way more sense than hating him for two dates more than a decade ago. I'd been afraid he'd been a sleazeball based on her reaction.

"Is now the time to mention, he's the new boyfriend Wren was telling me about?" I cautiously share. Her laughter catches me off guard. It's not quite the response I'd anticipated.

"Well, good for her! He's a decent man and not bad to look at either. And if memory serves, dude has moves." She continues to laugh, blushing slightly. My word, will the revelations never stop tonight. "Seriously though, I am happy for her. I've got no claims on him."

"Now that we've got that out of the way, tell me more about the case." Tipping my margarita up, I stare over the rim as Brad and Seb join us on the lanai. Perfect timing. Brad winks as he walks toward me, obviously having overheard our conversation. At my raised eyebrow, he shakes his head. Good, Seb didn't.

"Ugh! The ATF has so much information on Slug, Baek, and Diaz. Maltz seems to be an outlier with no connection. Baek and Diaz have been involved in several of the instances Darius mentioned at the town hall." She slipped and used his first name only, Seb side-eyes her but does not interrupt. Which answers my earlier question, no, he does not know she dated Agent Patton. "We have significantly underestimated all three of them. The crimes, while targeted, seemed randomly focused here. The paperwork in the briefcase was enlightening. But, sadly, that's where I draw the line on sharing. Cassidy and Mercer will have my badge if I tell you any more," she revels in it and I hate it. Stamping my feet, I groan, not caring if I look like a toddler on the verge of a tantrum. She leans back and gulps her margarita, seemingly unfazed.

"I don't have a great segue," Brad admits, "But...uhhh...how's the mirror shopping going?" I can't help laughing. He couldn't care less about the mirrors, and I am grateful for his attempt at a topic change.

"Well, no luck in the mirror department," Seb says with a smirk. "We've found a few other sparkly things." Chandra points at her ears, a dainty pair of diamond and ruby clusters twinkle in the light. I'd love to tease about any other shiny jewelry they've encountered, but don't want to embarrass them or put either on the spot. "There is an estate sale in the Keys that we'll check out when Chan has a few days off."

This gives us the conversation switch we'd all been seeking. I'm glad to have something else to talk about for a bit. I've got news of my own to share but decide tonight is not the night.

33

A Little Powder & a Little Paint

Leaning over, the paintbrush glides smoothly along the lower edge of the molding. Stretching to the maximum of my reach, I'm almost done with this section. Grunting, I reach a liittttlllle bit further and nearly fall from the ladder. The grunt turns into a screeching "OH NO!" Scrabbling for anything to grab hold of, my hands slip in the wet paint. In slow motion, the lean of the ladder increases, terrifyingly the back left leg lift from the ground. Suddenly, I'm officially falling, arms flailing, legs kicking. And then...I'm not.

Miraculously, Brad has caught me mid-air. His arms wrapped at an angle around my upper body and I'm hanging facing the floor. "Whew, babe, that was a close one!" He whistles, setting me down feet first and avoiding my paint covered hands. He holds my face between his palms, giving me a quick once over. His eyes are slightly wild, a mix of fear and concern. I splay my hands out, walking to the sink with the grace of Frankenstein, fighting off the vertigo caused by adrenaline. Brad gives me an assist, holding me by the elbow and steering me into the kitchen.

"Thought I was a goner for sure!" Giggling, I picture myself trapped in a modified football hold, dangling like a ragdoll from Brad's arms. Thank goodness he was able to catch me.

"Imagine if I'd left you alone to paint?" It's hard to tell if he's teasing or serious. Falling off the ladder, while funny, was also heart-poundingly terrifying. Painting at the community center felt fairly low stakes after all the hours I've recently spent at the cafe with a brush in hand. Yet again, over confidence nearly got me. Brad begins singing *I Got You Babe* as we enter the kitchen. A quick scrub of my hands, and he's twirling me, dancing through the empty dining room.

"Are we interrupting?" Moshe's voice booms from the doorway, a broad smile on his face. Peering around his back, I spot Linda, Desmond, Alfie, and Elena. They look like Meercats on a nature show. With a dramatic spin, Brad releases me and I pirouette toward our friends. We bow at their applause.

"You missed CiCi's new technique—" Brad points to the hand-prints in the wet paint and I hold out my splattered shirt.

"Learned a new dismount as well." The ladder rests at an angle, leaned against the wall. Grateful that it hadn't gouged any holes in the drywall, I grimace slightly. Checking where it had landed didn't occur to me in the aftermath. Reading my mind, Brad stands the ladder upright and lightly smooths a hand over the surface of the wall. All seems well, other than the stripes my hands made.

Sitting their supplies on the floor, the group looks around at our progress. Brad and I arrived an hour ahead and started prepping. The community center has needed this facelift for a while. We were the first volunteers on the list for painting. While we may not have picked the color, we can make sure it's done well. Other groups have tackled, cleaning, carpet repairs, bathroom updates. Turns out we had way more in the upkeep budget than we realized and there was no need to wait until next year. One of the other requests, purely driven by selfish motivation, is the installation of wall-mounted whiteboards in the conference room. Of course, none of us want another crime spree, but it never hurts to plan ahead.

"Let's get crackin'," Brad announces, "you stay off the ladder." Sticking my tongue out at him, I reach for my brush and wiggle it menacingly. I don't want to admit it, but there's no way I'm getting back on it anytime soon.

An hour in, we've made progress. Three walls are fully taped, with painting resumed on two of them. Desmond and Moshe are on roller duty while Brad and Alfie work on cutting in the upper. Linda, Elena, and I work around windows and outlets. It's tedious, but having our friends makes it more fun. The smell of pizza catches my attention. Who ordered pizza? We'd settled on snacks to keep us moving, afraid that if we stopped for dinner, we'd lose our momentum. Sniffing the air, I look around the room. No one else is reacting. Am I hallucinating? Maybe I hit my head earlier and didn't notice. Is this how brain injuries start?

Then the back door opens. Seb and Chandra walk in, carrying a mountain of boxes from their favorite pizza shop. Nearly dropping my cup of paint, I spring up from the floor. My stomach has been growling for the last fifteen minutes or so. I just hadn't wanted to be the first to call for a break.

"A little birdy told me you might be starving," Chandra says, holding a box of pizza toward me. Like a bloodhound, I trail the scent over to the covered table.

"Perfect timing," I say, tucking my cup and brush onto the counter.

"Plus, I needed to chat." She glances around the group painting and gestures toward the kitchen. Unusual that she wants to speak privately. If it's case related, most everyone in the room is up to date. Following her lead, I grab a slice and walk to the kitchen. Seb calls out to the others to take a break and join him. Eagerly, they step away from their tasks and dig into the pizza.

"What's the big secret?" My nerves won't let me wait much longer. Her words had the same effect as a text saying: *we need to talk.*

"Not a secret, but a couple quick updates that I'm not ready to share broadly yet." This must be good, I want to rush her but instead, I bite into the cheesy, hot pizza. "We've had some tips come in this afternoon. By some, I mean a lot.

"Were any of them helpful?" Please, please, please tell me they were.

"Oh yeah..." She grins and pauses, and I threaten to throw my pizza at her. "We got Baek and Maltz."

"Wait— define 'got'?" I squeak out.

"Just how it sounds, shug. We arrested Baek and Maltz. One of the calls was real time. The caller was eating lunch in their car and spotted the pair at the gas station over by the strip mall. They kept an eye on them until officers arrived. We had 'em rounded up in ten minutes." I slap her a quiet high-five. She grins broadly and continues, "You know how in cop movies, they always show the partners spilling their guts?" I nod enthusiastically. "They're selling out everyone but their mamas. It's a beautiful thing. I WISH I could tell you all the details, but for now, I wanted you to know. We're making big progress tonight!" I cannot believe it. Is this all finally coming to a close? Could we really be done with all this foolishness?

Dinner has a celebratory air, and we kick the painting into high gear afterward. Chandra may have to skimp on the details but we have enough information to boost our collective mood. Laughing, singing, and talking, the largest room is done in a flash. Standing back to survey our work, I am filled with pride and contentment. The soft color glows, enhanced by the new lighting fixtures that Brad and Seb have installed. Francie's cousin owns a lighting store back in Philly, he sent some over stock items to help with our renovation. Shell-shaped sconces have replaced the brass 1980s candle-style, a handful of ceiling mounted lights twinkle, the overall look creates an inviting, comforting space.

"I sent it," I say, glancing at Chandra out of the corner of my eye, continuing to peel strips of blue painter's tape from the trim, hopeful that she'll understand what I'm saying. She stays silent for a beat, twisting the end of one of her long braids.

"Your application?" she finally says, turning to look straight at me. I don't change my position, but instead only nod. "You'll be fine. The worst they can say is no." I stiffen, does she think it'll be rejected? "We both know that isn't going to happen though." Whew!

"The vote of confidence is appreciated, even if I've got my doubts." This time, I turn to face her. "If they say no, I can try again, right?" She nods her head and claps me on the back aggressively. Chandra demonstrates affection like a middle-aged man, back slaps, thumbs up, high fives. It's one of the nuances of her personality that I find hilarious and in contrast to her relationship with Seb. You can tell she was raised by grandparents and elderly aunts and uncles. "Wait— will this give me access to more information?" She rolls her eyes, and snaps an oversized trash bag open with a loud crack. I grin wickedly, knowing it will. I'll be able to know all those inside details.

Yet again, Chandra's fire alarm ringtone startles us all. A few gasps and chest clutches before she can find her phone and silence the call. Seb mutters, "You gotta change that babe, scares us every time." She swats at him with her free hand and answers with a terse, "Boudreaux." While she listens, she sticks out her tongue and spins on her heels, headed for the hallway.

Darn her, I wanted to listen in. Which is most likely why she's quickly retreating to the back of the building. Shrugging at the group, I return to picking at the remnants of blue tape. When I painted at the house, I got distracted during this part and it took my two years to finish getting all the bits of tape off the trim. Let me tell ya, it's way easier to remove now than years later. Faced with a particularly stubborn piece, I poke my tongue out of the corner of my mouth. I swear, it helps with tough tasks.

A tap on my shoulder distracts me. I quickly turn, and bite my tongue in the process. Irritated, I face a tense-looking Chandra. She waves for me to get up and follow her. Oddly, she isn't speaking. Cell phone glued to her head, she waves again for me to hurry, then walks off before I'm off the floor. Scrabbling to my feet, resembling a baby deer standing for the first time, I finally get up and half jog down the hallway behind her. My knee clicks with the first few steps and I have to kick to the side a bit to relax the joint. Brad watches me, a concerned expression on his face. Since my accident, he's been especially protective of me. Rightfully so, I was run down by criminals.

Chandra closes the door behind me when I reach the small conference room. She sits at the table, puts her phone on speaker, and inches it toward me. "Go ahead, Cassidy."

Blair Cassidy's Bostonian accent is particularly thick as her voice fills the room. "You can hear me okay?" Her voice drops a notch or two, she speaks in a harsh whisper.

"Yep, you're good," I tell her, assuming she's asking me, not Chandra.

"There have been some," pausing, her keyboard clicks as she types, "developments." Good Lord, she's acting like Chandra.

"She's looking peevish," Chandra chimes in. "Get to it, Cassidy." I give her a thumbs-up, was definitely getting that twinge of irritation starting to flare.

"I'm certain you're aware that Baek and Maltz have been apprehended and questioned. Through their interrogations, we've gained additional insights into the depths of the crimes, including eyes on who else is involved." She pauses again, sighing loudly. "I need to ask you a few questions, either now or in person." My eyes bug out, she certainly can't think I'm involved in all of this. "Do you have some time to chat?"

"Ye...yes..." I stutter out, looking at Chandra for reassurance and she smiles tightly. I mouth, "Should I get Brad?" She shakes her head and I relax slightly. Not much, but enough that I can listen again.

"How well do you know Melody Deluca?" Cassidy asks, keyboard clicking again. She's speaking louder and has slipped into cop mode, it's like a switch flipped.

"Not well. I'd met her through Bernice. We've only met in person the one time," I answer while rubbing my now sweaty palms on my paint covered shirt. "We were supposed to meet the day of my accident but we never made it. So I guess we actually met twice."

"Who arranged to meet that day?" she asks. Chandra nods for me to go on.

"Melody did. She'd come into the cafe while I was working. We agreed to catch up when I got off work. On my way out the door, I was talking about it and someone must have overheard me. I'm guessing it was one of Slug's crew?" I don't remember if we ever figured out who was listening and passed on the details. "We were supposed to meet downtown, but you remember what happened there."

Click, click, click. She types aggressively, every keystroke echoing through the phone. The urge to fill the silence is overwhelming. Struggling to stay quiet, I bounce my leg up and down, tapping my fingers on my knees. Whether she notices or not, Chandra doesn't acknowledge it.

"Tell me about the second time you met," Cassidy finally asks. I'm so relieved that I answer in a rush, sharing all I can remember of her coming to my house with bread and jam, her tearful apology, and the details of the weird events she and Malcolm had prior to the break-in. Neither of them speak, Cassidy types the whole time, occasionally muttering sounds to let me know she's listening.

"And that's about it. I haven't heard from her since. Now that I think about it, was she even at the Town Hall?"

"From what we know, she and Malcolm were not present," Cassidy's tone is so formal. It's a bit freaky that she can change so much depending on the circumstance. "Are there any other details you can share about Melody or Malcolm?"

Wracking my brain, I try to conjure any memories of interactions. All I see is from the day of the first robbery, Malcolm bouncing between sadness, despair, and aggression. His asking if I can stay while the police talked with them. Which at the time, all felt very normal and appropriate for the situation. Was it normal, though? Now I'm suspicious of his behavior and don't have a clue why.

Cassidy thanks me for my time and then I'm dismissed. Chandra does her best to seem relaxed, but it isn't genuine. Something has happened and her tension is through the roof. She'll tell me when and if she can, for the time being, I need to be patient and finish before the paint dries up.

34

Reckoning

Coffee mug frozen in place, halfway to my mouth, I stare at my ringing phone. It's lit up with MELODY, flashing across the screen. An image of her and a smiling Malcolm stares back at me. I should answer, but at this second have no idea what to say. After all of Cassidy's questions yesterday, I was up half the night overanalyzing every interaction I've had with Melody and Malcolm. Waking up this morning, I was grumpy and slightly paranoid. Seeing her incoming call ramps those emotions up to the roof. Panicking, I tap accept and raise the phone to my ear.

"Hey Melody," I answer, my voice is squeaky, high-pitched, and tight. Nothing says I'm relaxed and happy to hear from you quiet like a helium inflated, strangled voice. There's a chance she doesn't know how I really sound, maybe she won't notice.

"Oh hey, CiCi," she says, obvious hesitating. "You doing ok?" Oh cool, so she absolutely noticed.

Forcing a steadiness into my voice. "Not much of a morning person, ya know?" I attempt a joke to cover the remaining tension.

"Me either, girl! I hate those early mornings at the bakery. Plenty of days, I whine to Malcolm that we need new careers. But he's *super* committed to the bakery." While her tone is light, her words put me even more on edge. My palms are so sweaty that I'm worried the phone is going to slide right out of my hand. The heat of it against my face becomes unbearable. Squeezing like my life depends on it, I switch to speaker, holding the phone a few inches from my face. Melody continues to chatter on about her distaste for the bakery life, the hours, the heat, how hard it is to take a vacation. She's speaking so quickly that my undercaffeinated brain can't keep up. She sighs heavily and pauses, "That ship has sailed, I guess. There's no way Malcolm will leave now." That gets my attention.

"What's that supposed to mean?" I blurt and then grimace, not my best work. Mental note— work on my question intros. Bluntness won't get me anywhere.

To my surprise, she answers just as fast. "I was hoping after the break-in, we could close down and sell." Another dramatic sigh, but this one sounds more irritated than disheartened. "If anything, all this mess has made Malcolm even more committed to this *stupid* bakery." She hits that word, stupid, like she'd rather it be a swear word. I flinch slightly at the force of her words. Over the last few months, I'd never picked up her passionate hatred for the family business.

"Wow! I'm so sorry, I didn't realize how tough the bakery life was," I weakly begin. I've got no idea why she called and am completely unprepared for the direction the conversation has taken. "Is there anything I can do to help?" She snorts derisively, furthering my confusion.

"You've done plenty, trust me," not entirely sure what she means, "speaking of that, you're probably wondering why I've called." It's like she's read my mind or can see the look on my face. A sudden spike of anxiety makes me glance around the edge of the porch. She's not out there, right? I hate to sound so paranoid but this too weird. Rather than answer, I make some sort of non-committal sound. This seems to satisfy her and she plows right on through. "Granny Jenkins and my mother-in-law are planning a reopening and would love for you to be a guest of honor. You've been *so*," noting that same emphasis from moments ago, "instrumental in helping, the family wants to thank you." She stops speaking abruptly, making her thank you seem disingenuous. I stumble through a series of oh, um, thank you, and with telling her how honored I'd be. "Don't get a big head, there will be a group of you." Again, the tone doesn't match the words. It sounds almost as if she's mocking me, but attempting a teasing tone. "Could you come by this afternoon for some planning?" She lists out the time and instructs me to enter through the back door to avoid disrupting final preparations out front.

I haven't actually agreed when she disconnects the call. Something about this interaction puts my hackles up. There's no way I am meeting her without Brad and Chandra knowing.

***

The gravel crunches beneath my feet as I cross from the parking lot behind Azúcar over to the bakery. A breeze has kicked up since this morning, signaling rain is on the way. I'm bundled up to my chin and snuggle deeper into the down vest I'd thrown on over my thick sweater. As a native Floridian, I have no idea how to dress when the weather cools. Every single year, it catches me off guard and I'm shocked by how cold and damp some of the days get. I end up dressing in far too many layers. Cramming my hands in the fleece lined pockets, my hand wraps around a crumpled wad of bills, forgotten from the year before. Maybe today isn't going to be so bad! Finding $40 is a win.

Seb's cousins are back on duty and sit in the front seat of a shiny, black Tahoe. They nodded a subtle hello as I passed by, otherwise not acknowledging me. Grateful that I don't have to remove my hands, I dip my head in return and rush past them toward the back door of Gerardo's. Unfortunately, I have to remove my hands to readjust the larger than usual purse needed for today. While I'm at it, I slide my phone out and place into the front pocket, within easy reach if needed.

Knocking lightly on the door, I step back waiting for it to swing out toward me. Again, no response. I knock again and louder. No response. Several minutes have passed already and the sky has darkened with the impending storm. Taking a page from Agent Yoori Cho's book, I hammer on the door with the side of my closed fist. The door rattles in its frame with the impact. I'd love to be impressed by the move, but holy cow does that hurt. Is this a skill that toughs up your hands the more you do it?

Still no response. Checking the handle, I am shocked when the door opens easily. After all these thefts the door is unlocked?

"Melody? Malcolm?" I call inside, poking my head in a bit. The lights are on but the entryway by the door is dimly lit and the space is crowded with boxes. "Hey Melody? It's CiCi." Leaning into the space further, I hear the faint strains of music. Raising my volume, I try calling again, practically shouting Melody's name. There's still no answer. I'm cold and getting creeped out. An internal conversation stirs, back to the car or into the creepy storage room? Brad would tell me to grab one of the guards and have them look first. Chandra would tell me to get my butt to the car. My brain says to go on in, Melody knows I'm coming and maybe she's just lost track of time.

Obviously, I chose the last option. Why come out in this weather and only to bail? Plus, the rain has just started. I quickly send a message to Brad that I'm here and going in to meet Melody, intentionally keeping it light on the details.

Entering slowly through the creaking door, I step into the dim space. Wafts of freshly baked bread hit me as I step around a tower of boxes. Businesses need a lot of stuff, but this feels beyond excessive. A few of the stacks nearly touch the ceiling, it is also odd that most are the same size. Let's be real though, what point of reference do I have? I work as a barista, not a baker. And it's only been six months. Not as I've got years of experience to draw from.

Crossing the threshold of the kitchen, it's a relief to see the spotless, brightly lit room. The stainless counters gleam and the white walls reflect the overhead lights. Along the back wall, a series of proofing and baking ovens are filled with bread and rolls. I inhale deeply, fresh bread is the best smell in the world next to fresh coffee. Giving it another shot, I shout for Melody. Still nothing, but the music does seem a little louder. She has to be in the front. Reluctantly moving away from the bread, I give one last nose-whistling sniff to tide me over.

"Mel—" A whack across my shoulders takes me by surprise, I stumble forward, wheeling my arms. The strike was hard enough, that I gasp for breath. Crumbling to the floor, stunned, I attempt to struggle to my feet. A searing pain tears through my right knee and shoulder. I can't seem to coordinate my movements. Startled and in pain, I stay in place on the floor, my breaths short and noisy. The music has stopped and I'm surrounded by silence. "He...ll..o," finally able to speak, the words come out fractured. "Who's there?" Silence. I doubt I could hear over my own breathing in this moment anyway. Have they gone? I get my answer when the lights snap off, plunging the room into darkness, the only light coming in from the covered front windows.

Repositioning to sit on my butt, I scoot across the floor, aiming for the counter. With my back to it, I begin a modified three limb crab-walk. A foot crushes down onto the fingers of my left hand. I know it's a foot because my I stare in horror, the enormous black boot is still in place. Screaming from a mix of pain and terror, I attempt to yank my fingers free. No luck. They're stuck and the shoe grinds them into the floor. My right arm is useless and hangs at my side.

Turning to face my attacker, something hard and cold smacks into the side of my head. The room spins and goes black.

***

A high-pitched ringing assaults my ears, I shake my head and nearly throw up from the sharp pain that rips through and settles in my left temple. The lights around me sparkle like shattered glass, blinking does no good to clear it up. I have no idea where I am or why I can't move. Sitting still with eyes closed, I do a quick inventory. Head, right shoulder and knee, left hand. All three hurt in different ways and to different levels. What the heck is happening? I'm clear enough to recognize that this is exactly why those warnings exist. Don't go into dark, creepy places, alone. Why can I never listen?

Keeping as still as possible, I try to call for Melody again. "Melody? Are you here?" Still nothing. Onto the next step, "HELP!!!!!" I scream as loudly as I can. Which I realize is not as loud as it needs to be. Most of the businesses on the street are closed. Rallying with a deep breath, I scream "HELP ME!!!" again and again.

In the doorway, the shadow of an oversized man steps into view. I can't make out any details between the lighting and my distorted vision.

"Shout all you want, it won't do any good," the voice growls. Is it my imagination or is he proud of this?

"Why are you doing this?" I beg, shifting to get a better grasp of what I'm sitting on. Wrapping the fingers of my right hand around the edge, I feel rattan and a rim. It must be one of the dining chairs.

"Because you don't learn." His voice is mean. Not angry, just plain mean. "If you'd mind your own business, this could have ended months ago."

"Months ago? I don't know what you're talking about." Chair in the dining room, but where are the lights? In the scuffle, I lost my purse and cannot even guess where it is.

"Don't play stupid. You've proven that you aren't."

"I have no clue what you're talking about. Melody asked me to meet her for the reopening plan." Dread fills me. Oh God. Melody! Is she here too? Did he find her first? Is she dead?

"How do you think I knew you'd be here?" I can't see him, but I can hear the pleasure in his voice as revelation dawns. She told him I was coming to the bakery? "Why don't I save you the trouble of guessing who I am?" I hear movement as he steps toward me. His stench is overpowering— potent sweat, sour breath, and some sort of body spray. Defensively, I clamp my eyes closed tightly. Once I'm able to identify him, he'll kill me for sure. Every book I've read has this scene. How could I be so stupid? "Closing your eyes won't help, you aren't leaving here. So you might as well say hello." He stands so close, his knees press into mine. Pain flares again as he presses into my right knee. Roughly, he grabs the sides of my head and yanks it back so fast my neck makes a cracking sound. Is that his plan? He's going to break my neck? To my surprise, he places two fingers around each eye, digging the rest into the sides of my face. He stretches the skin around my eyes tight and pries them open. Screaming, I flail in an effort to fight him off. I do not want to see his face, either now or in nightmares later.

"Quite the fighter, aren't you?" The pressure increases as he tightens his grip. Tears flow from my eyes and he loses his grip. Taking this as an opportunity, I ram my left knee into his groin. He groans and bends forward. His skull crushes into my forehead, the force of his headbutt undoes any progress I've made at clearing my head. With a roar, he squeezes my head in his vice-like hands. The pressure is unbearable and I scream. He really means it, he intends to kill me.

"Enough," a female voice calls out from behind us. The hands release and he steps back. "You weren't told to kill her. Only to scare her, you buffoon." Who says buffoon anymore? I can't turn my head to look but the voice sounds familiar. "Forde only wanted her to back off." Forde? Forde? Think, CiCi. Your life literally depends on it. Between the spikes of pain and dizziness, my head feels heavy and dull. Thoughts collide but won't come together. "You've already crossed the line, he's not going to be pleased." Her words have cowed him. Through slitted eyes, I see him backing away toward the wall. Silence feels like the safest bet. I don't know if I can take another blow to the head and stay conscious. Staying awake feels necessary. They'll kill me for sure if I pass out.

"I did scare her, but she fought back, so what was I supposed to do?" A lame defense of his actions. He's beaten me nearly to a pulp. I've got one working leg and am not even sure how well it's working.

"Not okay, Diaz!" she barks. It's Arthur Diaz. Slug's buddy. He'd come into get coffee with Baek. He knows exactly who I am and likely has been watching me. Was it him that tried to run me over? "Don't touch her while I'm gone, I need to update Forde and figure out to do with her now. We can't very well like her leave." He once again offers my death as an acceptable solution. She tells him no and stalks away.

Menacingly, he pulls a stool over from the counter and sits a couple of feet from me. Continuing the farce of keeping my eyes closed, I watch him through the sliver hidden by my lashes. He leans, resting his elbows onto his knees, staring directly at me. Can he tell I'm looking at him? I have to relax and think. Incrementally, the brain fog is lifting, the white-hot spears of pain still rage, seeming to line up with my rapid heartbeat. Which feels like a bad sign.

A plan starts to form. "I won't say anything if you let me go." He snorts, reminding me of a warthog I'd seen in a nature show. "I'm really accident prone. I'll say I fell while out running or I can hit something with my car and tell the police that's what happened."

"You think the police can't tell a beating from a fall?" He leans back, crossing his beefy forearms over his chest. "Cops aren't as dumb as TV makes them seem. But don't worry, it will take them a long time to find your body. No one will even remember you by then." Terror makes my broken limbs go numb, temporarily relieving the pain. Refusing to relax, I use the reprieve to assess where I am and what's near me. The answer is nothing, my chair is in the center of an empty space on the floor. A strap or cord is around my waist, anchoring me in place. Clearly, I did not end up here accidentally. This was all planned. Starting with Melody's call this morning.

Subtly, I shake my left wrist. Thankfully nothing clatters against the chair. I've lost feeling in most of my fingers, but can still feel my wrist and forearm. Testing the waters, I shake a little harder. So far so good. I give a violent shake of my wrist, pain roars up my arm and into my chest. Hissing, I attempt to breathe through it. This grabs his attention.

"What are you trying to do? Get free? Good luck." His tone is so demeaning, anger flares inside.

"I'm pretty sure you've broken all my fingers, just assessing the damage," I lie, continuing to shake my wrist. The watch vibrates. Progress. Without speaking, I keep shaking my wrist and the buzzing increases.

"Knock it off, it's annoying," he barks and stands from his chair. With one final shake, bashing the edge of the watch on the chair, I rest my bruised and swollen hand in my lap, careful to place it palm up. Satisfied, he returns to the stool to watch me. "Settle in, you're in for the longest day of your soon to be short life." His smugness makes me want to spit nails. Or at least spit at him. I don't, my plan hinges on his confidence in my fear. Tears continue to fall from my eyes, rolling down my cheeks and off my chin. This part isn't an act. I couldn't stop the tears if I tried.

"As predicted, he is not happy," the woman says re-entering the room. Despite my cloudy vision, I risk taking a peek. A tiny gasp escapes and I flinch reflexively. Their attention is on the phone in her hand, whispering harshly, she points to the screen repeatedly. Not willing to chance it again, I close my eyes and watch through the slit. My watch continues to silently buzz on my wrist. I pray silently that it's worked.

35

Re-opening One Way or Another

Splintering wood and shattering glass herald my salvation.

The front door is bashed in. The SWAT team crashes through with their battering ram and armed officers flood the room, guns raised. I sob loudly as they rush forward, weapons trained on Diaz and Melody. Two officers divert and jog to me, guns lowered, flanked by the others. Reaching me they reassure me I'm safe. One officer supports me in the chair while the other cuts away the strap holding me in place. I hear myself whispering Brad's name over and over as I collapse into safety.

Diaz silently raises his hands, this isn't his first rodeo. Melody protests her innocence, shouting loudly that she found me this way. Pain and relief overtake me, I lapse into the unconsciousness I've fought for more than an hour.

***

The quiet beeping wakes me gently. A vast improvement of the high-pitched ring that turned into a squeal. Opening my eyes halfway, I glance around to check my surroundings. Just in case I imagined my rescue. Exhaling a sigh of relief, I spot the beige walls and a four-foot whiteboard with my name and the date on it.

"Babe?" I croak, my throat is dry and tight. It feels like those images of a cracked desert road. Brad jumps up from the chair at my bedside. He hovers above me where I can see him without moving. Everything feels heavy, even the light blanket.

"Hey beautiful, I'm right here." He gently kisses my forehead and brushes a thumb across my cheek. I wince slightly, my cheeks and eyes feel swollen and bruised. Recalling Diaz's thick fingers, prying my eyes open, I shiver. "Cold?" It's easier to say yes than explain. Brad wraps a soft throw around me. It's one that my sister crocheted for us last year. The weight and warmth are reassuring. My husband continues to stare down at me, tears in his eyes. "Can I get you anything?"

"Water, please," he calls for the nurse, letting them know I'm awake and thirsty. In a flash, two nurses and a doctor appear in my room.

"Welcome to the land of the living!" the gray-haired doctor calls out cheerfully, I squeak before bursting into tears. He looks chagrined and flushes, his gaze moves to the nurses who appear equally alarmed. For a moment, no one speaks as I calm myself and apologize. Again, explaining is too difficult right now. How could he know that my last memories are escaping my death? Brad gently wipes my face with a tissue, working his way around the oxygen tubing tucked into my nose. He makes soothing shushing noises while resting his free hand on my forehead. His face tells me it's the only non-bruised spot.

"I'm so sorry, my dear," the doctor apologizes, "My excitement got the best of me." I do my best to smile and nod. Realizing for the first time, there's a soft brace around my neck. The resulting nod is more of a bobble than any recognizable movement. "Are you feeling up to as asking a few questions and taking a peek at your dressings?" I have no idea what injuries were actually sustained, but readily agree.

"How long?" I begin, then lose my voice. Pausing and putting in more effort, I ask, "How long have I been here?" The pain on my husband's face nearly does me in. I'm hanging by a thread here.

"You've been recovering with us for three days," a sweet faced nurse with a long red braid says, leaning in to make eye contact. Her hair reminds me of a cartoon princess and I hold onto the peace of that. Three days?!? How has it been three days? I shift my gaze to Brad and see his quivering chin. Tears cascade from my eyes and roll back to pool in my ears and run down onto the cloth brace. The team sets to work, checking me over from head to toe, asking me a series of questions. Some I know, many I don't. Thankfully, the who questions come easily. My name and birthday, my husband's, our wedding anniversary, address are all correct. The staff doesn't think I notice them confirming each answer with Brad. The tension on his face lifts a little with each of the correct answers. The incorrect are tougher and simply don't have answers. There are some that I frown and refuse to answer. Those will take a while for me to say out loud. What happened? How long I was there?

As they finish lifting, poking, and prodding, the younger nurse with a blonde pixie cut asks if I'd like some company. Brad waits for me to answer. I agree but ask for only two at a time.

Visitors pour in. My mother and my sister, Cassi, tearful and relieved to see me. They collapse around me on the bed. Everyone cautioning my mother not to squeeze to hard. My sister refuses to leave. She says she's spent too many hours thinking I wouldn't wake up and can't bear leaving me for a moment. Mom takes one for the team and offers to bring coffee and snacks for them. I'm unfortunately only allowed water and Jell-O today. The doctor said my stomach needs to wake up before I can have anything else. Linda and Desmond with love and well-wishes from Karen, Moshe and Francine. Mirabel with Alfie and Elena. My bland room fills with flowers, balloons, and cards. I'm showered with kisses, told how much I'm loved, that it's a miracle to see me awake and talking. I soak in their love, letting it wash over me. I need it as much as the oxygen and pain medicine.

An hour passes and fatigue creeps in, I can't speak and Brad ushers everyone out to the lobby. Sister only leaves with Brad's reassurance they'll swap in an hour.

Yet, there's no Chandra or Seb. I begin to panic, did something happen to her and I don't know? Was she there the day I was taken? Brad senses my unease, even though he doesn't know the source. He quietly sits next to me, his hand resting with his fingers gently touching my left shoulder. His presence calms me, my heart rate and breathing slow. I need to know what injuries I have, there are plenty that I suspect but knowing will help.

"Top to bottom or bottom to top?" he asks. I gesture to my head. "Gnarly cut and bruising to the back of your head, oh and an impressive concussion. Broken right upper arm, bruised the bones in your shoulder and ribs. Crush injury to your left hand, he broke three of your fingers and bruised the bones in the others and back of your hand. Right knee seems like there's no new injury. Your fall, or what we assume happened, flared it up from your car accident." The phrase what we assumed happened makes my stomach hurt. Diaz and Melody aren't likely to spill the specifics of the afternoon. I'd passed out before telling anyone.

"I *need* to tell you." My words are strangled, catching in my throat. Brad holds the hand of my casted right arm, gently circling his thumb over my knuckles. "It's my fault and...." Brad interrupts with a murmured, "no, no, no" not realizing foolishness led me to the hospital room. I shake my head gently. "I knew better." He remains firm, jaw set.

"No matter what you were doing or why you were at the bakery, there is no excuse for what Diaz did to you. I will not let you blame yourself for the actions of a sociopath." His words take the sting from the guilt burning in my chest. "Not saying there aren't a few things I'd rather you would have done differently, but it is NOT your fault and I desperately need you to know that." The tears clinging to his lashes finally fall. I grasp his fingers with as many non-broken ones as I can. Nodding my head, tears fall. How many tears can one person hold? I've got to be running low by now or at least I hope so. A shuddering breath and I'm ready.

"Melody called me while I was having coffee on the porch," I say through sniffles. The story pours out. Every agonizing, painful, gut-wrenching blow. I needed him to be the one to hear it first. We cried, prayed, and finally Brad crawled into the bed to hold me while the tears flowed, hot and lavalike. Resting against his chest, the pull of sleep is overpowering and I drift off.

***

A soft, quickly whispered conversation wakes me. I'm alone in the bed and cold. Outlined at the foot of my bed are three people. From their shapes and voices. Brad, Cassi, and Chandra huddle. Furiously talking, making a poor attempt to stay quiet.

"What are we talking about?" I whisper loudly, successfully startling all three. They jump in unison and Cassi grabs her chest, stumbling back slightly. Their responses make me giggle.

"Sorry shug, we didn't mean to wake you," Chandra apologizes, squeezing my toes through the covers. Her sweet tone makes me sad, I don't want to be pitied right now. We have a crime to solve, I still haven't figured out how it's all connected.

"You think they'll let us use their board?" I suggest, trying to clear some of the thoughts in my head.

Chandra and Brad follow my gaze, Cassi looks confused. Chandra clucks her tongue and chuckles, withdrawing a tablet from her purse. "Will this work?" she asks, flipping the case open and illuminating the screen.

"You're going to need to write this time." I tip my head between the two casted limbs, smiling.

"I'll do it this time, cher, but laziness is no excuse from now on." The shine in her eyes conflicts with the teasing tone in her voice. She sits on the opposite side of bed, propping the tablet up where I can see. Her hands tremble faintly. "Now that I think of it, would you mind if Blair listened in?" Brad sighs and my sister rolls her eyes. Ah— this was what they'd been whispering about. Pausing before answering, I recognize that I am not in the best mental or physical shape. Yet, that doesn't invalidate the need to find answers. We've already lost three days. Brad stares at me, trying to see what I'll do. My gaze doesn't leave his for several heartbeats. The corner of his mouth quirks and he nods, coming to sit beside me. Sister sighs, throws up her hands and sits on the end of the bed, curling up under my untucked covers. Chandra takes the cue and dials Blair. Seconds later, she enters my room from the hall, half hidden behind an enormous bouquet. It's not surprising that she's here but I do wonder how long she's waited.

Red faced, she sits the flowers beside the window, saying, "From all of us." She slides a card to Brad before leaning against the window frame. "Please carry on," gesturing to our group. "I'm only here to listen." I appreciate that she's here as a friend and detective, but friend first.

"Cees, I know it may not be easy to talk about yet. Can you share what happened?"

Having talked through it with Brad hours before, the emotions are a bit less raw. I share the story from the call from Melody to when the SWAT team kicked in the door. What I don't share is the terror I felt, the utter dread at knowing Diaz would kill me without hesitation. That isn't necessary in the moment. Throughout the retelling, I cling to Brad, hiding against his chest when I tell the hardest parts. His heart races, his breaths quick, but he never falters. My sister sobs quietly, still wrapped around my legs, holding my feet like they're anchoring her in place. Tears stain our faces when I end with collapsing into the rescue team.

"I am in awe!" Blair pipes up. "You kept a level head. In a way that many trained officers wouldn't be capable of," She dabs her eyes with the sleeve of her sweater. "How did you know do to that with your watch?" This is a part of the day that I feel proud of.

"We all know I'm accident prone. When we got the watch and checked the features, I turned on the emergency detector settings. It's for falls and car accidents, so I figured this might be a good time to see what it could do. In theory, if the fall is hard enough and you don't respond, the watch connects to your emergency contacts. Before leaving, I reset the emergency contacts to Brad and Chandra, but they didn't know. Both knew that Melody and I were meeting at the bakery to go over the supposed re-opening plans. My gut said something was up..." staring at my crushed and casted hand, wondering if the fingers will ever work the same, "sure wish I listened."

"Don't worry, Melody got a grand re-opening," Chandra chimes in. "Probably not the kind she was envisioning, though." Goosebumps raise along my arms, the sound of the battering ram splintering wood replays in my mind. Shuddering, I scrunch under the blanket Brad brought from home.

"Alright, I'm calling it," Brad says, he stands and rubs his palms together, doubling down that it's time for everyone to go. Chandra and Blair leave together. My sister lingers filling me in on Coco and Aggie. She and Mom are staying there while we're at the hospital.

Seeing videos of their tiny faces makes me antsy to go home. Healing is better at home anyway. While they talk, I slowly drift off, already half dreaming of home.

When the physical therapist comes in the morning, I'm committed to getting out of here and put in more work than planned. Denying pain and pretending the skull splitting headache doesn't exist, I persevere. The sooner I'm on two feet, the sooner I'll go home. The biggest adjustment will be the lack of working arms. We chat strategies for the next six weeks or so until I'll be mostly healed. That wipes me out more than the workout.

36

Fresh Brews

Two days later, I am wheeled out into the sunshine. It is warm and soaks into my skin while we wait for Brad to bring the car. You'd think I've been hospitalized for years instead of five days. Free of the neck brace, I gently and slowly tip my head back to the let the sun on my face.

"We'll get you set up on the porch the minute we're home," Brad promises as he approaches my wheelchair. "Your mom has been cooking all day and is antsy for you to get there." She's not the only one, I'm itching to get to the house and relax in my own bed with the dogs. I've missed our routine. And good coffee.

Pulling into our driveway, I howl with laughter and tears. A banner proclaiming, "WELCOME HOME!! WE LOVE YOU, CiCi", brightly decorated with flowers. Our friends and neighbors surround it, clapping and cheering. Linda blows kisses as we roll to a stop. Coco and Aggie bolt from the porch, racing to the truck, barking maniacally. The second Brad opens my door, both dogs jump into the truck, slathering my face with kisses. Aggie climbs up, using my sling like scaffolding, tucking herself under my chin squealing with delight.

Brad, Alfie, and my brother-in-law help me down from the truck and into the house. Rather than a few seconds, it takes minutes to inch our way across the lawn. Our procession has turned into a spectacle, drawing more attention from others on the street. Even the Avalon's, Hubert, and Edna make an appearance, wishing me well on their parade around the neighborhood. For once, they're all pleasant, waving and smiling. I know death must have been close for Edna to be acting so nice.

Hours pass before I make it into bed, down comforter to my chin, pillows and ice packs supporting all my sore spots, and my mother hovering until my pain medication lulled me off to the verge of sleep. The final moments I'm awake, I feel the bed shifting under Brad's weight. He tucks the dogs in around me, then wraps his arm over my waist. I fall into the deepest sleep I've had all week.

***

The scent of fresh coffee and pastries wakes me. An attempt to stretch quickly reminds me of the situation. Using our smart speaker, I call out for Brad to help me. He whips the door open, flying into the room.

"Sorry! I just meant, can you help me get out of bed? I'm dying for coffee." Frantic apologies pour out when I see his face. His frown relaxes into a sweet grin.

He half-jogs to our bed, with an accented "ma' lady," then bows and sweeps the covers free. In a smooth motion, he sits me on the edge of the bed. Slightly dizzy and breathless, I brace myself with a hand on his chest. Fighting the room spinning, I take slow breaths in and out, those dang yoga breaths. I hate that they always help, but it could also be the scent of coffee that rights my senses.

"Coffee," I whisper, pretending to collapse. Using the waistband of my sweatpants, he hoists me into a standing position, somehow avoiding a power wedgie. Hobbling into the kitchen, a steaming mug of coffee with a straw awaits me. If I had two hands to rub together, I would. Instead, leaning forward like the tin man, inhaling the aroma of the blisteringly hot coffee.

As I sip, my mom and sister circle round each other, cooking in sync. Despite having grown up cooking with them, I've inherited none of their talent. Nibbling the bits of pastry that Brad hands me, we watch the magic unfold. Onions and garlic sizzled in the hot oil, spices are added in without measuring. The space smells even better as they stir, chop, and laugh. Through all of the prep, they joke and tell stories, catching us up on what has been missed over the last week. Even though this week has been one of the worst ever, this morning makes it seem less brutal.

In the midst of our relaxed morning, the doorbell rings, startling us all. Brad opens the camera app and shows me a porch full of law enforcement. My stomach drops.

Chief Mercer, Detective Cassidy, Chandra, and Agent Darius Patton file into our kitchen behind my husband. He grimaces and tips his head slightly. Not a single person is smiling, all appearing like they've had a glass of battery acid for breakfast. Way to avoid stressing us out.

Taking seats around the table, one by one they decline coffee and the sticky buns in the center of the table.

Clearing his throat, Chief Mercer is the first to speak, "I'd like to extend the well wishes of our entire department. Additionally, we made assurances for your safety and failed you. Please accept my heartfelt apology." He makes direct eye contact, in a genuine way, neither practiced nor forced.

"I appreciate that very much," I say, doing my best to smile. A good bit of the swelling and bruising has gone down, and the motion is more natural despite the purple and green fingerprints. "I don't feel any of this is the fault or failure of the department. Trust me, I knew going in there was stupid." This prompts smiles from our guests, their ramrod straight posture relaxes ever so slightly. "Are you sure you don't want coffee?" I ask again. Chandra raises an eyebrow, then winks at us. Brad stands for the pot while Cassi places four mugs on the table, giving them no option to decline. Agent Patton reaches for a mug, followed by Cassidy. Soon everyone is sipping happily.

"We'd also planned to fill you in on the case, but only if you're feeling up to it." Cassidy's tone is formal, but her face is pure mischief. There's not a chance I would pass this up. I encourage her to continue, and she launches into the arrest of Diaz and Melody on scene.

"Baek and Maltz had already filled in details on Slug's involvement and the reason they were in town. Slug, or Mr. Emory, to be correct, is the nephew of Mr. Alain Forde, leader of the briefcase brigade in town. When there was initial interest in acquiring properties downtown, Mr. Forde met Melody Deluca. She has a previously unknown hatred of small-business ownership, as well as the town of Palmetto Breeze. According to her statement, 'this town killed off any chance at living out my dreams.' A tad melodramatic, but it plays in. Forde was visiting businesses and met Melody. She was more than happy to discuss the prospect of selling. Mrs. Jenkins owned the bakery and several other commercial properties in town, including the buildings leased by Azúcar, the Coral Belle, and Sew It Is. She saw dollar signs and an escape plan. Her husband saw the opposite, loss of his dreams. He loves the family business, and our sweet little corner of Florida." She smiles when speaking about our town. Cassidy wasn't raised here, yet obviously feels the same way

Malcolm Deluca does. "Patton? You want to share? I don't need to have all the fun."

Patton lifts his mug in a salute, picking up the story, "We've had Alain Forde on our radar for a while. He's slippery, and always seems to be just out of reach. Lots of shady deals, property exchanges, with money that moves a little too freely. His actions trace back to a few suspicious fires over the last four years. We would be on the cusp of connecting, then lose the trail. We'd been keeping an eye on him in collaboration with local law enforcement and the FBI. This was the longest he's stuck around with a project. Likely, there's more we'll learn in the coming weeks. Notably, Mr. Emory, or as he's known by you, Slug, is the nephew of Forde. Baek, Maltz, and Diaz are buddies that he developed a tight working relationship with through a series of crimes sprinkled in the southeastern US."

"According to Baek, this got out of hand. Slug was desperate for his uncle's approval," Chief Mercer adds. "The original break-in was the starting point. Slug didn't get the response he'd anticipated, so he upped the game. Each occurrence, including your hit-and-run, were examples of those escalations. Diaz had grown frustrated by the lack of resolution. This led to the fight that ended Slug's life and your abduction. Diaz is a violent, dangerous man."

"Forde had Melody convinced that he only needed a little more time to make it happen, he promised he'd get Mrs. Jenkins to sell and she'd be free. Those promises led her down the rabbit hole. She began blaming you for the town banding together and fighting back." Chandra takes her turn. "The longer it took, the angrier she became."

"The good news is, we've arrested all five. Baek, Maltz, Diaz, Forde, and Melody. We're transferring to Federal custody this afternoon," Mercer says in conclusion. He drains his coffee and reaches for the pot. "Do you have any questions or want to know more details?"

My brain is buzzing. Already hindered by pain medicine, the revelations of the morning are overwhelming. "So all of this, the robberies, fires, drive by shootings, were because Forde wanted what wasn't his?"

"A succinct summary," Patton agrees. "As with much of organized crime, greed and selfishness are at the center. People trying to take from others."

"Is it over?" Brad asks, he's been leaning against the counter, silently listening.

"It appears so, all of the players in the game are in custody. The Jenkins and Deluca families are devastated by Melody's involvement and the damage done to the town. They're eager to move forward and help the town rebuild," Chief Mercer reassures.

"What can we do to help?" I ask.

"Shug, you need to heal. Then we'll talk," Chandra responds, slipping out of her professional tone and becoming more herself. I nod in agreement. Even if I wanted to help, the non-usable hands make it tougher than usual.

Chief Mercer stands, again expressing his appreciation of my bravery and the hope of a speedy recovery. The others follow suit, making their way to the door. On her way out, Chandra flashes a hand signal to call her.

We sit around the table, flabbergasted by the information shared. Relief floods me. The reign of terror has ended and our town can move forward now. A few weeks of healing will help me wrap my brain around the news and to figure out how I can help.

37

Time for a Change

Cast free and bundled up, I hit the pavement with Coco and Aggie. We've modified our walks to include a leash connected to my belt. The idea of a leash yanking on my freshly healed finger induces nausea.

Our first stop is Linda's. As usual, she's on the porch, waiting for us with human and canine snacks. When I sit, she throws her blanket over me, fussing that I might be cold and end up stiff. Promising her I'm bundled and toasty, we munch on cookies while filling each other in on the week. The upcoming re-opening celebration for downtown is this weekend and everyone is excited. Whether a business has re-opened already or not, we're all involved. Azúcar is sparkling, stocked, and staffed for the event. While I'm not back at work yet, I'm more than ready to join the party.

Dragging myself from the warmth of her porch, back into the freezing, fifty-degree morning, we trundle down the street. Talking to neighbors as we go. Desmond is backing out of his drive, intent on visiting Karen. He promises to give our love. Moshe and Francine are out of town for the birth of a great-grandchild. Mirabel is on a cruise with Alfie, Elena, and their children. The neighborhood feels emptier without them.

Passing the community center, I pause. The hours spent reviewing case notes, sharing what we'd found, discussing who we suspected. All fond memories. Part of me wonders what the future will hold. I hope the Porch Patrol can retire from sleuthing.

My letter came last night and I am still torn. Do I have it in me to become a Private Investigator? The internship will give me the chance to figure it out at least. Pulling my gloves off, I text Chandra.

Me: *Guess what?*

Acknowledgement

No story is ever the work of one person. It is through the efforts of many that it comes to life.

For all my readers, thank you for choosing my stories. You make this dream possible. I write these books for those who crave connection, laughter, and stories that feel like time with friends. To my ARC team and early readers, your encouragement, feedback, and enthusiasm carry me through every draft. You help shape these stories, and I'm so grateful for your time. Thank you for believing in this little world I've built. Ramona, my editor, thank you for putting in the work to strengthen my story and fix my grammar. My illustrator extraordinaire, Ki Charm, you've made my sticky note sketches come to life! I appreciate all the brainstorms, revisions, and collaboration.

Now for the mushy parts. My family and my husband. For my family, a heartfelt thank you for cheering me on, whether the pages are blank or the words are flowing. Your support, emergency read-throughs, responses to bizarre texts, and humor inspire me (and keep me on track). To my husband—my real life Brad, are there enough words? Thank you will never cover the days, nights, and all the car rides I've rambled through stories, plots, and picked your brain when I ran out of words. Couldn't do any of this without you in my corner.

About the
author

Kate Montgomery is a Georgia-based fiction writer. A lover of dogs, coffee, and the beach, she finds joy in the simple pleasures of life. With a deep appreciation for the outdoors, Kate draws inspiration from nature, weaving themes of family, faith, and friendship into her stories. She believes in the power of words to build communities and create meaningful connections.

Other works by Kate:

Light Roast Larceny- A Coastal Coffee Mystery

Southern Breeze & Mimosa Trees